# B

## “It re

## read me like a book?”

Claudia nodded in response to Billy’s question. “Frankly, yes.”

“So no one is allowed to have a secret?” he persisted.

“I believe in honesty,” she said.

“You don’t have any secrets, then.”

She hesitated a beat. “No.”

“How many men have you slept with?”

“Billy! Good God, that is none of your business.”

“I’m trying to prove a point. Everyone is allowed to privacy.”

“Everyone reads expression and body language. I just happen to be better at it than most people.”

“And I’m better at *not* being read than most people. So that means I’m dishonest? Lady, where do you get off?”

“There. That is the first honest emotion I’ve seen from you.”

“Stop reading me!”

“I can’t help it.” Her eyes inexplicably filled with tears.

“Here,” he said gruffly. “Read this.” He leaned across the gearshift, pulled up the parking brake and kissed her.

Dear Reader,

Many years ago, I attended a workshop on the art of reading faces and body language. Back then, it was considered a fringe science, right up there with astrology and palmistry. But I was fascinated with the subject, and I always knew someday I would create a character with this skill.

Now, copious research has proved that reading expressions and body language is a legitimate science. And I finally found the right story and the right character: psychologist Claudia Ellison, who was introduced in my first Project Justice book, *Taken to the Edge.* Claudia is known as the human lie detector. In fact, she doesn't feel safe unless she can "read" the people she deals with. Of course, the one man she can't read—investigator Billy Cantu, a man skilled at hiding his feelings—is the one she falls in love with. She skates the fine line between fascination and fear as they work together to try to save a woman on death row, a woman no one else seems to care about.

I hope you enjoy their adventure!

Sincerely,

Kara Lennox

PS—I like to hear from readers. Please contact me through my website, www.karalennox.com. And look for the next book in my Project Justice series—*Hidden Agenda,* available July 2012.

# For Just Cause

## *Kara Lennox*

TORONTO NEW YORK LONDON
AMSTERDAM PARIS SYDNEY HAMBURG
STOCKHOLM ATHENS TOKYO MILAN MADRID
PRAGUE WARSAW BUDAPEST AUCKLAND

ISBN-13: 978-0-373-71779-8

FOR JUST CAUSE



This edition published by arrangement with Harlequin Books S.A.

For questions and comments about the quality of this book please contact us at Customer_eCare@Harlequin.ca.



www.Harlequin.com

**Printed in U.S.A.**

## ABOUT THE AUTHOR

Kara Lennox has earned her living at various times as an art director, typesetter, textbook editor and reporter. She's worked in a boutique, a health club and an ad agency. She's been an antiques dealer, an artist and even a blackjack dealer. But no work has ever made her happier than writing romance novels. To date, she has written more than sixty books. Kara is a recent transplant to Southern California. When not writing, she indulges in an ever-changing array of hobbies. Her latest passions are bird-watching, long-distance bicycling, vintage jewelry and, by necessity, do-it-yourself home renovation. She loves to hear from readers. You can find her at www.karalennox.com.

### Books by Kara Lennox

#### HARLEQUIN SUPERROMANCE

1689—TAKEN TO THE EDGE‡
1695—NOTHING BUT THE TRUTH‡
1701—A SCORE TO SETTLE‡
1767—OUTSIDE THE LAW‡

#### HARLEQUIN AMERICAN ROMANCE

974—FORTUNE'S TWINS
990—THE MILLIONAIRE NEXT DOOR
1052—THE FORGOTTEN COWBOY
1068—HOMETOWN HONEY*
1081—DOWNTOWN DEBUTANTE*
1093—OUT OF TOWN BRIDE*
1146—THE FAMILY RESCUE**
1150—HER PERFECT HERO**
1154—AN HONORABLE MAN**
1180—ONE STUBBORN TEXAN
1195—GOOD HUSBAND MATERIAL
1216—RELUCTANT PARTNERS†
1240—THE PREGNANCY SURPRISE†
1256—THE GOOD FATHER†

‡Project Justice
*Blond Justice
**Firehouse 59
†Second Sons

Other titles by this author available in ebook format.

For my dear friend Marie Del Marco.
I can never thank you enough for luring me to Southern California and giving me such a warm welcome. Your relentless pursuit of your dreams is an inspiration to dreamers everywhere.

## *CHAPTER ONE*

THE WEIGHT ROOM AT PROJECT Justice smelled like gymnasiums everywhere—a hint of sweat, overlaid with eau de cleaning supplies. Claudia Ellison, dressed most inappropriately for the gym in a buttercup-yellow linen suit and cream leather heels, stood poised in the doorway observing her quarry.

He didn't see her. Billy Cantu sat on a bench doing reps with a barbell. His rippling biceps mesmerized her for several moments. She'd met Billy before, briefly, but she hadn't guessed how ripped he was underneath his neatly pressed shirts.

Wearing only a pair of gym shorts, Billy exposed an awful lot of skin, smooth and naturally tan due to his Hispanic heritage. Thick, almost-black hair, deep brown eyes, sensual lips parted slightly as he breathed from the exertion…

She stopped herself. Her job wasn't to catalog Billy's masculine assets, charming though they were. She was supposed to be reading his body language, gauging his mood. Would he be receptive to her proposal?

He'd better be. Billy was her last hope.

Billy's face was relaxed. His arm moved slowly, no jerky motions. He didn't appear to be pressed for time, given the leisurely way he returned his hand weight to the rack and selected another to work on his lats. This might be the best time to garner his undistracted attention.

She walked briskly into the room, stepping around a stationary bike and a rowing machine, making sufficient noise that she wouldn't startle him when she spoke.

He looked up, and the first thing she saw was blatant male appreciation—before he schooled his face. He controlled his features quickly, so quickly that only someone with her training would have caught that brief microexpression when he was unguarded.

"Dr. Ellison." He laid his weights on the bench and grabbed a towel, blotting the light sheen of perspiration on his face and neck. "You come to work out?"

She looked down at her suit and heels, then back up to find him grinning. She tried to mirror his teasing mood, calling up a smile of her own.

"Call me Claudia, please." She strode forward, hand outstretched. "It's nice to see you again."

His hand was large and calloused. It swallowed hers whole as they shook hands. She hadn't expected his touch to feel so…so personal, and now she was the one who had to arrange her face into a pleasant but neutral expression. Adopting whatever mask fit the situation was something she did very, very well.

"I hope you're not here to shrink *my* head."

"No, not at all. But I do have something to ask you."

He stood and walked over to an old-fashioned watercooler and filled a paper cup with spring water. She tried to gauge his reaction to her interrupting his workout. Was he irritated? Did he welcome the intrusion?

Strangely, she couldn't read anything into his posture or facial expression.

She didn't know a lot about Billy, only that he was

an ex-cop from Dallas who'd been working at Project Justice for about three years as an investigator, mostly operating in the background. According to Daniel, Billy had never been the point man on a case.

Now it was her job to convince him to do just that. An innocent woman's life depended on it.

She watched, fascinated, as he gulped down two cups of water, then crushed the cup in his hand. "You've got me curious. What is it you'd like to know?" Although he looked exotic, with his dramatic coloring and sultry, full lips, his speech bore no trace of a Spanish accent. He was a hundred percent Texan.

"Actually, I need your help. Do you remember the Eduardo Torres murder case?"

"Of course. Eduardo Torres was a key player in the Rio Grande Mafia. He was a murder suspect himself, killed some guy in a drug turf war. Then his wife offed him."

"Only she didn't. I was hired by the wife's defense attorney to do a psychological evaluation. I found Mary-Francis Torres to be deceptive on a number of issues. But not about the most important thing. When she said she didn't kill her husband, she was telling the truth."

"How do you know?" Billy sounded neither curious nor skeptical; the question was perfectly neutral.

"Well, that's what I do. I read body language and facial expressions, and with a high degree of accuracy I can tell when someone is lying."

"So, you believe the wife is innocent?"

"I believe she didn't kill her husband, and that she has no idea what happened to him. I testified to that effect."

"I guess the jury didn't believe you."

"Unfortunately, when the prosecutor cross-examined me, he focused on the lies Mary-Francis told. Most notably, she claimed her marriage to Eduardo was a happy one and that they hadn't quarreled. I had to point out to the jury, again and again, the instances in which I spotted deception. Sadly, I did her case more harm than good."

And she'd been racked with guilt about it ever since.

"I'm sorry to hear you were sliced-and-diced by the prosecutor. But I doubt you're to blame for the conviction. As I recall, the case was something of a slam dunk. They found about a gallon of Eduardo's blood in the bed he shared with his wife."

"But no body."

"The medical examiner testified he couldn't have survived that much blood loss."

"But someone else could have killed him."

"Maybe. But unless some new evidence has surfaced—"

"That's the thing. Mary-Francis knows I'm a consultant for Project Justice, so she contacted me—the only person who believed she was innocent, even if I wasn't much help in the courtroom. She claims to have new evidence."

"Hmm. What kind of evidence?"

"She couldn't explain it in the email. She doesn't write, spell or type very well. I told her I would come see her. But I'd like someone from Project Justice to come with me and evaluate whatever she has—from a law enforcement perspective."

"Me?"

She'd surprised him. At least she could read that much. But not much else. Billy Cantu was a blank canvas. She'd never met anyone so difficult to read.

"Why not you?"

"You can't just sneak in the back door like this. Surely you know how it works. There's an application process. Cases have to be evaluated. Then Daniel himself makes the final decision about which cases we accept."

"I talked to Daniel. He feels the case merits at least a preliminary investigation. But all of the lead investigators are stretched to the max right now. He said you're the only person who might be available."

"So, I'm your last choice?"

Was he teasing? She had no idea. "You're my only choice, Billy. And the only chance this poor woman has of getting off death row. Right now, I am the one person in the world who believes she didn't kill her husband. I have a responsibility to pursue this, or I can't live with myself."

Billy blew out a breath. "I'd like to help, Claudia. But I assist the other investigators. I don't take on my own cases." He moved to the weight machine, stacked up what looked like two hundred pounds, and started working his legs.

"Only because you don't want to." Claudia sat down on the adjacent station, so he would have to see her face. "Daniel says he offered to promote you to senior investigator, and you turned him down." And why was that? Claudia wondered. What normal man didn't want to be promoted, get a better title, a bigger paycheck and more prestige? But she didn't ask aloud. This meeting wasn't about making Billy uncomfortable.

"I like things the way they are."

Claudia sighed elaborately. "All right. I'll just have to tell Mary-Francis that you're too busy building muscles to save her life."

Billy let the weights drop with a clang. "Now, wait a

minute. I'm not just goofing off here. I'm on my lunch hour. Anyway, part of a cop's job is to stay in shape."

"You're not a cop. And if you're not working in the field, if the heaviest thing you lift is a phone—"

"I work in the field."

"Then come with me to interview Mary-Francis. C'mon, Billy, don't make me beg. You don't have to commit to the case. Just commit to the one interview. If it pans out, maybe Daniel will reconsider and assign it to someone else."

"You're not leaving me much choice," he groused as he resumed his reps. His thighs had muscles on muscles, and she had to force her gaze away.

"I never intended to. A woman's life, Billy."

"All right. One interview. But Mary-Francis better wow me. And just for the record? I'm not crazy about shrinks."

"All shrinks? Or me in particular?"

"Let's just say I'm a skeptic of your particular skill, and leave it at that."

She did her best not to show how insulted she felt. Most people, even cops, were impressed by her skills, or at least politely curious. "Fair enough. I'll call you as soon as I've set up the visit with Mary-Francis."

A ROAD TRIP WITH A BEAUTIFUL blonde sounded like heaven to Billy Cantu—unless the blonde spent four hours straight studying him like a particularly fascinating species of toe fungus.

"I know I'm good-lookin'," Billy finally said, "but do you think you could stop staring at me for five minutes?"

"Oh. Sorry." Claudia turned to look out the windshield at the parched midsummer fields. "It's an occupational habit."

"It's also kinda rude. I mean, when women stare at me, I want to at least pretend it's because they're trying to get inside my pants—not my brain."

"I don't want to be either place, thanks," she said tartly, and Billy grinned. A quick glance told him she was blushing.

"You've been awful quiet," Billy said. "How about you give me some more background on this woman we're going to see? I read the court transcript, but you must know stuff that's not public."

Claudia had a transcript in her lap, but she'd spent more time covertly studying Billy than looking at her notes. Maybe she'd thought he wouldn't notice, but he had excellent peripheral vision.

This interview was a waste of time. But Daniel wanted him to check it out, so here he was. Daniel had built Project Justice from the ground up and continued to choose which cases they took on. Apparently he trusted Claudia's opinion that Mary-Francis was innocent. Or he at least didn't want to offend her.

Billy preferred to work behind the scenes, supporting the other investigators. But lately Daniel had been pushing him out the door more and more.

"Mary-Francis isn't the most likable woman I've ever met," Claudia said. "She never should have taken the stand in her own defense."

"I'll say. The cross-examination was a bloodbath."

"And yet…I still believe she's telling the truth. Not about everything, maybe—but about not killing her husband, yes."

"Obviously, or you wouldn't have brought the case to Project Justice." As a psychologist on retainer with the foundation, she didn't normally bring in cases. She interviewed witnesses or analyzed interrogation or trial video. She was a nationally recognized expert on body language.

Which, if anyone asked Billy, was all a bunch of hooey.

Since nobody asked, he listened politely as she went through her notes. "Anytime she was questioned whether she knew where her husband was, or whether she'd killed him, or if she knew someone else had killed him, her body and face indicated her answers were truthful. If she were lying, her body would show more stress. But her shoulders were relaxed, her eyes wide and animated, her voice confident. However, she wasn't always truthful. She lied about some things."

"Like what?"

"Like her marriage. She tried to pretend everything was fine, that she and her husband were deeply in love. But any time that subject came up, she would pull her head in like a turtle and hide her hands in her lap. In fact, whenever anyone raised their voice or tried to intimidate her, she showed the classic body language of an abuse victim."

A squirrel darted out into the road. Billy swerved to miss it.

Claudia squeaked and grabbed on to the door. "God, Billy! What the hell are you doing?"

"Trying not to hit a squirrel."

"Oh. That shows great compassion. But I'd prefer one dead squirrel to a head-on with a semi."

"It was a reflex." He didn't like her assigning a motive to his actions. Great compassion. For a squirrel? Really? But he had a lot of hours to spend with her, and he didn't want to spend them arguing.

"So," he continued, "you're telling me someone does an imitation of a turtle, they're lying?"

Claudia released the door handle and seemed to gather her composure around her. "That was one of many signs that she felt threatened when certain subjects were broached. Each person is different, though. I have to observe a subject for some length of time to get a baseline of their usual body language, then note when that changes—"

"Yeah, okay."

"You don't believe me?"

He shrugged, unwilling to tell her what he really thought about hocus-pocus disguised as science. He much preferred the old-fashioned method of catching someone in a lie—breaking them down with tough interrogation.

"What I do is legitimate science, backed up by scores of studies—"

"Really, you don't have to convince me. It's not essential for me to understand your work to do my job, is it?"

"Well, no."

"You just want me to interrogate Mary-Francis so she'll tell us about this supposed new evidence, and you'll observe."

"*Interrogate* is rather a strong word. I don't want you to put too much pressure on her. It could completely shut her down or cause her to end the interview."

"Hmm." He had his own way of questioning a suspect, a way that usually worked, honed by his experience with the Dallas Police Department. He'd have to play it by ear. "Any idea what this evidence is?"

"Only that it's something shocking. But whatever it is, I want you to evaluate it from a cop's point of view."

"That means I ask hard questions."

"I know. Just don't bully her, or her stressed-out body language will override everything else."

"Got it."

They lapsed into silence. Claudia shifted in her seat, crossed and uncrossed her legs. Billy couldn't help looking at the bit of leg she revealed as her skirt slid up.

Damn, hard to keep your eyes on the road when something like that was sitting next to you.

"So you really don't believe in what I do," she finally said.

He grinned. "That really bugs you, huh?"

"Yes."

"Why? You must be used to skepticism."

"Usually not from people in my own camp. I thought Daniel only hired open-minded investigators."

"You're saying I have a closed mind?"

"I think you refuse to open your mind to something that goes against your deeply held beliefs. In my business we call that—"

"Stop right there. You are not allowed to analyze me. That's not part of the deal."

"You didn't object to my analysis during your initial employment screening."

"'Cause if I had, I wouldn't have gotten the job. My head is just fine, thanks. It doesn't need shrinking."

"Fine." The single word came out sharp and punchy as a quick right jab. But after a few moments of tense silence, she spoke again, sounding much more relaxed. "I apologize. Analyzing everybody I spend time with is automatic for me."

That was something Billy understood. Even now, years after his undercover work, he still evaluated every person he met in terms of potential threat. He still sat with his back to a wall. And he still kept a spare gun inside his boot.

Back in the day, he hadn't been completely safe anywhere, not even behind locked doors. Ingratiating himself with one party of drug dealers made him a target for the other. He'd had a price on his head when Sheila was killed. His superiors had agreed that relocation to a different city, where his face wasn't known, was the best course of action.

The Houston P.D. would have hired him, but he'd decided that he was done with police work. Getting the job with Project Justice had seemed like a godsend.

"Didn't mean to overreact. But if you're going to pick apart every word I say or every gesture I make, maybe you should keep your observations to yourself."

She raised an eyebrow. "Afraid of what you might hear?"

"Let's just say I don't want to have to defend myself against incorrect assumptions. I'm a lover, not a fighter." He smiled and hoped she took that in the spirit he'd intended—as a joke. Because even though he'd spent a good portion of his sleepless night last night fantasizing about her slender legs wrapped around his hips, he did not intend to become her lover.

Like most women, she would want way more from him than he was prepared to give.

BY THE TIME MARY-FRANCIS Torres was led into the interview room wearing handcuffs and leg irons, Claudia had set up her small video camera in one corner. She might want to analyze the video later, run it in slow motion to detect the rapid-fire expressions that were too fast for human eyes to catch.

Claudia had requested that she and Mary-Francis be seated face-to-face, no glass partition, no telephones, not even a table between them. The prison officials had reluctantly agreed after Daniel had intervened. Whatever people thought of Project Justice's efforts to free inmates who shouldn't be in prison, Daniel's name had clout.

"Remove her handcuffs, please," Claudia instructed the guard.

"I can't do that, ma'am."

"Yes, you can," she said smoothly. It was essential that Claudia observe Mary-Francis's entire body. Legs and feet often revealed a lot because people didn't monitor those body parts as much as hands and facial expression.

With a bit more prodding, the guard finally did as Claudia asked, though he cautioned her and Billy that no touching was allowed.

Finally they were left alone, and Claudia was able to inspect her subject.

Mary-Francis Torres was forty-three years old, slightly overweight, with black-and-silver hair scraped into a tight ponytail. Before imprisonment she'd worn it in a bun, but she probably wasn't allowed hairpins.

She looked as if she was holding up pretty well. But death row inmates, isolated from the rest of the population, didn't have to worry about fights, or other inmates stealing their food. They were allowed books, sometimes a radio and an hour of outdoor recreation a day.

It was probably the most comfortable way to spend

time in a maximum-security prison, not that Claudia would recommend it.

Prison had not yet humbled this woman. She still wore a belligerent expression, a subtle sneer that had not impressed the jury at her trial.

Claudia supposed she would be belligerent, too, if someone unjustly accused her of killing her husband. Assuming, of course, that she had a husband.

"Hello, Mary-Francis." Claudia used her most soothing voice. "How are you doing?"

"How do you think?" Mary-Francis spoke with only a slight accent. She had emigrated to the U.S. when she was fifteen, Eduardo Torres's child bride.

"Is there something you need?" Claudia asked. "Toiletries or books?"

Mary-Francis declined to answer the question, and instead looked pointedly at Billy. "Who is he?"

"Billy is my associate from Project Justice. He'll be helping me evaluate whatever evidence you present."

"He's staring at me. Tell him to stop staring at me."

Billy didn't look away. He said nothing. Claudia wished he would try to put Mary-Francis at ease. A relaxed subject was much easier to read.

"Let's get down to business, shall we?" Claudia said. "You said in your email that you have new evidence that will prove your innocence."

Mary-Francis shot another look at Billy. "Not in front of him."

"He *has* to be here," Claudia said. "He is the only one who can decide whether Project Justice will take on your case."

Mary-Francis pursed her lips in disapproval. "I have no patient-doctor privilege with him. This information can't get out. It can't go public. If certain people find out what I'm going to tell you, they could have me killed."

*Evidence of paranoia.* That wasn't a good sign. Claudia hoped this wasn't a fool's errand.

"Billy is entirely trustworthy," Claudia said. "He would never reveal sensitive information to an outsider."

"Not even for a lot of money? A *whole* lot of money? He might be wearing a nice shirt, but he looks like a gangbanger to me. The kind who would pop an old lady in the head and steal the rings right off her dead fingers."

Claudia watched carefully for a reaction from Billy. But he took the insult as if Mary-Francis had been commenting on the weather. Which was one of the main reasons the man unnerved her, and why she'd been studying him on the way to Mountain View Correctional Facility. He showed nothing of his true feelings—not a single nonverbal clue. His every gesture and facial expression were carefully choreographed to project only what he wanted others to see. In her experience, only sociopaths could disguise their feelings so completely, and only because they didn't have genuine feelings. All of which made Billy both challenging and scary.

"Look, Ms. Torres," Billy said, finally breaking his silence, "you either have to talk with me here, or this interview is over. It's not Dr. Ellison's decision."

Mary-Francis shot Billy a look of pure venom. "Fine. I will talk." She sounded as if she was bestowing upon them a great honor. "The other day, my daughter, Angie, came to visit me. She *never* visits me, so I knew right away something was up."

"You and your daughter aren't close?" Billy asked, smoothly taking over the questioning.

"She thought I murdered her father. She wouldn't speak one word to me. Now, suddenly, everything has changed. Eduardo must have contacted her."

Claudia was shocked—and disappointed. Eduardo couldn't possibly be alive. Was this simply a last-ditch, desperate effort of a condemned woman to stir something up?

Billy didn't look shocked. "So you think your husband is alive? Because your daughter came to visit."

"I know he is."

"Maybe Angie simply had a change of heart." Billy flashed a charming, completely phony smile. "Your execution has been scheduled. It could have made her realize she's about to become an orphan."

Claudia watched for variations in her subject's posture, or telltale gestures that might indicate stress.

But everything remained the same. Mary-Francis faced them squarely, her hands folded on her lap, her shoulders down and relaxed.

"Angie asked me about something that was a secret between Eduardo and me. Something we agreed she shouldn't know about. Since I never told Angie, Eduardo must have."

Billy looked confused. "Maybe he told Angie this secret before he died."

"If he had," Mary-Francis said, "Angie would have come to me long before now. I know my daughter. She is an addict, and she would steal anything valuable and sell it for drug money."

"So this secret between you and Eduardo," Billy said. "It involves money?"

"It involves something valuable, yes..."

Ah, now Claudia could see it. Not deception per se, but evasiveness. Mary-Francis was uncomfortable talking about this secret, whatever it was. Claudia made a note of Mary-Francis's tight mouth.

"Well, what is it?" Billy asked.

Mary-Francis seemed to be weighing her options. Finally she came to a decision. "Coins. We had a coin collection worth a good deal of money. After we caught Angie stealing from us, I worried she might discover the coins and try to pawn them. So I gave them to my sister, Theresa, for safekeeping. I told no one, not even Eduardo."

"Why not Eduardo?" Billy wanted to know. "Didn't you trust him?"

"Of course I trusted him! I was going to tell him, but it slipped my mind. And then he disappeared."

*Hand to the neck. Eyes squinting. Shoulders raised. Voice at a slightly higher pitch.* Any one of those things could be a sign of deception. Together, Claudia felt absolutely confident they indicated Mary-Francis was lying.

"Ma'am," Billy said, "excuse me for saying so, but your story is ridiculous."

"I'll explain better, then," Mary-Francis said, losing her composure for the first time. "Eduardo was suspected of killing some drug dealer. The FBI was closing in, and Eduardo was scared of going to prison. I believe he fled to Mexico, thinking he would take the coins with him and sell them, so he could start over in comfort. But then he couldn't find them because I'd moved them, and he couldn't very well ask me about the matter. I was supposed to think he was dead."

"Your loving husband wanted you to think he was dead?" Billy asked.

"He must have thought that would be better than going to prison," she grumbled. "He knew the police would question me, and he figured I couldn't tell them where he'd gone if I didn't know.

"Later, he got in touch with Angie somehow, thinking she would help him find the coins." Her words were rushed, a little desperate. "Maybe he promised her some money—Angie would believe anything he told her. She would do anything for him.

"But Angie couldn't find the coins, either, so she came to me, thinking she could weasel where I'd hidden them, said she wanted to keep the coins safe, put them in a safe-deposit box, but that makes me laugh. She would turn them over to her father. Or sell them, probably for far less than they're worth. My daughter is not the smartest—"

"How much *are* they worth?" Billy's interruption halted Mary-Francis's avalanche of words.

Her body language changed abruptly. While telling her story she had been leaning forward, her face open and animated, gesticulating with her hands. Now she pulled into herself and smoothed her hair, another self-soothing gesture.

"I don't really know."

Billy glanced at Claudia. She shook her head slightly.

"So your daughter asks about the coins," Billy says, "and you draw the conclusion that your husband is alive." He leaned back and folded his arms, a classic male territorial display designed to intimidate.

"You're not getting it," Mary-Francis said. "My daughter absolutely did not know about those coins before Eduardo disappeared. Now suddenly she's full of questions. She knows. Because Eduardo told her."

"So what do you want us to do?" Billy challenged.

"Should we tell the police to let you out of jail because your daughter mentioned a coin collection? It's preposterous."

"I want you to find Eduardo. I *know* he is alive, and you must find him. He's probably running out of money by now, and he's desperate for the coins. Maybe you could set a trap. I can give you the names of friends and relatives he has both here and in Mexico. But first, I need for you to warn my sister. Sooner or later Angie will figure out I gave the coins to Theresa. Tell her to hide them well."

"Why can't you contact Theresa yourself?" Billy asked. "Advise her to move the coins to a safe-deposit box."

"I can't get hold of her. She doesn't respond." Tears sprang to Mary-Francis's eyes. "She has my…oh, what is the word, where she can sign my name?"

"Power of attorney," Billy supplied.

Mary-Francis nodded vigorously. "I am afraid she has turned her back on me like Angie."

"If Eduardo is alive," Claudia asked softly, "how do you explain all that blood?"

"Evidence can lie," Mary-Francis said. "The police are corrupt."

Billy was still stuck on the coins. "Mary-Francis, how valuable are those coins?" he asked again. "You must have some idea."

Mary-Francis hesitated. "I'm not sure. They are old Spanish escudos, from sunken ships. Maybe a million dollars?"

## *CHAPTER TWO*

"A MILLION BUCKS' WORTH of old Spanish coins?" Billy said once they were safely back in his truck. "It better be Jean Lafitte's treasure."

"If they're gold," Claudia said, "they could be pretty pricey just based on the meltdown value alone. Historical significance would add to their value. She could be right."

"I guess it doesn't really matter what the coins are worth," Billy said. "The question that concerns us is, does she really believe Eduardo is alive? If so, is she deluding herself?"

"She seems sincere to me." Claudia sounded tired. "I'm starving. Can we stop somewhere and eat?"

"Sure. Any suggestions?" Billy didn't recall seeing much in the way of classy restaurants in the closest town, Gatesville. Though it was the county seat and "the spur capital of the world," it was definitely a small town.

"Any place is— Oh, look, a Tubby's. Let's go there."

"Tubby's? You're kidding, right?" Claudia Ellison wanted to eat lunch at a greasy spoon with a gravel parking lot filled with beater cars and trucks?

"I have…fond childhood memories. But if you'd rather eat someplace else—"

"No, this is fine." Billy tried to picture what Claudia's childhood might have been like. He assumed she'd come from wealth. She had an aristocratic bearing and a way of speaking that he associated with old money. No Texas twang, so he doubted she came from around here. Maybe she'd eaten at Tubby's while on a family vacation?

He had a hard time picturing little Claudia with her upper-class family, dining on ribs or chicken-fried steak. The mental image wouldn't gel.

"I thought you'd be more of an upscale-French-restaurant sort of person," he said once they were inside and seated at a booth with a faded green Formica table between them. Out of habit, Billy had selected the table and placed his back toward the wall, where he had a good view of the front door and a plate-glass window into the parking lot.

"*Mais oui,* I love ze French food. But this place… they have the best banana splits here." She opened one of the plastic menus the waitress had dropped in front of them and gravely looked over the offerings as if about to make a decision of importance.

After a minute or two she looked up at him. "What? Why are you smiling?"

"I just never expected a Tubby's restaurant to delight you, of all people."

She suddenly became self-conscious, and he wished he hadn't ribbed her about her lunch choice. "I guess I needed something happy to focus on after being in that prison." She shivered delicately. "What an awful place."

"And Tubby's is a happy place?"

She looked around, perhaps assessing it through her adult eyes. The restaurant was half-filled, mostly with men in work clothes and a couple of tables of boisterous teenagers.

"Yes, it's happy," she declared. "These men are so relieved to sit in the air-conditioning for a few minutes' break from their construction jobs. And those kids—blowing their allowance money on burgers and ice cream, flirting, away from parental control—yeah, happy."

But her smile was slightly bittersweet.

"You ready?" the waitress asked.

"Yes, I'll have the chicken finger basket and a Diet Coke."

Billy ordered a standard burger and fries and the waitress left.

"No banana split?"

"It probably wouldn't be as good as I remember. Now. About Mary-Francis."

"I think she's a lying schemer. Please, can't we write this one off? No way could her husband be alive."

"Ah, sorry. She was telling the truth—about some things, anyway. The coins exist. She believes they're worth a million dollars, and her daughter did visit. She believes Eduardo has been in contact with Angie. All that's true. She was lying about one thing, though."

"What?"

"She didn't merely 'forget' to tell Eduardo about giving the coins to her sister. I think she deliberately kept the information from him. Their marriage was on the skids. But she couldn't just divorce him—he was violent. She might have wanted to keep those coins for herself, so she could escape and make her own fresh start."

"Forgive me for pointing this out, but a million-dollar coin collection is a nice motive for murder."

"She believes he's alive," Claudia said flatly.

"Then she's delusional. The blood evidence was

clear-cut. Maybe she had some sort of psychotic break and she forgot she murdered him."

"Give me some credit. I think I would notice if the subject was psychotic."

Their food arrived, and for a time they didn't speak, focusing on filling their empty stomachs. Once Billy had taken a few bites to dull the edge of his hunger, he sat back and observed Claudia as she devoured her chicken fingers, coating each one with a few dribbles of ranch dressing. She took small bites, closing her eyes to savor each one.

He again wondered why this place was special to her. He tried once more to picture her as a little girl. Long blond hair in pigtails, maybe. She had such a slight build now, she'd probably been thin as a child, all knees and elbows. Had she been a tomboy, or a Little Miss Priss? Probably the latter.

"You're smiling again."

Billy quickly schooled his features. Damn, that was careless of him, letting his musings show on his face. His life no longer depended on hiding his true self every waking minute. But he still preferred to keep his feelings out of public view, and the one person he ought to be more careful around was Claudia Ellison. He might not believe in her body-language junk science, but she was perceptive.

They finished and paid with a company Visa, then headed back into the sizzling hot afternoon. Claudia removed her pale blue suit jacket. Her blouse was damp, clinging to her breasts in a way that made Billy's mouth go dry despite the huge soft drink he'd just sucked down.

"So you're going to recommend Project Justice not take on this case?" Claudia asked.

"It's kind of fantastical."

"Yes...but don't you think we should at least check a few things out? For example, let's sic Mitch on Eduardo. If the guy is alive, he's leaving signs of his presence somewhere in cyberspace. Mitch is so amazing when it comes to that, and we have that list of friends and associates Mary-Francis gave us."

"I guess that would be okay, if Mitch doesn't mind." Mitch Delacroix was Project Justice's resident computer geek and missing person locator. "I can put Daniel off about a decision for a few days."

"And I want to visit Theresa and see what she has to say about this illustrious coin collection."

"Yeah, I'll admit I'm curious. If Theresa has some supervaluable artifacts in her home, we should advise her to take them to the bank and put 'em in a vault. Especially if her drug-addict niece wants them."

As Claudia climbed into the passenger seat of Billy's truck, she offered him a healthy flash of thigh, and his heart leaped into his throat...was that her panties he just saw? Then he realized she was wearing a lacy-edged slip.

How Victorian. How...intriguing.

"She was definitely concealing something," Claudia said once they were back on the road. "She gave at least a dozen signs of it."

"A dozen? Come on." No one could give themselves away that thoroughly.

"*You* knew she was lying. How did you come to that conclusion?"

"'Cause she told a stupid story about a million-dollar treasure and a dead husband come back to life. Doesn't take an expert to figure out it's a crock."

"My hunch is, you read all the body-language signals on a subconscious level—the direction of her feet, the angle of her body, voice inflection, how fast she talked, where she looked, what she did with her hands, nostrils, lips, whether she swallowed a lot—"

"It would take me a year to catalog all that. Isn't it easier just to listen to what a suspect says?" Yet merely listening to the words someone spoke hadn't always told him what he needed to know. He'd missed some vital clues during that last operation with Sheila.

Just thinking about Sheila filled him with a profound sadness. "Hey, Claudia, can you tell what I'm thinking now?"

"I read body language, not minds," she said tartly.

"What's my body language telling you?"

She actually took him seriously, studying him from head to toe in a slow perusal that made him hot—checking him out the way a woman does at a bar when she wants you to return the favor. If he was as good as he thought he was, though, Claudia would have no idea how badly he'd like to kiss those moist, full lips of hers and muss up that elegant blond hair.

"You're bored," she finally said. "You don't like this assignment, you don't like Mary-Francis, and you'd rather be working on something else."

"Uncanny," he said as relief washed through him. He still had it. He could still hide his true feelings.

"I'm not so ready to wash my hands of Mary-Francis," Claudia said, abruptly returning to business. "I'm going to talk to Angie. If she's in contact with her supposedly dead father—"

"Whoa, wait, Claudia. You probably shouldn't confront her. She could be dangerous."

Claudia seemed insulted. "I know how to deal with

addicts, even violent ones. I've had clients come at me with knives, try to choke me with drapery cords—"

"In a clinical situation, where I'm guessing you have a panic button, or people waiting in the next room who'll come running if you scream." Jeez, and he thought *his* job was dangerous.

"I know a little something about dangerous people," she said. "I wouldn't be dumb enough to confront her in an unsafe environment."

"I'll go with you," he said, surprised at how happy it made him to have an excuse to spend more time with Claudia. Now that he knew for sure she couldn't see inside his head as though it was a fishbowl, he wouldn't be so irritated if he caught her studying him again. In fact, he might not be irritated at all. Did she always wear lacy slips? What was that about?

"I'm sure you have better things—"

"Once Daniel makes up his mind to check out a potential client, he wants it done right. It's my job to run around interviewing people connected with the case. It's what I'm being paid to do."

"I'm on a hefty retainer," Claudia reminded him.

"Then we'll confront Angie together," he said, settling the matter.

"GOOD MORNING, CELESTE," Claudia said as she entered the Project Justice lobby the next morning. "I'm here to meet Billy Cantu."

Celeste Boggs, Project Justice's office manager and self-proclaimed head of security, looked up from her *Soldier of Fortune* magazine with a stern expression and pointed to a clipboard. "Sign in there, please."

"Oh, but I'm not—"

Celeste tapped the clipboard with one impatient

finger and glared, daring Claudia to complete her argument.

Claudia signed in. It was hard to defy Celeste. Though the former Houston cop was in her seventies, she was one scary mama who claimed to know fourteen ways to kill someone with her bare hands. Celeste dressed as if she were auditioning for the role of World's Most Eccentric Senior Citizen, but Claudia wasn't fooled by the flamboyant red, ostrich-feather-trimmed shirt or the huge earrings made from shotgun shells.

Celeste meant business, and no one got past her into the rest of the building unless she let them.

"Billy," Celeste said into the phone, "your date is here. I hope you bought a corsage for her."

Is that how Claudia appeared to Celeste? she wondered with some alarm. Like a high-school girl all primped for a date with the quarterback? She'd opted for a more casual look today, a pale peach linen sundress with a wide brass belt. The skirt was one of her shorter ones...had she subconsciously dressed provocatively for Billy's sake?

The possibility was troubling.

A loud clanging of metal and a snort coming from the vicinity of Celeste's feet interrupted Claudia's uncomfortable musing. "What's that noise?"

"Oh, that's just Buster."

"You have a dog down there?"

"No, not a dog." Celeste tried and failed to hide a mischievous smile. "Want to see him? He's a beauty." She leaned down and grabbed on to something that turned out to be a metal cage. As she hefted it up, Claudia saw that inside the cage was a large, furry, fierce-looking…pig? It was excitedly trying to dig its way through the steel bars with sharp, cloven hooves.

Claudia took an instinctive step back. "Oh, my God, what in the hell is that thing?"

"It's a javelina! Haven't you ever seen one before?"

"In a zoo, maybe. What's it doing here?"

"It was in my backyard, and it kept digging up my vegetables. I caught it. My grandson's school mascot is a javelina and their previous one died—or maybe they ate it. So I'm donating this one to the school."

"You're donating a vicious wild animal to a school?" That did not sound like a wise plan.

"He's not vicious. I've been taming him down. Watch, he'll let me pet him now."

"Uh, are you sure that's a good idea?" Claudia took a few more steps back.

Celeste opened the cage door. "Don't worry, he's really rather sweet. Aren't you, Buster?" Celeste petted the animal on the head, then scratched it behind one ear.

The beast didn't look as if it enjoyed the attention. In fact, it was frozen in a classic defense posture designed to make it invisible. Its next move would be to bolt for freedom. *Freeze, fight or flight.*

A frosted glass partition separated the lobby from the rest of the building. Just as Celeste withdrew her hand and was about to close the cage, Billy burst through the glass door like a freight train.

"Good morning, Claudia!"

The wild animal bolted out of the cage at the speed of light, sliding across the polished surface of the reception desk, plopping to the floor and wiggling right past Billy's feet and through the door before it closed.

Claudia screamed just from the sheer surprise, and

Billy backed up against a wall, his right hand automatically reaching under his jacket for a weapon.

"Holy crap, what was that thing?"

Celeste was the only one who didn't look perturbed. "A javelina, what did it look like?" She calmly picked up the phone and pushed the intercom button. "Attention, all staff. Please be advised there is a small, hairy, piglike animal loose in the building. If you see it, would you mind calling the front desk so I can catch it?"

"You brought a live javelina to work?" Billy asked, as if wanting to be sure he'd heard right.

"It would have been fine if you hadn't scared it."

Billy looked at Claudia. "Now would be a good time to leave."

"Sign out! Both of you."

Once they were out the door and heading for Claudia's car, they burst out laughing.

"What the hell was that about?" Billy asked. "Celeste's new pet?"

"She caught it in her yard," Claudia said, "and she's donating it to her grandson's school because they need a mascot."

"Her grandson? Celeste doesn't have any children. She never married. You must mean her great-nephew."

"She said grandson. I'm sure of it."

Billy shrugged one muscular shoulder. "She must have misspoken, then."

Elderly ladies didn't normally speak of grandchildren they didn't have. How odd.

As they approached Claudia's silver-green Nissan Roadster, she used her remote to unlock the doors.

Billy whistled appreciatively. "Sweet ride."

"Thanks." She'd insisted on driving for two reasons. First, it gave her something to do with her hands, somewhere to focus her attention besides on Billy so she wouldn't give away her roiling emotions. And second, she wanted—no, *needed*—to have control of something. Relinquishing the driving all day long yesterday to Billy had been a tough challenge, particularly since she hadn't felt she'd had a strong grip on anything else, especially her own feelings.

She glanced over at him as he fastened his seat belt. A lot of men would balk at allowing a woman to drive them anyplace. But Billy was obviously secure enough in his masculinity that it didn't bother him. Or maybe it bothered him and she wasn't able to tell.

Why wouldn't he be secure? Lord, he was handsome in a striped button shirt and a lightweight summer jacket, worn to disguise the fact that he carried a sidearm in a shoulder holster. A crisp pair of boot-cut Levi's, the ostrich-skin boots to go with them and a white straw Stetson completed the picture.

He took his hat off and settled it on his lap, then donned reflective mirror sunglasses.

One reason cops wore mirrored sunglasses was so they wouldn't telegraph their actions with their eyes. Was it possible he deliberately hid behind those opaque lenses to make it harder for her to read him? Did he really not want her to know who he was?

She supposed that was only fair. She didn't exactly go out of her way to broadcast her true self, either. She punched Angie Torres's address into her GPS, then slid her car smoothly into downtown morning traffic.

Angie Torres lived in a run-down area of Harrisburg Boulevard in Magnolia Park, a hundred-year-old neighborhood of Houston in the early stages of rehabilitation. But this block hadn't yet been gentrified;

the apartment was above a strip of white-brick stores, most of which were boarded up.

Mary-Francis had said her daughter worked in a medical office, leading Claudia to believe she was a functional addict, but this looked to be the sort of place where the near-homeless, prostitutes and other victims of society ended up.

Claudia and Billy climbed a dark staircase into an equally dim hallway, alive with roaches and smelling of urine. Billy placed his body between Claudia and the door as he rang the bell. Though it was a simple display of caveman machismo, it had an undeniable effect on her. His protectiveness made her skin tingle with warmth. Few people in her life had ever put her safety and well-being above their own, even casually.

No one answered. Billy knocked, then pressed his ear against the door and listened.

"I don't think there's anyone inside. I don't hear voices or a TV, not even sounds of a pet. Let's check around the back. There's probably a fire escape or something."

Once outside, Claudia was grateful for a breath of fresh air. She tried to follow Billy on his quest to find a back door, but the tangled, thorny brush behind the small, two-story building proved a bit much for her leather sandals and bare legs, so she waited for him in the shade of a tattered store awning, welcoming the small breather. Being around Billy was a lot of work.

She couldn't even tell whether he was attracted to her. Normally she could discern in a heartbeat if a man was interested in her, at least on a physical level. The signs were so obvious—the covert studying of her body, the way an interested man leaned in when speaking to her, the length of eye contact, the way his gaze would move from face to breast to legs, then back, and that unique male shifting of weight to accommodate a burgeoning erection.

Billy had flirted with her, but flirting was automatic with him. He'd have probably flirted with Celeste if he hadn't been so surprised by the javelina. But Claudia absolutely couldn't tell if anything lurked behind the flirting.

With Billy, she was drowning in a sea of unknowns, confused about where she stood. For the first time in years, the ball of fear in her stomach just wouldn't go away. Her built-in alarm system was warning her of *Danger!* in flashing red letters.

Unfortunately, the same thing that made Billy a mystery also made him undeniably exciting. What if he could read her attraction to him? How awful would that be?

She had some control over the physical signals she broadcast to the world, but she couldn't do anything about the pheromones that were undoubtedly wafting from her body in waves.

As she waited for Billy, a young, skinny Hispanic man covered with tattoos exited from the door that led upstairs.

He noticed her as he walked toward a beat-up truck, and did a double take, this time perusing her up and down, his expression at first hostile, then more curious.

Claudia slid her hand into her pocket where she kept a small device that, with the push of a button, would emit a piercing siren. She never went anywhere without it.

*"¿Qué pasa, mama?"*

*"Hola, señor."* Her Spanish was limited, but she

knew enough to have a stilted conversation if necessary. "Do you speak English?"

"You want me to speak English, I speak English," he said with almost no accent.

"My partner and I are looking for Angie Torres." She hoped the use of the word *partner* would cause the man to think she was a cop.

He smiled slowly. "Police? You?" He laughed and shook his head. Then he continued in perfectly good English, "No cop I know dresses like that."

"Do you know Angie?" she persisted.

The man leaned against a post and crossed his ankles as he lit a cigarette. The signs said he was flirting, not dangerous. She slipped her hand out of her pocket.

"Yeah, I know her." And didn't care for her, apparently, judging from the way he flashed a slight sneer. "She moved out. She inherited a house. Her mom murdered her dad and went to prison for it. She was a piece of work, that girl." The man closed his eyes and shook his head.

"Why do you say that?"

"Always carping about how selfish her parents were, that they were rich and never gave her a dime. But who could blame them? Any money they gave her went up in smoke. I wouldn't put it past her to kill her dad and blame it on her mama so she could get hold of their money."

An alarming possibility, one they should probably look into, though Angie's only criminal record consisted of a couple of misdemeanor possession charges.

"What kind of drugs did she use?"

The young man took a long drag on his cigarette and blew it out slowly—a classic move someone took to collect his thoughts before speaking. "Anything she could get her hands on. Got fired from her last job for stealing Vicodin."

That would explain why she wasn't working at the medical office anymore.

"Thanks. I appreciate the information."

"No problem." He flicked his ash into the breeze. "You busy later?"

Lord, she hoped so. She cast a glance toward the back of the building. "Um, my partner is really jealous. You probably don't want him to see us talking."

The man gave her a regretful look, then turned and sauntered away.

Billy reappeared around the corner. "No fire escape. This building is a code inspector's nightmare. Who was that guy you were talking to?"

"A neighbor. He says we'll find Angie at her parents' house, which she now considers hers."

"Probably at least half of it is. Mary-Francis wouldn't have been allowed to keep the profits from her crime—in this case, her half of the community property. Was there a will?"

"I don't know."

"Let's check out the house." He paused just before getting into the Roadster. "There's no reason you have to waste your whole day running around checking out leads. You can drop me at the office and get back to your work. I can do this on my own."

"I want to meet Angie," Claudia said firmly as she opened the car door. It had sat in the sun only a few minutes, but hot air wafted out, and she waited for it to cool off slightly before she climbed inside. "I want to see for myself how she acts when we bring up the coins...and her father."

Billy's eyebrows lifted. "You don't trust me. You don't think I can handle it."

"Oh, no, Billy, it's not that. I just…I feel so responsible for Mary-Francis ending up on death row. The prosecution used certain parts of my evaluation to make things worse for her. If there's any chance of saving her…I just want to do my part, that's all."

"You did your part. You drew the case to our attention. We can take it—"

"Billy, don't be difficult. I want to go with you to interview Angie."

"So you can do your hocus-pocus on her."

"My assessment could be of value to you. Why don't you just accept my help?"

"I work better alone."

"If I hadn't been here, if I hadn't talked to that neighbor, you wouldn't even know where to find Angie."

"I would have figured it out."

"We don't have all day. If Angie finds the coins—"

"If the coins even exist."

"They do. Mary-Francis was telling the truth about that, though not necessarily about the particulars."

He rolled his eyes. "Fine. You can come with me. But I don't want to have to look out for your safety all the time, okay? I almost had a heart attack when I saw you talking to that lowlife just now, and I realized I shouldn't have left you alone."

"I was fine. That guy was not dangerous. Just because he's poor and has tattoos doesn't mean—"

"Save me from a lecture about stereotypes. I'm a former cop and I can smell trouble. That guy was no angel."

"We won't be going anywhere dangerous," Claudia

persisted. Even though she was the one with the car keys, Billy had taken firm control of the reins.

"Angie could be dangerous. She has something to lose, if she thinks we might be challenging her right to her parents' stuff. Addicts do desperate things when they're cornered."

Claudia couldn't argue about that.

She should have just climbed behind the wheel, rather than debating with Billy over the roof of her car. But she felt compelled to make him agree with her. "It'll be fine."

"If I sense any danger, we're getting out of there. You'll do what I tell you to do. Is that clear?"

"Man, who pushed your macho button?" But she had to admit, he looked magnificent making his male dominance display. He leaned against the roof of the car, arms widespread, muscles tense, jaw firm. Any second now he would start beating those impressive pecs of his.

Her heart gave a flutter. At least *that* wasn't on display for anyone to see.

"I can call Daniel," Billy said. "He'll back me up."

"All right, I get it. Your word is the law where our personal safety is concerned. This is your case. I'm along to observe and assist. Is that good enough?"

The split-second expression of triumph on his face made her grind her teeth. But at least he'd shown her *something.*

## *CHAPTER THREE*

EDUARDO AND MARY-FRANCIS Torres had lived in a solidly upper-middle-class neighborhood in Conroe, a Houston suburb. Their subdivision wasn't quite uppity enough to be a gated community—but close. Tall limestone-brick walls flanked the subdivision entrance with a carved stone sign that read Pecan Grove. The cookie-cutter houses, built in the '90s, were all too large for their tiny lots, but the saplings planted by the neighborhood developers had grown into mature trees and the homes were well maintained.

The Torres house was on Apple Blossom Court, a peculiar name for a street in a climate where apples couldn't grow.

Out of habit, Billy paid close attention to the configuration of streets so he knew the fastest way to the nearest exit.

Claudia thought he was being macho, but he wasn't kidding about the danger. Angie was a drug-addicted woman in a dramatic family situation who undoubtedly felt stressed and could erupt into violence at any time. He stood a better chance of surviving unscathed if he didn't have to worry about a companion's safety before his own.

But he couldn't deny it felt great to be back out in the field.

When he'd first hired on with Project Justice, he'd

told Daniel he was no longer comfortable facing danger on a daily basis. Daniel had responded by saying he wouldn't require anything of Billy that he wasn't ready to deal with.

Somehow, after three years on the job, Daniel knew Billy was ready. Billy could have said no to this assignment. But though he'd made a few token objections, he'd eventually accepted the responsibility of unraveling the puzzle.

Claudia's onboard GPS found the Torres home with no trouble. The house was tan brick, just like all the others, but the lawn was yellow and scraggly and the landscaping hadn't been tended to in months. A for-sale sign featuring the photo of a smiling female Realtor advertised that the property had four bedrooms and a pool.

Claudia pulled up to the curb just as a woman stepped out the front door, her cell phone wedged between her ear and shoulder. She frowned as Billy and Claudia climbed out.

"If you're here about the car, it's already sold," she said. She was tall and painfully thin, with toothpick legs sticking out of her cutoff shorts. She had stringy, shoulder-length hair clumsily streaked with reddish-blond stripes. Her skin was pasty, and overall she had a look of ill health about her. Billy would have pegged her as a crack addict even if he hadn't already known she had a drug problem.

She returned her attention back to her caller. "Sorry, I was talking to someone." She opened the mailbox and pulled out a wad of envelopes that looked an awful lot like bills. Billy could just make out the *FINAL NOTICE* in large red letters on one envelope. Angie riffled through the mail and picked out one envelope to rip open. She turned her back on Billy and Claudia and headed back indoors.

"Excuse me. Ms. Torres?"

"I'll have to call you back," she said into the phone as she paused and turned to narrow her eyes at Billy. "What?"

"I'm Billy Cantu with Project Justice. This is my associate, Claudia Ellison. We need to talk to you about your mother."

"Are you those people who get criminals out of jail?"

"We free innocent people who have been unjustly imprisoned," he corrected her.

"Please don't tell me you think my mom is innocent."

"We have some questions, that's all," Claudia said. "Could we go inside and talk for just a few minutes?"

"I'm kind of busy here."

"Busy selling all of your parents' stuff?" Billy said. "Because I'm pretty sure you don't have the legal right to do that, and in about five minutes I could get a court injunction and a locksmith over here to change the locks."

Angie folded her arms, looking scared for a moment before she decided to brazen it out. "How am I supposed to pay the bills on this place without any money, huh?"

"Nice deal for you," Billy said as he strolled up the walkway toward the front door without invitation. "Living here rent free and getting all the drug money you need listing stuff on Craigslist or eBay. Bet your mom had some nice jewelry. That was probably the first to go. Am I right?" He took the two steps to the front porch and headed inside the house.

"Hey!" Angie was right behind him. He turned to see Claudia bringing up the rear, looking perplexed by his high-handedness. But he suspected Angie wouldn't give them the time of day unless they strong-armed her.

The inside of the house was stripped—no furniture, no pictures on the walls. But the air-conditioning ran full blast. Billy made his way to the kitchen, which was piled high with dirty dishes and empty pizza boxes. The trash can overflowed.

He whipped around to face Angie as an uncomfortable thought occurred to him. He'd just made a stupid mistake; he hadn't cleared the house before assuming Angie was here by herself. "Are you living here alone?"

"None of your business. Get out before I call the cops."

"No, you don't want to do that." He took out his cell phone. "I've got Judge Thomas Wilkes's number on speed dial. He'll issue the injunction on my say-so. You and whoever else is sponging off you will be out on your asses in a matter of an hour, maybe two."

Just then another person showed up, a scrawny guy with the same kind of pasty complexion as Angie. But he held a gun in one shaky hand.

"Who the hell are you people?"

Billy broke a cold sweat as he stepped in front of Claudia, shielding her from the shooter. His carelessness had just come back to haunt him.

He needed to defuse this situation fast. "Put the gun down now, okay? We're not cops, we're friends of Angie's mother."

"For God's sake, Jimmy, put the damn gun away."

Angie didn't sound terribly nervous about the threat. "I can handle this. Go…go clean the pool or something."

The man named Jimmy gave one parting snarl before he shoved his small handgun into the pocket of his baggy shorts and sauntered away.

Billy let out the breath he'd been holding, almost sick with relief. He stepped aside so he could look Claudia in the eye. "Not a dangerous situation, huh?"

"You're the one who made the situation dangerous," she countered, "by entering the house uninvited. We should go."

"Go wait in the car. I'll be out in a minute."

Claudia folded her arms, obviously not budging. Billy wished she wouldn't do that—it accentuated her breasts, which distracted him at a moment he needed all of his attention on Angie.

"What do you want?" Angie asked wearily. "They're gonna show the house this afternoon. I need to clean up."

That was an understatement.

"Who was that guy?" Billy asked.

"My boyfriend."

Claudia watched with hyperalert eyes.

"Recently you visited your mother in prison. You asked her about some coins. What was that about?"

"My dad's coin collection," she answered warily. "Did Mom say anything about it? Did she say where she'd put it? It's important that I find those coins." Angie nearly salivated with eagerness.

"Your mother put them away for safekeeping."

"They're not valuable," Angie said too quickly. "It's just a few coins that have been in the family."

"You know, Angie, you don't seem like the sentimental type to me. Why do you want them? And how did you find out about them?"

She flashed a superior look at him. "I don't have to tell you that. What matters is that the coins are mine. My father wanted me to have them. Mom has no right to hide them from me." Angie thrust her chin out in a show of false courage.

"How do you know Daddy wanted you to have the coins?"

"He told me so."

"When was that?"

"Right before he was murdered. He said he and Mom were going to split up and he wanted to give me some things before the divorce lawyers got it all. But he never got the chance."

"So why did you wait all this time to ask your mother about the collection?"

"I…didn't think about it until now. Like I said, it's not that valuable."

Claudia shared a look with Billy, then shook her head slightly. She obviously thought Angie was lying. Though Claudia had clearly been unnerved at having a gun pulled on her, she was still doing her job. His respect for her inched up another notch.

"You know what I think?" Billy was about to go out on a limb here, but he wanted to confront Angie with his suspicions while she was off balance—before she got the chance to get her story straight. "I think *you* killed your father and let your mother take the blame. Because they had money, and they wouldn't share it with you."

She did not appear disturbed by the accusation. "You can think whatever you want, but a jury says my mom did it. And if you know where those coins are, you better tell me. I know people, too. I have a lawyer."

"You're gonna need one," Billy said. "If you didn't kill your father, then maybe he's not dead. Maybe he recently told you about the coins, and that's why you took a sudden interest in them."

Angie laughed, but it sounded forced. "If he's alive, then how do you explain all that blood found at the crime scene?"

"There are ways," Billy said, wondering if there really were. "I have evidence people working on that right now, taking a closer look at that blood." Or he would, as soon as one of the lawyers at Project Justice officially became Mary-Francis's attorney of record and made a formal request to the Montgomery County Sheriff's Department to review the physical evidence.

Billy wasn't sure when he'd decided this case had merit, but there was something here. Something off-kilter. In good conscience he couldn't wash his hands of Mary-Francis.

"It's his blood," Angie said stubbornly. "DNA proved it."

"We'll see. Meanwhile, if I were you, I'd be waiting for a knock on the door from the police. Until your father's estate has been legally awarded to you, you don't own anything of his—including that coin collection. Unless you're using the proceeds to pay your mother's legal costs…"

"That's what I'm doing!" Angie said quickly, grabbing on to the lifeline he'd handed her.

"What does your aunt Theresa have to say about all this? Your mother gave her sister power of attorney. Not you."

At the mention of Theresa's name, a look of panic

briefly crossed Angie's features before she caught it. "She said it was fine for me to sell stuff. Hey, Jimmy! Get in here."

Claudia tugged on Billy's sleeve. "For God's sake, let's go."

"I'm not lying," Angie shrieked, though no one had accused her. "I'm not. I'm just doing what I have to do to pay bills, pay lawyers."

"Yeah, whatever." Billy ushered Claudia toward the front door and out into the still, late-morning heat, having no desire to face Jimmy and his shaky gun hand. Neither of them said anything until they were back in the car with the air-conditioning on.

Then Claudia started to tremble—violently. Probably a delayed reaction to the gun.

"Hey, it's okay." Billy put a hand on her shoulder. She reminded him of a scared bird vibrating beneath his hand. "We're safe now."

"He wouldn't have shot us," Claudia said. "I could see it in his face. It was all bravado, an empty threat. Still…"

Billy wasn't so sure.

"He would have been justified, you know," Claudia continued. "We practically committed a home invasion. It's legal to protect your domicile with deadly force."

"It all turned out okay."

She turned toward him, suddenly fierce. "Don't ever do that again. Not when I'm along for the ride."

"Now you see why I didn't want you to come with me?"

"You shouldn't be allowed to roam around loose without a handler. You're dangerous." She took a deep breath, started the car and pulled away from the curb. "Angie was lying."

"No kidding. I don't have to be a body language expert to figure that out. Maybe she *did* kill her father and frame her mother. She's clearly a sociopath."

"No, not a sociopath. Sociopaths are better liars." She said this with such assurance, it made Billy wonder if she had more than just clinical knowledge to back up her claim.

"Still, she's a bad seed," he said.

"I'll agree with you there. Not a pleasant person." Claudia paused, weighing her words. "She didn't kill her father—she was telling the truth about that. But she was definitely hiding something. Maybe it's just her drug use, but maybe it's something else."

"If I could get her in an interrogation room, I could break her. Your body language tricks only take us so far. A confession would be a whole lot more useful."

"Can we get her arrested?"

Billy thought for a moment, then shook his head. "Doubtful. If we'd seen any obvious evidence of drugs sitting around, we could call the cops and have her hauled in. But we didn't."

"She's stealing from her father's estate."

"Unless Theresa really did give her permission to sell the stuff. If she's mad at her sister, she might have."

"She didn't. I'd bet my career on it."

Billy wasn't so sure, and the police wouldn't take Claudia's word for it.

"Let's go talk to Theresa and see what she knows about the estate, or old coins, or whatever." Claudia seemed recovered now from her fright. The pink had returned to her cheeks, and she had the gleam of excitement in her eyes. Billy knew that gleam. She was on the hunt.

He glanced at his watch. "I should get back to the office."

Her shoulders slumped with disappointment. "It's your call."

He grinned. "I'm kidding. I am dying to find those coins now."

"Damn it, Billy."

"What? Why are you mad?"

They were still in the Pecan Grove subdivision; Claudia had been turning on streets randomly. Now she pulled over to the curb again and reached for her Day-Timer, flipping pages of her notes. "I'm not mad at you. I'm mad at me for not catching on that you were teasing. It should be child's play. Ah, here it is, Theresa's address." She plugged it into the GPS. "It's not far, only a couple of miles."

"It really bugs you that you can't read me like a book, doesn't it?"

"Frankly, yes."

"Did it ever occur to you that some people don't like to be read?"

"Only people who have things to hide."

Maybe he did have things to hide. Or at least, things he didn't want every random stranger to know about. Was that so wrong?

"So no one is allowed to have a secret?" he argued. "Everyone has to be completely up-front about every single part of their past, every single thought that goes through their heads?"

"I believe in honesty," she said.

"You don't have any secrets, then."

She hesitated a beat. "No."

"Nothing in your past that you'd prefer people didn't know about."

"I'm not ashamed about anything I've done."

"How many men have you slept with?"

"Billy! Good God, that is none of your business."

"Wow, must be a lot."

"I don't believe you! How could you even— That is so inappropriate—" She sputtered to a stop.

"I'm just trying to prove a point! Everyone is allowed privacy—in their homes and inside their heads."

"And I say if it's on their face or in their gestures or their posture, and I'm adept at figuring it out, then the information is fair game. Everyone reads expression and body language. I just happen to be better at it than most people."

"And I'm better at *not* being read than most people. So that means I'm dishonest? Lady, where do you get off?"

"There, right there. That is the first honest emotion I've seen from you. You're in perfect congruence—chest thrust forward, arms splayed to take up as much room as possible in a classic male territorial display—"

"Stop reading me!"

"And you just crossed the line from irritated to really angry."

"Ya think? And yet you don't stop."

"I can't help it." Her eyes inexplicably filled with tears.

"Here," he said gruffly. "Read this." He leaned across the gear shift, pulled up the parking brake and kissed her.

CLAUDIA'S SENSES SWAM as she leaned in to the kiss. Billy might have thought he was unreadable, but she'd seen the kiss coming a split second before he'd carried through with his intention.

And she'd welcomed it.

That was just crazy; she was mad at Billy. They were having an argument. And yet she'd felt this insane need to connect with him. He'd shown her only a tiny sliver of his true self just then, the self he wanted to protect from her prying eyes, and all at once she'd felt simultaneously guilty and turned on.

She believed very few people had seen what she'd just seen—the real Billy Cantu. And she wanted more.

He reached up to tunnel his fingers through her hair, settling his hand on the back of her head so he could hold her a willing prisoner.

She inhaled sharply as his tongue invaded her mouth. Of course his kiss would not be tentative. Billy didn't have a tentative bone in his body.

Or maybe he did; what the hell did she know? He was a mystery she desperately needed to unravel. How could she feel such a profound attraction to someone she didn't even know?

Though she would have been happy to make out in the front seat of her car for the rest of the morning, Billy gradually pulled away, ending the kiss with a series of gentle nibbles. They separated, but only by an inch or two, and she studied his eyes, trying to figure out his motive here.

Was this a display of dominance? Or had he really wanted to kiss her?

His pupils were dilated. She thought she saw desire there, but maybe she was seeing only what she wanted to see.

"Can you read me now?" he demanded.

"No." The word came out a whisper.

He released her and sat back in his seat, and she almost whimpered at the loss of his touch. "Good. 'Cause you'd probably slap me."

"Are you going to tell me what *that* was about?"

"No. You need to be off balance once in a while. For your own good."

He was wrong about that. She'd spent the first half of her life off center, shuffled into the care of one ambivalent adult after another, never sure if the new place would be a safe haven or a house of horrors.

Off balance wasn't where she cared to be.

And yet...the excitement generated by her uncertainty felt good in a deeply visceral way.

She pulled herself together, straightened her hair, blotted away the smeared lipstick with a tissue and added fresh. Finally she got back to the business of driving, following the instructions of the by-now-impatient GPS.

"Destination on the left," the bland voice informed them as Claudia cruised slowly past.

Theresa Esteve obviously hadn't achieved the level of wealth her sister had. This nameless neighborhood wasn't nearly as grand as Pecan Grove. The small ranch houses had probably been built in the 1960s, and the residents here likely mowed their own grass and trimmed their own bushes.

But there was something wildly askew about Theresa's house. The front window was boarded up with plywood.

Claudia double-checked her Day-Timer. "That's the house, 1642 Baxter Avenue. What do you suppose happened here?" She turned the car around, pulled up to the curb and stopped.

"Stay in the car." Billy manually unlocked his door. "I'll check it out."

Claudia ignored him. "It's a vacant house. I doubt we'll face any gunmen here."

As they approached the front porch, Billy took a detour to examine a flash of yellow he saw on the picket fence that separated the house from the one next door. "Hey, Claudia, look at this. Crime scene tape."

"Oh, my God. This might explain why Theresa won't answer Mary-Francis's calls."

"I'm going to call a buddy of mine that works for the Montgomery County Sheriff's Department. Maybe he can tell us what happened here."

Claudia nodded and sat down on the edge of a brick planter filled with thirsty-looking azaleas. What was going on here? What had started as a simple request from a condemned woman had turned into a crazy scavenger hunt featuring a drug addict, her gun-toting boyfriend and a lost million-dollar coin collection. And now another possible crime victim.

She did not envy Billy his job right now.

Maybe it was time for her to wash her hands of this mess. She had dutifully turned over the information she had to Project Justice. She could write up her final report tonight, including data from both interviews. Once she finished that, the ball was in their court.

Except…except she was still the only person who was sure Mary-Francis didn't kill her husband or know of his current whereabouts. The poor woman had no one to fight for her now. Certainly not her daughter, and now it appeared something had happened to her sister.

Antsy, Claudia stood again. She walked to the driveway, which was empty except for a few oil spots. The garage door had no windows, so she couldn't look to see if there was a car. She ambled to the side of the house, where a short section of weathered wooden privacy fence guarded the backyard. But one of the slats was broken, and she peeked in.

A woman dressed in a bright pink track suit was busy digging around in a parched, overgrown garden. Could that be Theresa? It would explain why no one had answered the door.

"Hello, there!" Claudia called out.

The woman froze, then hightailed it to a back corner of the yard and disappeared through a gate.

Claudia rejoined Billy just as he was finishing his call. "You're not gonna like this."

"What?"

"We're too late to warn Theresa. She was the victim of a home invasion. Someone broke in, roughed her up, then tore the house up, but no one knows what they took because the only person who could tell them—Theresa—is in a coma."

# *CHAPTER FOUR*

"THERE WERE NO PRINTS left behind, no trace evidence at all," Billy continued. "The cops don't have a clue."

Claudia felt sick to her stomach. "When did this happen?"

"A few days ago."

This crime couldn't be unrelated, could it? Theresa's neighborhood wasn't top drawer, but neither was it a hotbed of violent crime.

"There was someone in the backyard just now, digging around in the dirt," she said. "I called out, but whoever it was ran off, scared."

Billy's eyebrows raised in obvious interest. He turned and climbed the stairs to the front porch to have a closer look at the plywood patch covering the window. He pushed on a corner, which gave slightly.

"Billy, that would be breaking and entering."

"No one will care. The police are done with the crime scene. We're just going to look around." With a quick glance left and right to be sure no one was watching, he heaved his shoulder into the plywood.

With a shriek of nails pulling free, the board came loose.

Billy knocked it all the way to the floor inside, then climbed in. "I'll let you in through the front door."

Claudia considered going to sit in her car. An arrest for B & E could jeopardize her entire practice and cause Project Justice considerable embarrassment. But probably no one *would* care if they looked around, and she couldn't contain her own curiosity, so when Billy opened the front door, she stepped across the threshold.

It was like a brick oven inside; Claudia's skin immediately dampened with perspiration. Her dress stuck to her, clinging to her thighs and breasts.

She wasn't sure whether to be grateful or miffed when Billy ignored her, flipping on some lights, first in the entry way, then the living room, and going into search mode.

The place was a wreck—furniture overturned or ripped open, drawers and cabinets emptied. Here and there, black fingerprint powder marred surfaces.

Theresa was obviously a devout woman. Pictures of Jesus, the Virgin Mary and several saints adorned the walls. Over the red plaid sofa hung a huge print of da Vinci's *The Last Supper.* And on the brick hearth was a statue of Jesus as well as an angel, a monk—maybe St. Francis—and a couple of other saints Claudia couldn't identify.

"Whoever did this trashed the place to make it look like a random crime," Billy said. "But I worked in property crimes on the Dallas P.D. for a while. Burglars don't just destroy stuff for the hell of it. They take what they want and leave. This much damage is overkill."

"As if the perpetrator had an emotional connection to the victim?"

"Possibly."

Billy and Claudia quickly checked the rest of the house. Every room had been assaulted and vandalized.

"Let's check out the backyard," Claudia said. "I want to know why that woman was digging around."

"Digging for buried treasure? Maybe she heard something about the missing coins."

In the early summer heat, it wouldn't take long for an unwatered garden to wither and die. The backyard looked as if it had once been lovingly cultivated with flowers and a vegetable patch. Now, most everything was dead or dying. Green had turned to yellow and beige. The tall weeds rattled in the light breeze.

"If Theresa ever comes home," Claudia said, "she'll be horrified by what's happened to her yard." She walked over to where the mystery woman had been turning up the earth. Several large holes had been dug up in one corner of the garden. "I wonder what that woman was looking for?"

Billy squatted down and examined the other plants in the vegetable patch. "Potatoes. And onions."

"How can you tell?"

He gave her a pitying look. "I take it you don't garden."

"I have a landscaping service that does all that. Do you have a garden?"

"Sure. I grow all kinds of stuff in big pots on my patio—tomatoes, peppers, onions, squash. Growing up, if my mom hadn't grown vegetables, we'd have gone hungry. Now I just do it 'cause there's nothing quite like a home-grown tomato."

She never would have pegged him as a gardener. But she was more surprised that he'd shared something from his personal life with her.

"Hey, you!"

Claudia jumped and looked for the source of the voice. The woman in pink, wearing a large brimmed hat and sunglasses, was peering at them over the privacy fence. Unless she was seven feet tall, she was on a ladder.

"You're trespassing!" the woman screeched. "You better not be taking those vegetables."

"No, ma'am," Billy said. "We're with the sheriff's department, doing some follow-up on the crime that took place here. Did anyone talk to you about that?"

He lied with perfect assurance. If Claudia had been called upon to spot his lies, she would have failed miserably.

The woman, though obviously the suspicious type, didn't even ask to see a badge.

"Of course they did," the woman replied indignantly. "I live next door and I know everything that goes on in this neighborhood. We all watch out for each other here."

"Did you see what happened that night?" Billy prompted.

"It was late at night. I was asleep." She dared him to contradict her. "It's all in the statement I gave. Patty Dorsey is my name."

"We saw you stealing Theresa's vegetables," Billy said.

Patty whipped off her sunglasses. Her eyes narrowed dangerously. "Theresa wouldn't want her vegetables to go to waste. We share all the time. I give her peaches from my trees. What did you say your name was?"

"Sergeant Billy Cantu. You wouldn't happen to be digging around because you know something valuable is buried out here, would you?"

She shifted from angry to curious. "What kind of something valuable?"

"Coins, maybe?"

Her eyes widened with surprise and delight. "Her brother-in-law's coins? Theresa told me he'd stolen a pirate's treasure, gold doubloons or some nonsense. I didn't believe it at the time." She surveyed the backyard with new eyes, perhaps seeing something a lot more valuable than a few filched potatoes.

"Don't be digging around here anymore," Billy warned her. "I don't want to bust you for trespassing, but I will."

"Humph."

"If you discover the location of any stolen pirate's treasure, it's your civic duty to turn it over to the police—or become an accessory. Have a nice day, Patty." Billy tipped an imaginary hat and turned to head back inside.

Claudia followed, her heart pounding, until they were safely inside. "Lying to that woman goes against everything I believe in. Isn't it a pretty serious crime, impersonating a police officer?"

"She doesn't suspect. And even if she does, she's too busy thinking about buried treasure to report me. Maybe we'll luck out, and she'll find the coins for us."

"You just like playing games with people's heads." Another thought occurred to her. "You're obviously a skilled investigator, good at teasing information out of people. How come you don't like field work?"

He froze. "How do you know that about me?"

"During your original evaluation. You said you didn't want to work in the field. You told me then you were tired of it. And because Daniel asked me if there was any reason, in my professional opinion, that I thought you weren't fit for active duty, so to speak.

At the time I didn't know you were a lunatic, so I said no, no reason, that you were just ready for a change."

"We almost got our heads blown off today, and you want to know why I don't like field work?"

They ended up back in the living room. Claudia spotted a bloodstain on the carpet, probably from Theresa's assault. Her stomach turned, and their earlier confrontation with a loaded gun barged back into her mind.

What she recalled most clearly was how Billy had again put himself between her and danger.

She wandered back to the fireplace and noticed something she hadn't seen before. Lying on the bricks was a hunk of ceramic material, about the size of a poker chip but curved. It bore a bright blue glaze. She picked it up and studied it.

"Watcha got there?"

"A fragment of something. It doesn't belong to anything in the vicinity."

Billy studied the area where the fragment had lain. "Hey, look at this. There's a spot here on the hearth that's not as dusty as everything else."

Now that she looked more closely, she realized the arrangement of statues was unbalanced. "You think another statue used to be here?"

"Could be." He picked up the statue of St. Francis and flipped it upside down, examining the bottom. He did the same with the angel. "These statues are hollow inside."

"A good place to hide coins?" Claudia ventured.

Billy nodded. "It's an old drug-smuggler trick, hiding stuff inside statues." He thought about it some more. "I like it. But why wouldn't Mary-Francis just tell us that?"

"Maybe she didn't know exactly where her sister put the coins. Or she doesn't trust us. She's still hoping to keep the coins for herself when—if—she gets out of prison."

"And the robbers beat Theresa until she told them where the coins were hidden."

Claudia shivered at the thought of what that poor woman must have gone through—the terror, the pain. "Let's just get out of here, okay?"

"A woman's life is at stake," he reminded her. "We owe it to her to be thorough. Why are you so nervous? You told me you face down violent offenders in your work pretty often, right?" Billy checked the contents of two drawers in the coffee table that had been overlooked.

"That's different. That's in a controlled setting, when I'm squarely on the right side of the law. This is breaking and entering, and I for one don't relish explaining to Daniel how we got ourselves arrested."

Billy didn't seem bothered by their straying into unlawfulness. "Hey, Claudia, check this out." He held up a small white box that she at first thought was a pack of cigarettes or a deck of cards.

Claudia looked longingly toward the front door. "Billy, please."

His face softened, probably sensing her distress. She didn't make any attempt to hide it. "Okay." He tucked the item into his pocket.

Claudia didn't take a full breath until they were back in her car. She started the engine, again turning on the A/C full blast.

"You okay?"

She waved away his concern. "I'm fine, considering I just committed my first felony."

"Misdemeanor trespassing, tops."

"How comforting. What was that thing you found in the drawer?"

"Probably nothing important. It was one of those Flip video cameras. You ready for some lunch?"

How could he act so normal after all they'd been through? After seeing the visceral evidence of a violent crime? Then again, he was a former cop. She knew some homicide cops could literally eat a sandwich while standing over a bloody corpse.

"I could at least use something cold to drink," she said.

She hadn't planned on sharing another meal with Billy. Last time, she'd spotted Tubby's and gotten all sentimental, probably revealing more about herself than she'd intended. But Tubby's did make her think about one of the happier times in her life. At age thirteen she'd been placed in a foster home with another girl close to her age, and they'd become inseparable. One of their hangouts had been Tubby's. Marlene, who'd been pretty and popular, had shared her clothes and makeup and had made sure Claudia was accepted into her "in" group of kids.

For the first time in her life Claudia had felt like an accepted member of a peer group. She had *belonged.*

After about six months, Marlene's real mother had regained custody, and the friendship had ended abruptly—along with Claudia's acceptance. It turned out her "peer group" had only been putting up with Claudia for Marlene's sake.

"You like Mexican food?" Billy asked. "I saw an El Fenix on the way over here."

"Sure, that's fine."

Billy gave her directions, and five minutes later she

was pulling into the parking lot, the lunch crowd thinning out by now.

Once they were seated in the blessedly well air-conditioned restaurant with a basket of chips and hot sauce between them, Billy took the tiny video camera from his pocket.

Claudia couldn't bring herself to order an actual meal, so she requested an iced tea. Billy gave her a disapproving frown, ordered a plate of beef enchiladas, then returned his attention to the camera, fiddling with the buttons.

"Theresa took quite a few movies. Does she have kids, grandkids?" He looked at the screen and grinned. "Aw, cute baby."

"I saw some family photos at the house, so, yes, I'm sure she has children. Mary-Francis said her sister was a widow."

A baby's laughter issued from the camera's tiny speaker. Billy pushed more buttons. "Now we have what looks like a Little League baseball game. And this one…an elderly lady's birthday party and…someone who apparently just got a new car."

"Sounds riveting. Will the Academy of Motion Pictures be calling?"

"Same baby again. This time he's walking." Billy smiled a really sweet, unguarded smile, and her heart swelled. He continually surprised her. Sure, she could tell herself the kiss they'd shared earlier was an isolated incident, that it would never happen again. But the desire she felt for him wasn't going away.

Not until she figured him out.

Claudia was great at coaching her clients on relationship matters, but the fact was, she'd never had a successful romantic relationship, just a few spectacular failures—like Raymond Bass.

He'd been executed last year.

It seemed every man she met had an angle in wanting to date her, and she always figured it out much too easily. If they were interested in sex and nothing else, she always knew it, no matter *what* they told her or how sweet they appeared to be. They were so painfully transparent.

Then there were the ones who wanted free therapy. Pass.

Her abysmal love life was a failing on her part. She couldn't put the blame on anyone else. Because part of her strained to learn every detail about a potential boyfriend so that she could feel safe; then she lost interest when no mystery remained.

Billy's motives for kissing her were impossible to read. He was mysterious…exciting…dangerous…and she ought to be running as far and fast as she could in the opposite direction. Instead, she was intrigued.

"Oh, now here's something interesting."

"What?"

He studied the tiny screen intently for a few moments. "Claudia. I think this is a memorial service for Eduardo."

"Let me see."

He turned the camera partway in her direction, but as they both leaned across the table to look, neither of them could see very well. Without thinking much about it, Claudia slid out of her side of the booth and into his.

Big mistake.

"Start it over." She struggled to make her voice sound calm, as if their contact, from her thighs all the way up to her shoulder, didn't affect her at all, as if her heart hadn't started beating like a drum solo and her insides hadn't clenched up in anticipation of something that would never happen.

Apparently her efforts succeeded. Billy obliged, turning up the volume.

An elderly priest stood informally before a group of people seated in folding chairs. "This is Theresa's house." Claudia recognized the large sofa painting of *The Last Supper.* "I wonder why the service was held there?"

"Because the Torres home was a crime scene?"

"Now we can at least see what the house looked like before the break-in."

The priest talked about Eduardo's sterling qualities, how he gave generously to the church and sponsored a poor village in Mexico—the village where his wife's parents still lived.

"There's something funny about that priest," Claudia said.

"Funny, how?"

"He keeps glancing at the fireplace. He's definitely distracted by something over there. See how he bounces up on his toes?"

"Like a kid who needs to pee," Billy said.

"Or he's nervous. Stimulated somehow, anyway."

"Maybe he thinks Eduardo left the church something in his will," Billy joked.

"I'm serious here."

"Claudia, he's just looking around."

She shook her head and returned her attention to the video. "That's Theresa, there on the front row dressed in black. She was in the courtroom every day."

"Where's Mary-Francis?"

"Already in custody. They arrested her very quickly after she reported her husband missing and they found the blood."

"The older lady next to Theresa is the one from the birthday video," Billy said. "Is that their mother?"

"Eduardo's mother. Mary-Francis's parents are still in Mexico."

"The sisters' families must have been very close."

The camera now panned around the room, taking in all of the mourners, sometimes zooming into a face, sometimes pulling out for a wide-angle shot.

When the camera panned to take in the fireplace, Claudia noted something interesting. "Can you freeze it for a second?"

Billy did.

"Look, there on the hearth."

"Hmm."

There by the fireplace, where they'd seen the blank spot, was a large statue of the Virgin Mary. She stood at least three feet tall and wore a bright blue cloak.

"I don't recall seeing that statue at Theresa's house, do you?"

"No. But it matches that ceramic fragment you found."

Claudia didn't know if the excitement rising up inside her chest was because they'd discovered a clue or due to her proximity to Billy; either way, she needed to move away from him without letting him know how hot and bothered he made her.

The waitress arrived with Billy's meal and gave them a knowing smirk, as if she thought they simply couldn't keep their hands off each other. This was Claudia's cue to slide away and return to her own seat.

"Need anything else?" the waitress asked, her voice rife with innuendo.

"Can you bring an extra plate, *por favor?*" Billy asked.

"Sure thing, sugar."

They were alone again before Claudia realized he intended to share his meal with her. "That's not really necessary." She didn't enjoy sharing a meal. It always called to mind a certain foster home she'd stayed in where there was never enough food. Any time there was "sharing" involved, Claudia usually lost out because she was the smallest.

"You gotta eat. Daniel has a thing about not letting his people go hungry. Food fuels the brain, and we have some serious figuring out to do."

With that, Billy tucked into his enchiladas. Claudia grabbed a tortilla chip from the basket on the table and nibbled at it, and by the time the plate arrived, her appetite was returning. "How's your meal?"

"Not as good as my mama makes, but no one makes an enchilada like Rosa Cantu." Billy scooped one of his enchiladas onto the plate, then added some rice and beans. He gave her exactly half of everything, which she thought exceedingly generous on his part, given he was nearly twice as big as she was. Her heart warmed another degree toward Billy Cantu.

"Thanks," Claudia said. She hadn't thought she was hungry, but she had to admit Billy's choice wasn't half-bad. She surprised herself by polishing off her portion of the meal.

After their table was cleared, Billy again phoned the detective in charge of the Theresa Esteve home invasion case. He put the guy, Sergeant Hudson Vale, on speakerphone.

"My associate and I paid a visit to the crime scene this morning," Billy began. "We have an idea of what the robbers might have stolen."

Claudia cringed at the casual confession, but Sergeant Vale obviously didn't think it odd.

"I'd be grateful for any observations or ideas," Hudson said. "'Cause this case is going nowhere."

"There used to be a big statue of the Virgin Mary sitting by the fireplace. Now it's gone."

"A statue? There was a lot of religious stuff there, I remember. Was it valuable?"

"I only saw it on a video. It just looks like one of those painted chalk statues you see at flea markets and outdoor shrines. I think my mom has a similar one. But here's the deal. We think it might have been stuffed with valuable coins—gold coins. Spanish escudos, recovered from Spanish treasure ships, probably off the Mexican coast."

"I guess I can check around and see if anything like that's been fenced lately, or if anyone tried to sell old Spanish gold."

"Thanks. Think we could get a look at the crime scene photos?"

"Sure, stop by anytime."

They finished up the conversation. Billy collected their bill and paid for their lunch as Claudia pondered what the missing statue might mean. If Eduardo was behind the home invasion, and the robbers had gotten their hands on the coins, they'd never see Eduardo again.

"What's next?" she asked as they got back in the car.

"We talk to Daniel. I'll schedule a meeting for tomorrow morning, if you can make it."

"I'll clear my calendar."

There was no good reason for Claudia to continue her involvement in this case. She'd done her duty, turning her suspicions over to Daniel and convincing Billy there was something here to investigate. But she felt so invested in the case now, she didn't want to turn it loose.

She wanted to find those elusive coins. She wanted to bring the home invaders to justice. She wanted to stop Angie from stealing her father's estate blind. But most of all, she wanted to find Eduardo Torres alive and save Mary-Francis's life.

As a psychologist, Claudia wasn't supposed to get emotionally involved in any client's case. Her skill depended on objectivity and an ability to see the big picture. But like it or not, her emotions were all over this case. Maybe it was because she felt guilty over her part in Mary-Francis's conviction. Maybe it was the gorgeous ex-cop sitting next to her. Either way, she was deliriously happy Billy hadn't shut her out.

When he finally got around to saying, *Okay, little lady, we'll handle things from here,* she would take it hard.

## *CHAPTER FIVE*

"BILLY," DANIEL SAID from the wall-size video screen in the Project Justice conference room, "looks like we're all present and accounted for. The floor is yours."

*Daniel's impatient,* Claudia thought, *maybe because of that muscle spasm on the left side of his neck.* That Daniel blinked and kept tipping his head to the right told Claudia everything she needed to know about his mood. He wanted to get on to something else, possibly an appointment with his masseuse, so anything she could do to speed this meeting along would be a good thing.

Billy had prepared well for the meeting. Dressed in what looked like crisp new jeans and a starched, dark blue shirt, his almost-black hair neatly combed, he gave a brief overview of the case against Mary-Francis, the interview at the prison and the investigation he'd done so far.

Claudia noted that he didn't mention the fact he'd illegally entered Theresa's house, or that he'd bulldozed his way into the Torres home uninvited. He didn't mention Jimmy and the gun, either, no doubt suspecting Daniel would have his head on a pike if he found out Billy had endangered himself and Claudia.

Raleigh Benedict, head of Legal, sat at the mahogany table with them, leaning slightly forward as she jotted notes on her iPhone.

*She's already intrigued.* The slight flaring of her nostrils gave the pretty attorney away.

"You think Eduardo could actually still be alive?" Raleigh asked.

"I followed this case," put in Beth McClelland, who ran the Project Justice evidence lab. "The medical examiner testified that Eduardo couldn't have survived that much blood loss."

*She's skeptical.* That eyebrow lifting up just on one side was as good as a flashing neon sign.

Claudia couldn't help herself; her habit of reading the body language of everyone in the room—everyone she came into contact with—was so deeply ingrained that she found it impossible to turn it off. It wasn't as if reading the people in this room would keep her safe; she had nothing to fear from them. She'd been dealing with them on an almost weekly basis for several years. But she read them anyway.

Mitch Delacroix, the foundation's tech expert and resident computer hacker, sat next to Beth. His body language was always a piece of cake to read: he was lusting for Beth. Claudia had seen the romance building between those two months before anyone else. She hadn't been at all surprised to learn they'd hooked up while working together.

Then there was Billy: impossible to read, as usual. When she studied his body language, she got nothing but a jumble of mixed signals that never failed to frustrate her. He disapproved of the way she used her skills. Did he go out of his way to confuse her, or was this just how he was, in his natural state?

That was one thing that made him different from Raymond. Raymond had projected a false image. Billy seemed to simply be cautious of revealing too much of himself.

Thankfully no one else in the room could read body language the way she could, or they might see something in *her* expression she didn't want revealed. Mitch wasn't the only horny person at the table. Just watching Billy, or listening to him speak, made her think about tangled sheets and sweaty skin on a hot summer night. He made her think about the kind of sex "nice" girls who looked like Claudia didn't have.

She struggled to pull her mind out of the gutter and back to business.

"Beth," Daniel said, "is there any way around the blood evidence?"

Beth pondered the problem for a moment. "Maybe the CSI was sloppy and only tested one portion of the blood stain," she said, "and assumed their results applied to the whole stain."

"But there's an outside chance all that blood wasn't his?" Claudia asked.

Beth nodded. "I suppose so."

Claudia's gaze slid to Billy. There, she caught a microexpression of satisfaction. Did that mean he wanted to pursue this case as badly as she did? If so, he'd changed his mind from that first day.

"Wasn't Eduardo Torres a crime boss or something?" Mitch asked.

"He was alleged to be some kind of kingpin in the Rio Grande Mafia drug cartel," Claudia said. "He could easily have been a murder target. Someone could have shot Eduardo in his bed then buried the body where no one would ever find it. No body, no murder charge. If Mary-Francis is innocent, that's the most likely scenario."

"Is that what you believe?" Daniel asked.

"The one thing I'm certain of is that Mary-Francis didn't kill her husband. I suspected so before, but now that I've interviewed her again, and with this business of valuable coins and the assault on Theresa..."

"We only have her word that her daughter didn't previously know about the coins," Beth observed.

"Maybe. But something is seriously out of whack," Billy said. "To use the technical term."

Everyone in the conference room looked at the video screen, which made it almost appear as if Daniel was in the room with them.

He made his decision quickly. "Raleigh, Mary-Francis has already signed the necessary papers to make you her attorney of record, correct?"

"Yes, that's all taken care of," Raleigh replied.

"Good. Request an immediate review of all physical evidence. Beth, see what you can find out about how the blood evidence was collected and analyzed on that case."

"Okay. I have a friend I can call at the Montgomery County lab. She'll give me the unofficial lowdown even before I get my hands on the evidence."

"Good. Mitch, try to find Eduardo. If not him, then his associates."

"I have a list of his friends, relatives and employees." Claudia dug into her briefcase to find the piece of paper Mary-Francis had given her at the end of their visit.

Everyone started gathering their belongings, eager to get to work. The meeting was over.

Claudia should have felt elated, or at least pleased, but instead she felt a slight letdown, like someone had just stuck a pin in the balloon that lived inside her chest.

She glanced at Billy, hoping he would seek her out. Hoping he would want her to continue investigating with him. She could play the body-language card, insist that her skills could help him sort fact from fiction as he worked in the field.

But since Billy didn't believe in her "voodoo," as he called it, her argument wouldn't carry much weight.

"Claudia, I'd like to talk to you privately, please."

Claudia jerked her attention back to the video screen. Apparently Daniel wasn't finished with her yet. Alarm bells went off in her head. What was this about? Had he seen something, something in the way she dealt with Billy, that he didn't like? Next to her, Daniel was the most observant person she knew. Having successfully proved his innocence after spending six years on death row, he knew a lot about human nature.

But he wasn't opposed to office romance, so if he suspected some chemistry growing between her and Billy, he wouldn't care.

She would know soon enough.

Once the room cleared, Claudia smiled at Daniel. "Now, what's this all about?"

"Billy seem okay to you?"

"Okay, how?"

"Does he seem comfortable working in the field? Is he making appropriate decisions?"

Her answer should have been a flat-out no. Twice in one day he had committed illegal acts in the name of getting at the truth. But Daniel wasn't exactly a choir boy himself, so his definition of *appropriate* might be different from hers.

"I feel uncomfortable discussing Billy behind his back this way," she said.

"It's important. If I've pushed him out the door before he's ready, the consequences will be on my conscience. Does he seem unduly stressed?"

Daniel's reasoning seemed sound, so she answered truthfully. "No, not at all. He seems to be enjoying himself."

"Good. Just the same, can you keep an eye on him?"

Claudia laughed, until she realized Daniel was serious. "You want me to babysit Billy?"

"You're already part of the investigation. And unless I miss my guess, you'd like to continue. Billy isn't the only one enjoying himself."

*Busted.* "I'm not sure Billy will want me around, cramping his style."

"I'll tell him it's my idea. I feel it's important to have a second set of eyes looking out for liars, since there's a lot of deception surrounding this case. That's the truth, by the way. But you already knew that." He grinned.

"I'll see what I can do. Why is he so reticent to work in the field? When he told me he was tired of chasing down bad guys and getting shot at, I believed him. But now I'm not so sure."

"I'm not at liberty to say." With that, the video screen went blank, as if Daniel was afraid he might give away secrets if he remained face-to-face with her for too long.

"I HOPE YOU DON'T MIND my tagging along," Claudia said as she climbed into Billy's truck later that day. She'd spent the rest of the morning and early afternoon squeezing in a few patients, the ones who really needed her. Others, she had rescheduled, clearing her calendar to work with Billy.

"I'm gettin' used to having a sidekick," he drawled. "But even if I objected, Daniel wants you here. Why is that, do you suppose?"

She didn't answer right away as she fumbled with the seat belt and silently cursed the two men who were putting her in the middle of their machinations. She couldn't tell some things to Daniel because she didn't feel it was her place. Billy wasn't her patient, but he trusted her on some level, or he wouldn't have opened up even a little. And she couldn't tell Billy of her conversation with Daniel, because Daniel was her client, to whom she owed confidentiality.

"Daniel said he thought my expertise would be of value, since clearly a lot of people are lying," she finally said.

"People are always lying, on all of the cases the foundation takes on," he countered as he whipped out of the parking lot. "You know what I think?"

"I'm sure you'll enlighten me."

"I think Daniel wants to hire you on full-time. None of this retainer B.S. He thinks by giving you a taste of how we work, and what your day-to-day job would be like, you'll be more interested."

She was relieved Billy hadn't guessed the real reason for her presence. But what if he was right? What if Daniel had overstated his concern for Billy, and his real motivation was to get her onboard at Project Justice full-time?

Considering motive was one of the things she was trained to do, and she couldn't help look at all the possibilities.

"I'm not sure I'd want to give up my private practice," Claudia said. "I like helping people, one-on-one. When you help a client through a crisis, and you mark their progress and see them come out on the other side, it's very rewarding."

"Yeah, but it's also rewarding to get people out of prison who don't belong there. Save their lives, sometimes."

"Is that what you like about the work? The end result?" She was far more comfortable turning the conversation back on him.

But he spotted her trick too easily. "Nah-ah, none of that what-do-*you*-think garbage. We were talking about you."

"I'm content with the status quo. I like being on retainer, but I also like running my own business. I don't want to be an employee."

"Daniel treats his employees really well."

"I'm sure he does. He seems to attract and keep some brilliant, capable people."

"With me being the exception." He said this with a good-natured laugh. "That's what you said the other day. I'm an idiot 'cause I'm not a disciple of your body-language—"

"Do not call my work voodoo again."

"I was gonna say *theories.* Don't get all bent out of shape."

"They're not just theories," she huffed under her breath. But the twinkle in his dark brown eyes soothed the irritation she wanted to feel. He was deliberately teasing her. "You know, teasing is a sign of affection. Among junior-high boys, anyway."

"Now you're saying I'm socially stunted."

"I was saying you secretly like me, or you wouldn't give me so much grief."

He didn't deny it, which pleased her no end. She couldn't remember the last time any man challenged her the way Billy did. Even Raymond hadn't really challenged her. He'd said what she wanted to hear; he'd played the part of the perfect boyfriend at a stressful time in her life.

Billy had rolled his sleeves up in deference to the heat. He wore his shoulder holster, his gun tucked under his left arm, but he'd laid his jacket in the back-seat.

Her hands itched to touch Billy's tanned biceps, to connect somehow on a physical level to let him know she was teasing, too. She didn't think he was dumb. Or socially stunted. He was at least smart enough to get the best of her.

They were headed to the sheriff's office in Conroe, the Montgomery County seat, on the northern edge of the Houston metroplex. Sergeant Hudson Vale wanted to meet with them; he had quickly run out of leads on the Theresa Esteve case, and he was hoping Project Justice's investigation might reinvigorate his own.

The mention of valuable coins had piqued his interest, too.

The criminal justice center was north of town in a flat, featureless, semirural area with clumps of trees here and there, but mostly parched pastures. The one-story white building didn't call attention to itself. Its one redeeming feature was a parking lot with plenty of spaces.

Hudson Vale met them at the front desk. If Claudia had seen him anywhere besides the sheriff's office, she would have pegged him as a California surfer boy rather than a seasoned detective. He wore his sun-bleached blond hair a little longer than regulation, and the tails of his loud Hawaiian-print shirt were untucked and paired with a disreputable pair of khakis.

"Sorry for the ultracasual look," he said after the formalities. "Just got back from doing a little undercover sting operation."

In an unusually unguarded moment, Billy's eyes lit with interest. "Narcotics?"

Hudson shook his head. "Vice. Personally I hate working on stuff like that, but when the working girls start getting too thick downtown..." He shrugged. "I drew the short stick, had to play bumbling college boy looking for a good time."

The working girls probably flocked to get a shot at him.

"Anyway, come on back. I'm happy to show you what I have if you can come up with fresh ideas."

Hudson's office was a cubicle in the detective division. Large by cubicle standards, there was room for an L-shaped desk, credenza and three chairs. He indicated they should sit down, then offered them cold drinks from a dorm fridge in the corner.

"Handy," Billy commented as he popped the top on an orange soda. Claudia already had her own bottle of water.

"Makes my office real popular on a hot afternoon," Hudson said with a smile. "For whatever reason, the staff break room and vending machines are all the way on the other side of the building. Since I have an incurable Mountain Dew habit, I worked out this system." He opened a bottle of his beverage of choice and took his own chair. "Here's the file on the Esteve case." He pointed to a pitifully thin folder at the end of his desk. "Have a look, if you like."

"Thanks." Billy started reading the incident report,

but Claudia couldn't resist the crime scene photos. Although most police departments had gone to digital photos, they almost always made prints right away as a more permanent, tangible way to store evidence. Digital pictures could be tampered with, altered or erased, by accident or on purpose.

The crime scene looked much messier than when Billy and Claudia had visited two days ago. The floor was covered with stuff that had been swept off tables and shelves. Furniture was knocked over, pictures ripped from the walls. Someone had obviously come in and cleaned up after the cops got done.

The cops wouldn't have tidied up. Nor had a professional service, or they would have done something about the bloodstain on the carpet.

"Where are Theresa's children?" Claudia asked.

"She has just the one son, divorced and living in Arizona. He came for a couple of days when notified of his mother's situation, but he had to get back—kids, a job, you know."

"Could he have tried to have her killed for the inheritance?" Billy asked.

"I pretty much ruled that out. Theresa doesn't have much, and the son isn't doing bad financially. Plus, this didn't appear to be the work of professional killers, unless they were particularly inept."

"You keep referring to 'them' and 'they,'" Claudia noted. "Why do you think there was more than one perpetrator?"

"No fingerprints or DNA, that's for sure. But two sets of shoe prints in the mud below the broken window."

"Shoe prints?"

"Unfortunately not enough detail to even determine

what kind of shoe. Just enough to get an approximate size. One guy was size thirteen; the other about a ten and very wide. That is the sum total of our physical evidence."

"At least you know it was two males. That rules out the niece, although her boyfriend could have gotten a buddy to help him do the deed. Angie and Jimmy are selling off everything that's not nailed down. Maybe Theresa was getting in the way of that profitable enterprise."

Nothing Claudia said seemed to surprise Hudson. He was on top of things. "You mean because her aunt has power of attorney over her mother's affairs? I questioned Angie and her boyfriend. Nothing stuck. They both have alibis, and I didn't get a sense either of them was lying. Plus, neither has the financial resources to hire someone to do the deed."

"Maybe Angie promised cash after the fact," Claudia said. "She did sell her mother's car."

"I'm on it. She deposited the check into her account and didn't make any large withdrawals. Instead, she makes small withdrawals from the ATM every couple of days."

"She could be withholding payment because her aunt isn't dead," Billy suggested. "The job wasn't properly done."

"Honestly? I'm not seeing Angie as the guilty party here. She seemed genuinely shocked when told of the break-in. Cried real tears."

"Any other suspects?" Billy asked.

"No one."

"What about the neighbor? Patty Dorsey?"

Hudson rolled his eyes. "The neighbor from hell, apparently. Everyone on the street loathes her. Gladys

Kravitz on steroids. She claims to 'mind her own business' one minute, and to know everything going on in the neighborhood the next. She's the one who called in the crime. Saw her neighbor's broken front window, went to investigate and found Theresa lying there. She probably saved Theresa's life, so I'm not liking her for a suspect."

"Unless they argued. Things got out of hand. Patty bashes Theresa with a lamp or something, did more damage than she meant to, so she calls the cops. Stages a home invasion."

"The crime scene does look staged to me," Claudia said as she continued to study the photos.

"Patty didn't make those footprints," Hudson reminded them. "Whoever did this came in through that window. Left a bit of mud on the sill and the carpet."

Billy deflated right along with his theory.

"So tell me about the coins," Hudson said.

While Billy recounted their interview with Mary-Francis, their conversation with Angie and their theory about the coins being hidden inside a statue of the Virgin Mary, Claudia continued to study the photos with her most critical eye, hoping to see something others had overlooked.

When she finally saw it, it was so obvious she laughed out loud. How could she have not noticed immediately?

"Claudia?" Billy looked over, curious.

She handed one of the photos to Billy. "Take a look at the mantel. What do you see?"

"Holy cow."

"What?" Hudson sounded anxious.

"The Virgin Mary statue. It's still here, in the crime scene photos. The home invaders didn't take it."

## *CHAPTER SIX*

HUDSON TOOK THE PHOTO and studied it. "Oh, yeah, I remember that now. I didn't pay any attention to it, beyond looking at it briefly to see if it was the assault weapon. It did seem heavier than the others, but at the time that fact didn't register as odd."

"So your people didn't collect it as evidence?"

"We collected a few things for possible DNA and fingerprints, none of which panned out. But not that statue."

"Then where did the statue go? Who had access after you guys finished with it?"

Hudson thought for a moment. "The son. He's not good for the assault, but I guess he could have taken the statue after we released the crime scene. Then there's Patty, the neighbor. She had a key. I assume she let you in."

Billy reached up and tugged his collar, which wasn't tight to begin with since he didn't wear a tie. "We, um, let ourselves in."

Claudia gave him points for honesty.

Hudson laughed. "You're lucky nosy Patty didn't call the cops on you."

"We almost called the cops on her," Claudia put in. "She was digging around in the backyard when we arrived, and when I called to her she ran like she had something to hide."

Hudson's eyes widened with obvious interest. "Maybe I'll question her again."

"If you do," Billy said, "she thinks we're cops."

Hudson laughed again. "You got a set of big brass ones, I'll give you that." Then he seemed to remember Claudia was there. "Not you, of course."

Claudia shrugged. "I'd walk funny if I did."

Hudson looked at his watch. "You guys want to go grab a bite?"

Claudia was about to say she'd love to when Billy abruptly stood. "I think we better get going, but thanks. Maybe we can catch a game, tip a few. Sometime." The invitation was so imprecise, it sounded like a brush-off to her.

Hudson didn't see it that way. "It's July Fourth weekend on Lake Conroe. You guys like to water-ski?"

"Sure," Claudia said, being agreeable. She'd never tried water-skiing, but since it was something affluent people did—people with boats and lake houses—she pretended to know something about it.

It was a habit with her, but one she really ought to break. She had a spotless professional reputation to rely on now; she didn't need for people to think she came from the "right" sort of background.

They shook hands all around and exchanged cards, then Billy and Claudia left. She knew she should probably leave it alone, but she couldn't resist asking. "Why were you in such a hurry to leave? It's well after lunchtime, and I'm hungry."

"I just want to keep working, that's all. And what is it with you and food? For an extremely slender woman, you eat a lot."

"Well, excuse me. I like food, and you're the one who said we have to keep our bodies and brains fueled, blah blah blah." Something about Billy's manner bugged her. "You don't like Hudson?"

"I like him okay. Do *you* like him?"

"I don't really know him well enough to form an opinion."

"Oh, come on. As a psychologist, you know people form opinions about other people the second they meet. He must have made an impression on you."

"Fair enough. From what I saw, yes, I liked him. He's friendly, has a sense of humor, seemed willing to share information with us, unlike some of the cops I've encountered who get very territorial about their investigations. He seems to genuinely care about the victim, and he wants to see justice done."

"And he's good-looking, right?"

"Very. But a little young for me." Or at least young-looking. "What does that have to do with anything? I try not to let people's looks bias my opinion of their character."

"I thought maybe I saw a little spark there. Hudson was flirting with you."

She looked at him as if he'd just announced the Rapture was imminent. "Flirting?"

Billy shrugged one shoulder in a deliberately unconvincing manner. "Looked that way to me."

"So what if he was? Maybe I wanted to have lunch with him, and you hustled us out of there like you thought the place was sprinkled with anthrax."

Billy slammed on the brakes hard enough to make Claudia's shoulder harness catch and jerk her back. "I can take you back if you want. I'm sure Vale would give you a ride back to the office. If you'd rather waste time on a leisurely lunch than help prove Mary-Francis's innocence—"

"Now you're just being silly. Step on the gas, please, there's a line forming behind you."

He eased the car forward, gripping the steering wheel hard enough that his knuckles turned white.

"You are acting really weird."

Billy loosened his death grip and took a deep breath, obviously trying to shake off whatever had made him mad. "You're right. Being around Vale—I guess it brought up a few memories that aren't so pleasant."

"How do you know Hudson?"

"We worked together on a joint investigation several years ago. Drugs were coming through Houston to a dealer in Conroe, then sliding through the pipeline straight to Dallas."

"Sounds like you didn't really like working Narcotics, if just the reminder of it can put you on edge."

He shook his head. "Let's just drop it, okay?"

"It might help you to talk about—"

"No head-shrinking allowed, remember?"

"Have you ever been to therapy?"

"Yes. Been there, done that, all better. And if I did need a shrink, it wouldn't be you."

Claudia leaned back in her seat, hurt. She was surprised how much his insult stung, like steel wool on a sunburn. "I know you don't have much faith in the body-language thing, but I hadn't realized you think I'm a complete incompetent."

"No, Claudia, that's not it. I wasn't trying to dis you. I just don't want that kind of relationship with you."

The question begged to be asked: What kind of relationship *did* he want? She was too chicken to ask out loud.

"I could fix you and Vale up, if you're interested."

They were back to that? "No, thanks. I'll solicit my own dates."

"Do you?"

"Do I what?"

"Date."

"Sometimes." She squirmed in her seat and adjusted the visor to block the sun from her eyes. Probing other people's personal lives was endlessly fascinating to her, but she didn't like it when the tables were turned.

Still, she stuck with the conversation out of blatant curiosity. Where was he going with this?

"Are you involved with anyone now?" he asked.

"No. Are you?" She'd already figured out he wasn't, because there'd been no signs of a wife or girlfriend—no phone calls, no references to a particular woman, nothing calling him home at the end of the day. Unless he was one of those guys who so severely compartmentalized his life that he could lock a woman out of even his thoughts while he was working.

"No one special. So why not Vale? It wouldn't have to be a fix up. A group of us could get together to watch baseball—"

"I'm not interested in Hudson Vale." Then, feeling she needed to justify herself, she added, "He's not my type."

"You don't date cops?"

"I have nothing against cops."

"Who's your type, then?"

She had no idea. So far, no particular "type" had ever worked out for her. Maybe her type was bossy, Hispanic ex-cops who drove big pickup trucks and had an uncanny ability to hide secrets from her.

"I don't have a type."

"Then why not—"

"I'm not going out with Hudson Vale. Even if he was interested, which he wasn't."

"How do you know?"

"I can always tell when men are interested in me. It's child's play for someone with my training."

He latched on to a single word. "Always?"

The air hung heavy with that word, but finally she responded. "Maybe not always."

"So Vale is out?"

She sighed with exasperation. "He is awful cute. And we only just met. Maybe I should give it a shot. When's the next baseball game? We could invite a group to that bar you guys like—Pacifica, I think it's called?"

"We have work to do." He was suddenly cranky again.

"Oh, my God." She should have seen it before.

"What?"

"You're jealous."

"That's ridiculous. Why would I be jealous of Hudson Vale? I got a better job at twice the pay, and I'm better lookin'..." He glanced over to see if she knew he was kidding.

She refused to let him defuse the situation with humor. "You're jealous because he paid attention to me. You think because you and I shared one kiss you have some kind of hold on me—"

"Whoa, whoa, whoa." He pulled into a strip mall parking lot, found the only spot in the shade, turned off the engine and opened the windows. "For the record, I don't harbor any illusions that I have rights to you because we locked lips. Once. And for the record...yeah, maybe I'm jealous. He flirted like that with my partner in Dallas, and she flirted back, and…and I didn't like it, that's all."

"Oh. I'm sorry, that must have been uncomfortable."

"Don't feed me therapy dialogue, okay? Nothing ever came of it because Vale wasn't seriously interested. But it just gets in my craw that your type is always interested in his—"

"Excuse me? My *type?* What type is that, Billy?"

"You know…"

"Enlighten me."

"Rich. Educated. Sophisticated."

How ironic that all the qualities she'd strived for her whole life, the image she'd struggled to project, was the very thing driving a wedge between her and a man she was starting to care for. "You're making some pretty big assumptions about me."

"Yeah?"

"I'll give you educated, because I have a PhD. But rich? I'm still paying off student loans. My condo is mortgaged to the hilt and my car isn't paid for. As for sophisticated…it's a facade. I buy my clothes at outlet stores, my designer purse is a fake, I can't tell a good French Bordeaux from Ripple, and I've never set foot outside the United States.

"Even my accent is fake." She'd quickly realized her Texas twang marked her as a hick when she'd started college at Dartmouth, and in no time she'd picked up a Boston accent. "And the blond hair? Straight out of a bottle. Although my skin is on the fair side, I think my father might have been Puerto Rican, just from little things my mom would say when she was drunk, but I never laid eyes on him, so I don't know."

She'd clearly surprised him. He studied her as if she'd sprouted scales and cloven hooves.

Claudia shrugged. “Now you know. So don’t presume things about me again, okay? And how about some air-conditioning?” She deliberately returned to the accent she’d had in childhood, so he’d know she wasn’t making things up. “I’m feeling ’bout as parched as a toad on a brick patio in August.”

BILLY FELT AS IF HE’D BEEN hit in the head with a brick bat. He turned on the engine, ran up the windows and turned the A/C back on, as requested, then eased out of the parking space and resumed their journey home.

Neither of them said anything for a long time.

Apparently Claudia wasn’t at all what he’d believed. The “cool blonde” was as fake as her knockoff handbag.

It should have turned him off. But oddly, he was even more drawn to her. What disadvantages must she have overcome? No father, drunk mother, clearly not rich, if she had all that debt.

He wanted to ask Claudia questions. Where had she grown up? Where was her mother now? How had she managed an Ivy League education if she grew up poor? And what was her natural hair color?

Most important, why did she feel it was important to disguise who she really was?

Of course, the outer trappings weren’t what made her an extraordinary human being. Her intelligence, her compassion, her work ethic—those were the qualities that truly attracted him, he realized with a start. The superficial crush based on blond hair and long legs had evolved into something much deeper, richer.

And that kiss…

She didn’t want to talk about the kiss. Maybe she was embarrassed that she’d made out with a poor boy from the barrio. That would make sense, since she tried to hide everything else that might cause others to mark her as low class.

He finally decided he needed to say something. "I'm sorry, Claudia. For that whole business with Hudson, for the assumptions, everything." Maybe even the kiss.

"You don't have to apologize. I deliberately mislead people. If others make incorrect assumptions, I have only myself to blame."

"Why do you do it? Are you afraid people wouldn't like the real Claudia? Claudia is your real name, right?"

She grinned at him. "Now who's sounding like a therapist? I think we've played enough true confessions for one day. Let's give it a rest, huh?"

He didn't blame her. The more she revealed of herself, the more she would expect him to reciprocate. She was still a shrink, and she still wanted to get inside his head, a place he didn't invite guests.

She would wait a long time for him to spill his guts. He'd already told her about Sheila's crush on Vale, which was more than he normally told anyone. Especially about Sheila.

"You still hungry?" he asked.

"I thought we didn't have time to eat."

"You know I just said that because I didn't want you to eat lunch with Vale. Yeah, maybe I'm jealous."

He couldn't be sure, but he thought she'd started to smile just then. "I'm starving," she said. "I could go for some ribs."

"There's a Smokestack Barbecue close to the office. Ever been there?"

"Nope. Let's go for it."

TELLING THE TRUTH TO Billy was like taking off a tight pair of shoes that pinched her toes. For the first time in years, Claudia felt free to be herself. She didn't have to ruthlessly squelch her Texas drawl or pretend a "classiness" that wasn't native to her.

And she could dig into a big plate of barbecued ribs, something she hadn't done since she was a kid in foster care. And this time, she wouldn't have to growl like a jungle cat to get even one rib. When Billy suggested they share a rack of baby backs, she actually admitted she wanted her own.

Instead of being horrified by her indelicate appetite, he laughed and told her to order whatever she wanted. He ended up with a pulled pork sandwich.

She gnawed on those ribs like a true Texan, and she even licked her fingers, all the while knowing Billy was watching her—not with revulsion, but with a quiet amusement he didn't attempt to hide.

"I never would have pegged you as a rib girl," he said as she ripped off another rib to gnaw on.

"I like stuffed jalapeno peppers, too. I guess when I decide to let it all hang out, I do a bang-up job of it. Disappointed?"

"Of course not. I'm actually touched that you trust me enough to just be yourself."

"You're not going to tell everybody, are you?" Daniel knew of her humble background, and she imagined Mitch Delacroix did, too, since he was probably the one who'd done the extensive background check Daniel required of anyone who did work for Project Justice.

"My lips are sealed. For a price." He waggled one eyebrow at her suggestively, and she had just enough time to squelch the frisson of desire that swept up her body before Beth McClelland swooped down on their table and grabbed a chair.

"Hey, Billy, I thought I might find you here." Beth nodded toward Claudia as she swiped a cold French fry from Billy. "Good to see you again, Claudia."

"Nice to see you, too." Claudia liked Beth. She had an irrepressible optimism about her, reflected in her brightly colored, slightly eccentric clothing, her wild, curly brown hair and a ready smile. Beth was also painfully easy to read. She had almost no ability to hide her feelings and probably had never lied successfully in her life.

"Were you looking for me?" Billy asked.

"I was." Beth grabbed an abandoned menu from an adjacent table and quickly perused it. "But I figured I'd just join you for lunch, since I was hungry. I have good news. Or at least, interesting news. Unless..." She looked back and forth between Billy and Claudia. "Unless I'm interrupting something?"

"No, not at all," Billy answered, running right over Claudia's weaker objection. Now that she and Billy weren't arguing, she'd been enjoying her alone time with him. Probably far more than was healthy.

A waiter stopped by their table, and Beth ordered a barbecued chicken sandwich with coleslaw. Her order seemed positively dietetic compared to Claudia's big ol' slab of ribs, which she'd come close to finishing.

"So, spill it," Billy said. "What's the news?"

"My buddy in Montgomery County did an end run for me and couriered over a box of evidence from the Torres case. I dived right in, started running tests on the bloody mattress cover. Besides getting a DNA profile, I tested it for everything I could think of."

Claudia pushed her plate away. "I'm done." No

matter how long she worked with Project Justice, she would never get used to their casual discussion of murder scenes. Bugs and bodily fluid didn't go well with meals, in her opinion. She wiped her hands on a moist towelette provided by the restaurant.

"That was really fast," Billy said. "And...?"

"It's Eduardo's blood, all right. No wiggle room there. But here's the interesting thing. The blood contained sodium citrate, an anticoagulant."

"So he was taking heart medicine or something?" Claudia asked, drawn into the discussion despite herself.

"Sodium citrate is used to preserve blood in test tubes and other vessels outside the body. It would never appear in blood in its natural state." She waited, and it took a few seconds for the implications to sink in.

Claudia slapped a hand over her mouth to keep from shrieking in shock.

"Oh, my God," Billy said. "Eduardo faked his own death."

## *CHAPTER SEVEN*

BILLY'S VOICE WAS TINGED with amazement. "He stockpiled some of his own blood over some extended period of time, enough to convince a medical examiner that he couldn't have survived."

"Angie worked in a medical office," Claudia said. "She could have drawn his blood, or stolen the equipment he would need to do it. The anticoagulants were necessary to keep the blood from spoiling before he could use it."

Billy was nodding. "Then he dumped it in the bed to frame his own wife, let it dry, put the sheets back on so Mary-Francis wouldn't notice."

"Why didn't the police crime lab find the anticoagulants?" Claudia asked.

"It's not something they would normally test for," Beth explained. "They probably didn't do a tox screen. They went straight to DNA."

"That Eduardo is one sick bastard," Claudia couldn't help saying. The man sounded depraved, and given the hordes of mentally unstable people she'd encountered over the years, that was saying something.

"He needed to disappear to avoid a pending murder charge," Billy said. "But he couldn't stand the thought of letting Mary-Francis have all of their accumulated wealth, not when they'd been heading for divorce. So he figured out a way to prevent her from benefiting from his supposed death."

"Why wouldn't he just syphon off all of their assets and disappear to some country that doesn't have an extradition treaty with the U.S.?" Claudia asked.

Billy shrugged. "Sending his wife to death row was the ultimate revenge, I guess. We might never know his motive, but it doesn't matter. This constitutes a strong suggestion that Eduardo is still alive. This should be enough to reopen Mary-Francis's case. I'll schedule an appointment with the Montgomery County D.A."

"When?" Claudia asked. "Can I come?"

Billy seemed a little surprised by her eagerness. "I'll meet with him as soon as he can see me. But I thought I'd probably take Beth, since she's the one who can talk at length about the blood analysis. And I don't want to overwhelm the guy with a mob in his office."

"Of course," Claudia said quickly. "I guess I'm a little overanxious. I've consulted on several cases for you guys that have resulted in overturned convictions, but I've never been this invested in a case before. It's exciting. I'm beginning to understand why you all love your jobs so much."

"It's rewarding work," Beth agreed. "Have you ever thought about working at Project Justice full-time?"

Hmm, that was the second time today she'd been asked that very question. "Did Daniel tell you to ask me that?"

"What?" Beth looked surprised and confused. "No. But I think he would like the idea of having a psychologist on staff, especially if it was you. I mean, you've been very accommodating with your schedule, but if you were there all the time… Sorry, I get carried away."

"No, that's okay. I'm flattered. Maybe I should talk to Daniel about it."

Beth wasn't lying, that was for sure. Which meant Claudia was being paranoid about Daniel trying to manipulate her. She wished she could be more trusting, especially with people she'd known for years and had no reason to distrust.

Claudia excused herself to the ladies' room. When she returned, their party had grown again. Mitch Delacroix had joined them, and he and Beth—who were so in love they would use any excuse to get closer—were squeezed into one side of their booth.

Claudia slid in next to Billy, but she hovered at the edge of her seat, leery of sitting too close to him. Even a healthy distance away she could feel his body heat radiating toward her.

"Hey, Mitch."

"Hey, Claudia. I was just telling Billy about my search for Eduardo."

"And…"

"Unfortunately, I've turned up almost nothing. If this guy is alive, he's good. His Social Security number hasn't turned up anywhere. He's made no attempt to access any bank accounts or retirement funds. He hasn't used any credit cards. He hasn't used his cell phone."

"It's gotta be tough," Mitch said. "For a man of his standing, used to living at a certain level, it must be hard not to touch his own assets."

"His personal assets are frozen," Billy said. "Until his estate is settled. Maybe he *can't* touch anything."

"He hasn't tried. I've checked into the financial activities of all his known associates, including his most trusted men. I've talked to some of them. They think he's dead. They honestly believe it. It appears that the Rio Grande Mafia is falling apart without his leadership."

"He's probably been living on funds from his illicit activities," Claudia said. "But as those ran out, maybe he became more desperate to find the coins. Which would explain Angie's sudden interest in locating them."

"Coins?" Beth and Mitch asked at the same time.

Billy explained about the missing coin collection.

"Why don't you let me take a crack at Eduardo's buddies," Claudia suggested. "I can tell whether they're hiding something or not."

"That's not necessary," Billy said quickly. "The blood analysis will be enough to prove Eduardo is alive. Or at least that he didn't die the way everyone thought he did."

Mitch, who had stolen half of Beth's sandwich, stopped midbite. "Look, Billy, I know you don't believe in…that is, I know you're, um, skeptical—"

Beth had apparently kicked him under the table. She glanced over with disapproval evident on her face.

"It's okay," Claudia said. "I know Billy doesn't have a lot of faith in my abilities."

"That's not the point," Billy said. "I just don't want to waste Claudia's time. She's already shuffled around a lot of her patients to help us."

She was about to say that it was no imposition, but the implacable look on Billy's face stopped her. This was his case, he didn't want her talking to Eduardo's associates, and nothing was going to change his mind. Why butt heads with him over it?

She'd thought he was starting to come around regarding her skills, but apparently she'd been wrong.

"I better get going," Claudia said, hopping out of the booth. "I have appointments this afternoon. Billy, do let me know what the D.A. says."

"Of course."

Over Billy's objections Claudia left some cash to pay for her meal—the foundation had picked up a number of her meals already, and she felt she ought to do her share. With a faux cheerful goodbye to Beth and Mitch, she got out of there.

Just when she was starting to think she had a grip on Billy, she realized she didn't. Really, it was time for her to back off. For good this time.

Even if Daniel really was amenable to her working full-time at Project Justice, she wasn't interested. Seeing Billy every day would send her right to the nearest asylum.

"IS SOMETHING GOING ON with you two?" Beth asked innocently after Claudia had left the restaurant.

"Beth," Mitch said in a warning voice. "That's none of our business."

"No, there's nothing going on," Billy answered in a way that would guarantee they'd buy it. And it wasn't too far from the truth—unless you counted one mind-blowing kiss.

Beth pushed the last bit of coleslaw around with her fork. "She just seemed a little flustered, or huffy, or something when she left."

"Yeah, because Big-mouth here had to bring up the fact that I have no faith in her life's work." Billy made it sound as though he didn't really care one way or another if Claudia was offended.

"Do you really think it's a bunch of bull?" Beth asked.

Billy shrugged. "I'll admit she's pretty good at analyzing what someone says and figuring out motivations. And *maybe* she can spot a lie. Sometimes. But the whole thing with microexpressions, and that it means something if someone folds their arms or scratches their head—I mean, maybe they're just cold, or they have an itch. I'm surprised any jury buys her song and dance."

Billy was overstating his skepticism. He'd actually started to develop a grudging respect for Claudia's cagey interrogation skills, which even he could admit got results when his strong-arm tactics might not.

But he didn't want Mitch and Beth to think he'd gone soft in the head.

"You don't believe in the whole body language thing, do you, Beth? You're a scientist. Don't you think what she does is junk science?"

"No, not at all," Beth said. "I've reviewed the research on microexpressions and all that goes with it. It's the real deal, and so is she."

"Huh. But it doesn't compare to, say, DNA, does it?"

"Nothing compares to DNA," Beth admitted. "That's the gold standard."

"Well, then." Billy acted as if he'd scored a point in their discussion. "She's certainly not proved herself reading me. She's way off."

"Really?" Mitch said. "I'd think reading you would be easy. Anyone can see you've got the hots for her."

"You've got sex on the brain," Billy said with a laugh, though inside he felt the first stirrings of panic. Of course he had the hots for Claudia, but *no one* should have been able to spot it.

"No, Mitch is right," Beth said. "I saw how you

looked at her when she left for the ladies' room. Like you wanted to devour her and protect her from the whole world, all at the same time."

*Good God.* If even Beth could read his thoughts, he was terminally messed up. The skills he'd developed during years as an undercover operative—the skills that had kept him safe, kept him alive—were slipping. All because one cool-but-vulnerable blonde had gotten under his skin and wouldn't let go.

BILLY GOT THE CALL AT 6:00 a.m., before he'd even stumbled out of bed toward the coffeepot. "Billy, it's me, Beth. I'm so sorry, but I've come down with something awful, something contagious. I can't go with you today to Montgomery County."

He sat up and shook off the last vestiges of sleep. "You're sick?"

"Horribly. It's some kind of vicious virus. Can you reschedule?"

"Yes, of course." Except that the Montgomery County D.A. was leaving the country tomorrow, going on a two-week Mediterranean cruise with his wife. The guy had gone out of his way to clear thirty minutes from his frantic schedule today; it was now or never.

Billy would figure something out. "Just focus on getting better. The world will keep turning without you for at least a couple of days."

"Thanks."

He thought about his dilemma all during his shower and while he mindlessly chowed down on a bowl of Cheerios. He could go to the appointment alone. But he'd promised scientific data that would blow D.A.

Warren Fitz away, and Daniel wasn't sure he could explain Beth's laboratory findings in any convincing way.

Science was his absolute worst subject. He understood what Beth had told him about the blood evidence, but he wasn't sure he could even pronounce *anticoagulant* in a way others would understand.

He could call on Beth's lab assistant, Cassie. She was capable. But she was extremely young, and she looked about sixteen. The D.A. was old-school and would probably laugh poor Cassie right out of his office.

That left one choice.

"Claudia. Hope I didn't wake you."

"No, of course not."

He'd just caught the good doctor in a lie, because her voice was decidedly sleep-muzzy. If she wasn't still in bed, she hadn't had her first cup of coffee. An enticing picture floated through his mind of Claudia in a sexy negligee, or maybe wrapped in a sheet, her normally sleek blond hair tousled from her pillow, or from him running his fingers through it…

"What can I do for you?" she prompted when he'd gone too long without talking.

"Beth's sick as a dog. I need someone to come with me to the D.A.'s office and explain, with some degree of intelligence and eloquence, the blood evidence."

"Billy, I'm no expert on physical evidence."

"Yeah, but you understand what Beth told us yesterday, right?"

"Yes. She did a good job explaining."

"You're a doctor. You testify in court as an expert witness all the time."

"A PhD," she reminded him. "I testify about psychology."

"Warren Fitz doesn't have to know that."

"Billy, are you suggesting we lie to a district attorney?"

"No, no, of course not. No lies. But he won't ask for your credentials. He's a busy man. Just introduce yourself as Dr. Claudia Ellison, tell him about the blood, use all the big words, and you're done."

"I'm happy to help," she said at last. "But I'll have to tell him who I really am."

"Okay, whatever. But I want you there. You *should* be there. You've been there from the beginning, and you can plead this case better than anyone, including me."

"Thanks, Billy." Her voice sounded warm, almost intimate, and Billy took a deep breath to savor it. "Tell me where and when to show up, and I'll be there."

MONTGOMERY COUNTY DISTRICT Attorney Warren Fitz was one scary dude. At six foot six and probably three hundred pounds, he looked more like an NFL linebacker than a prosecuting attorney.

Claudia had heard that he'd played ball in college. She'd also heard that he was old-fashioned and didn't like to be trifled with.

She had readily agreed to help Billy convince the D.A. that the Eduardo Torres case needed to be reopened, and that Mary-Francis's conviction should be overturned. But now that she was face-to-face with him, she wondered whether she'd made a sound decision.

District attorneys did not like having their cases overturned, because it meant they had to admit to the whole world they'd made a mistake, that the justice system had failed. And in a case such as this one—much publicized, very emotional—Mr. Fitz would have to admit that he'd sent an innocent woman to death row.

But the evidence was compelling, extremely so.

If Mary-Francis had shot or stabbed her husband in their bed, and he had bled to death, that blood would not have contained anticoagulants. There was no room for interpretation. If Mary-Francis had killed Eduardo, she'd done the deed in some other way—a way that no evidence pointed to.

They were in Fitz's office. He sat behind his desk, arms folded, lips pressed together in a thin line. This was not a good way to begin.

Billy introduced Claudia, then allowed her to present the report Beth's assistant, Cassie, had sent via email that morning. The report was full of big words and scientific jargon that could either impress or bore. Claudia tried to strike just the right balance between authoritative and animated. She knew a lot about testifying in court, and she pretended she was on the witness stand, facing a hostile cross-examination.

But Fitz didn't cross-examine her. He hadn't questioned her credentials, even though she'd made it clear she was a psychologist. He seemed to be merely waiting for her to be done.

Taking her cue, she wrapped up quickly, having made what she thought was a strong, compelling case for taking another look at this supposed murder.

"That's all very interesting," Fitz finally said. "But no telling where that blood sample has been since it was first tested. Maybe contaminants were introduced during the original examination."

"Ms. McClelland used a fresh sample from the mattress cover," Billy said. "It hadn't previously been swabbed or—"

"How do you know that? Were you there at the lab? As I understand it, the samples arrived in a box at your office."

"With a detailed chain of custody attached," Billy tried again, but Claudia could already tell this was a lost cause.

"Maybe Mrs. Torres contaminated the blood herself, with cleaning products or some such," he said with finality. "They put all kinds of chemicals in those spray bottles, including some ingredients that might coagulate blood. And if Mr. Torres is still alive, then where is he?" Fitz challenged them. "There hasn't been a whisper out in the world to indicate he's alive."

"We think he's been hiding in Mexico, where he has family," Billy said.

"Then find him. Because nothing short of seeing Eduardo Torres walking and talking will convince me that Mary-Francis didn't kill him."

Billy started to object again, but Claudia subtly shook her head—a signal he was getting pretty good at reading from her. He clamped his mouth shut, took a deep breath and finally spoke again.

"Then we'll find him. Thank you for your time, sir." He spun on the heel of his boot and stalked out of the office.

Claudia followed. Neither of them stopped until they were outside the building, in the parking lot, where the oppressive heat seemed to soak any remaining energy right out of her. She paused at the bottom of the steps, grabbing on to the handrail.

"Claudia? You okay?"

"I'm so sorry, Billy. I'm so sorry I couldn't convince him."

"Don't be sorry. You did great in there."

"I sucked. I made it too technical."

Billy put his arm around her and led her to a stone bench in the shade of a live oak tree. Her legs felt heavy and sluggish, no longer capable of supporting her. She sank onto the cool stone of the bench. To her mortification, her eyes filled with tears.

He sat next to her, his arm still around her, his hand splayed at her waist, branding her with his heat right through her clothes. "You can't blame yourself. His mind was made up before we opened our mouths."

She wished she knew why her reaction to this case was so emotional. If Mary-Francis was even a little bit nice or likable, Claudia could understand it better. But maybe it was the woman's abrasiveness that moved Claudia. What was she hiding? What was she protecting? Had she ever loved her husband? Her daughter?

"She must feel so betrayed…so alone…and now we can't help her."

"We haven't lost yet."

"But before, I thought we'd won." She looked up at Billy. "It was my fault Mary-Francis got convicted in the first place."

"Excuse me? Did you put that blood in her bed?"

"It was my evaluation of her. I should have advised the defense counsel to bury it. Yes, I testified that she was telling the truth about not killing her husband, but I also introduced the idea that she was lying about other things. Once they branded her as a liar, the jury hated her. It was over."

"You had to tell the truth on the stand."

"I know, but I shouldn't have taken the stand."

"Mary-Francis's lawyer was the one who made that decision. He should have known your opinion could be used against his client."

"On an intellectual level I know all that. But that doesn't change the fact that my testimony harmed Mary-Francis more than it helped. She's innocent, and I helped put her on death row."

"I understand." He smoothed a strand of hair from her face, the gesture both sweet and intimate. How could she feel such intense desire for him even when she felt so wretched in every other respect?

"Do you really understand?" she asked. "Have you ever made a bad decision that cost someone their life?"

In that split-second delay he took in replying, Claudia saw the answer on his face. *Yes.* He believed he'd caused someone's death.

But with his next breath, he went into heavy-duty denial. "No, I never have. So maybe I don't know exactly how you feel. But I can imagine. I'm sorry you feel responsible."

Now, on top of everything else, she felt a crushing disappointment that he wouldn't confide in her. She wanted to press him because that's what therapists did, but her instincts told her to back off.

She turned the conversation back on herself, to keep him at ease. "That's one reason I've pushed to stay involved. I want to make this right. Even though my testimony harmed her, Mary-Francis still put her trust in me. I was the only person who believed in her innocence. She's put her life into my hands, and that's a big responsibility, and something I don't take lightly."

"But what if you can't make it right? What do you do if there's no way to make amends, no way to atone?"

Claudia had a strong feeling he was no longer talking about her situation. "I guess then it becomes a matter of self-forgiveness."

"What if I can't—" He stopped, seeming to remember himself. "You don't have to forgive yourself. You did nothing wrong. And anyway, Mary-Francis is still alive, and we're not done yet. We have more stuff to check out."

"You were going to say something else, a minute ago," Claudia said, unable to stop herself from trying to wedge herself into the tiny crack he'd opened. "What is it you can't forgive yourself for?"

His face hardened. "Nice try. But did you forget the rules? No crawling inside my head. I don't want you to be my shrink."

Claudia started to pull back, stung by his sudden change of tone.

He immediately softened and pulled up a grin. "I'd much rather you be my lover."

# *CHAPTER EIGHT*

HAD HE JUST SAID THAT out loud?

Judging from Claudia's expression, he had. She had that deer-in-headlights, what-am-I-supposed-to-do-now look on her face that meant she was either about to slap him—or kiss him.

"You can just tell me to go to hell," he said. "I won't take offense."

"That is exactly what I *should* say. You coming on to me—it's very unprofessional. It could even constitute sexual harassment."

"Then say it. 'Billy Cantu, you giant dirtbag, go to hell.'"

She sighed. "I can't. It wouldn't be fair."

"What does fairness have to do with anything?"

"You only said what I've been thinking all day."

He blinked a couple of times. He'd thrown out that "lover" line to distract her. Not that it wasn't true, but he'd never expected her to give it serious consideration. Now he didn't know what to say.

Claudia stood abruptly. "I need air-conditioning. Meet me at my office in thirty minutes."

"Thirty… What?"

"Unless you didn't mean it. About wanting to be lovers."

"You think I'm bluffing? That I just said that for effect or something?" Um, yeah. That was exactly the case.

"I certainly hope not. My office. Thirty minutes."

"Why your office?"

"It's closer than your house or mine. And I have a comfy couch."

She turned and strode toward her Roadster, aiming for nonchalance. But she couldn't quite hide the tension in her gait.

Did she actually think he would back down?

Yeah, he got her game. She'd tried to show him some compassion and he'd shut down, closed off his feelings and turned the conversation in a direction that suited him.

He'd expected her to be flustered enough that she would walk away, forgetting all about her oh-so-sensitive desire to force him to spill his guts about his *feelings.*

But she'd called his bluff.

He damn sure wasn't going to blink first. When she'd admitted she'd been thinking about sex, with him, his whole body had gone rock hard. She'd planted a picture in his mind, and it was there to stay—her, him, on the therapist's couch doing a lot more than analyzing dreams or looking at inkblots.

It suddenly occurred to him he didn't know where her office was. He'd never been there.

Her engine was revving. He hurried to his truck, jumped inside, started it up and followed Claudia out of the parking lot.

She drove like a woman on a mission, darting deftly in and out of freeway traffic. Billy had to run one deeply yellow light and cut off a Hummer to keep her in his sights.

It took nearly the whole thirty minutes to get to her building in a classy neighborhood near West University and Bellaire. When she used a passkey to get into the parking garage, Billy whipped around the corner and found an empty spot at the curb. After feeding some quarters into the meter—would two hours be enough?—he headed for the building's front door.

Claudia Ellison, PhD, had her office on the fifth floor of the posh medical building. Billy rode the elevator up, questioning his own sanity. Was he really going to make love to Claudia? He was almost positive she had some agenda other than that. It seemed out of character for coolly professional Claudia to want to boff him on her office couch. But he had to know, and she probably knew that about him.

Only an elevator ride separated them now. Guess he'd soon find out her game.

Her outer office was decorated in shades of mossy-green and slate-gray, probably aimed at calming anxious patients as they waited for their appointment times. The chairs were wide and deep and well padded. Tea and coffee were available from a table in the corner. But the room was empty, no patients waiting.

That was good.

He went to the reception window, where a cute redhead manned the phone and a large appointment book. Billy waited until she'd finished a conversation and looked up at him.

"May I help you, sir?" Her metal name tag identified her as Kimmy.

"I'm here to see Claudia. Dr. Ellison," he amended, because probably Claudia wouldn't want her office staff to know their appointment was of a personal nature.

Kimmy's lips made a silent "Oh" as she looked at

him with concern and sympathy. "You must be Mr. Cantu."

"Yeah..."

"Please, sit down. Everything's going to be fine, I promise. Dr. Ellison is...well, she's just remarkable. I'll tell her you're here." Kimmy closed the glass partition that separated her area from the waiting room. He could hear her muffled voice as she said something into the phone, but he couldn't understand her words.

So, Claudia's receptionist thought she was remarkable. At what? he wondered. What had Claudia told her about him? Kimmy had clearly been expecting him.

He was too antsy to sit, instead pacing slowly around the room, studying the paintings on the wall—innocuous pastoral scenes, also intended to be calming, he imagined.

Frankly, nothing was going to calm him down. His heart was racing, his blood pumping. The suspense was killing him.

Their setback at the D.A.'s office drifted to the back of his mind. He would have to come up with a new plan of action soon, because he wasn't giving up, not when it meant so much to Claudia. And Mary-Francis, of course. But right now, more urgent matters clamored for his attention.

Before he'd left his truck, he'd dug into his gym bag, which he kept behind the front seat, and plucked out a small, foil packet. He'd put the condom in his jacket pocket—just in case.

"Billy."

His heart nearly stopped at the sound of her voice. She'd taken a few moments to freshen up. He could tell she'd brushed her hair and put on a fresh coat of pale, frosty-strawberry lip gloss.

"Hey."

"Come on back."

He followed her into the inner sanctum. The office was a stark contrast to the generic waiting room. While some professional had probably been responsible for the grays and greens and dull art outside, this room felt much more personal.

Not that it wasn't neat and professional, but it also had touches of warmth that made it comforting. An oak roll-top desk stood in one corner, but the rest of the room featured more cozy-looking chairs in brown and dark orange and an old, slightly worn Persian rug underfoot. Everything was softly lit by lamps with stained-glass shades.

There was, indeed, a sofa against one wall. It was at least eight feet long and decorated with several big, soft-looking pillows in silky fabrics, the colors deep and mysterious.

For a few moments, he couldn't take his eyes off it, but finally he dragged his gaze back to her. She was watching him expectantly.

"Why did you bring me here?" he asked. "The truth."

Here in her den, she wasn't going to be easy to fluster. She removed her turquoise suit jacket, kicked off her bronze-colored heels and sat down on the sofa. "In this room, I feel safe. Kind of ironic, since I've been physically assaulted twice in here by my own patients. But if I could choose any place to be vulnerable, this would be it."

"So you plan to be vulnerable?"

"When a woman allows a man to have sex with her, it's about as vulnerable as she can get."

Billy's skin tingled. "So you're serious."

"You said you wanted to be lovers. Were *you* serious?"

"Yes. But...don't get me wrong, I'm not changing my mind. But it was a heat-of-the-moment sort of blurt-out."

"The sort of impulsive statement that often leads to an initial intimate encounter. It had the desired effect on me, and if I could have allowed myself to be swept away right then and there, I would have."

He had to laugh at how clinical she made it sound. Maybe that was how she rationalized feelings that couldn't be pinned down, measured and labeled.

"Why are you laughing? It's not like we could just do it in the Montgomery County Justice Center parking lot."

"You're something else." He took off his own jacket and sat beside her, still wary of the situation. Wary and really, really hard. Just the sight of her bare feet, with pink-polished toenails, turned him on.

"Billy, not many people know about me. The things I told you about my childhood. I work hard to maintain a certain image. I've set myself up as an expert in my field. In order for people to put their lives, and their clients' lives, in my hands, they have to believe I'm competent, the consummate professional. I can't show any chinks in my armor.

"But it's exhausting, being Claudia Ellison, PhD, all the time. I wasn't always professional. I didn't always wear designer clothes and sport perfectly manicured fingernails. I learned all these behaviors that helped me in my career. But sometimes I just need to be me. Carol Sue Calhoun from Homer, Texas.

"I feel like I can be that person around you. You won't judge me harshly for it."

"That's your real name? Carol Sue?" She so did not strike him as a Carol Sue. But the name sounded familiar. He searched his memory banks, but nothing popped up right away.

"I legally changed it because I needed to divorce myself from the past," she said. "But she's part of me." Her soft Texas drawl drew him in.

He leaned back and stretched his arms along the back of the sofa. "I need to know what you expect from me, *cielito.*" The endearment slipped out. It was something his father called his mother, sometimes.

"Right now, I'm hoping for an hour of smutty sex with the first man to excite me and challenge me in years. After that, I don't know."

His mouth went dry as a box of saltines. "I could do that."

He'd said he could do it, but no matter what her background, she still didn't look like the kind of woman a man had "smutty sex" with. She was so delicate, so feminine. Even the bones of her face, her small, perfectly formed nose and sharp cheekbones, looked fragile.

He touched her hand, then let his fingers slide up her forearm, which was dusted with light blond hair.

She watched the progress of his fingers. When they reached the edge of her short sleeve, she took his hand and placed it against her breast, then covered it with hers.

He inhaled sharply. It was all he could do not to grab her and throw her down on the couch cushions, to tear her clothes off and savor every inch of her skin with his hands, his mouth.

"You're still not sure I mean it?" Her voice sounded husky. "It's not a trick, Billy. It really is uncomplicated. I need to forget about things. If you don't want to, under those circumstances—"

"*Querida,* I'd want to make love with you under just about any circumstances you could imagine. If there was a live javelina roaming your office, it probably wouldn't stop me."

"Then..."

He slid his hand from her breast, across her collarbone, to her slender neck until he finally cupped her chin and leaned in to kiss her. "Just don't want to rush things, that's all. Sex is something I like to savor," he said just before their lips touched.

Kissing Claudia was like diving into a cold, clear pool of water—exciting, bracing, but smooth as satin against his skin. She came alive under his hands. So reserved and controlled in other situations, she appeared to hold nothing back in his arms. She managed to unbutton his shirt with her right hand and her blouse with her left.

He realized he was still wearing his shoulder holster; he pulled away from her long enough to yank it over his head and lay it on the rug. Even when he was with a woman, he always had a gun within easy reach. Locked doors were no match for...

*No.* He swept those disturbing memories from his mind and focused his full attention on Claudia, who was busy taking his shirt off as fast as she could manage the buttons.

"What if your office help decides to check on you?"

"Kimmy thinks you're a suicidal patient and we're having an intense one-on-one session. She wouldn't interrupt me unless the building was on fire or the president was on line one. Or if I scream, of course. I'll try to control that." She rose from the sofa and stood before him in her snug, bottom-cupping skirt and a bra made of pale peach silk and trimmed in lace—superhot but with a Victorian feel. Like that slip she was wearing the other day.

The combination of naughty and nice made his insides quiver with anticipation. "Have I ever told you you're the sexiest woman to walk the earth?"

She smiled faintly. "Nice, but pretty words aren't necessary."

"I didn't say them because I thought I had to." Just the same, he took the hint and shut up. For the next little while, the beautiful woman was his.

He pulled her back down to the sofa and kissed her again, harder this time, testing the softness of her skin where her breasts bulged above the cup of her bra. Her breasts were small, but rounded like ripe mangos. They fit perfectly in his hands, and he wanted—no, needed—to feel them without the barrier of fabric blocking access.

It had been a while since he'd removed a woman's bra with one hand—high school, maybe. The women he'd dated—and there had been a fair number—had mostly been eager and sophisticated enough about sex to strip the second foreplay started. Claudia was obviously eager, but it was a turn-on that she left some undressing for him to do.

Some skills a man never lost. He flicked open the front closure of her bra and her breasts sprang free.

With a low groan he dipped his head and closed his lips around one taut nipple.

"Oh, yeah," she whispered. "Feels so…feels so…"

Right, no words could describe it. She actually tasted sweet, as if she perspired honey. He swirled his tongue around her nipple and she squirmed beneath him. As her spine softened she fell slowly onto the cushions.

Her skirt fastened on the side, and she reached down and unzipped it slowly, the sound reverberating in the quiet, restful office.

Billy had never realized how erotic the rustle of clothing could be. He helped her wiggle out of the skirt and slip and watched as they whispered down her silky bare legs. He pulled away from her long enough that he could admire how pretty she looked in those barely there panties—peach silk, just like the bra—then hooked his fingers on either side of the elastic at the top and dragged them down, feasting his eyes on each inch of skin revealed. The curls that protected her femininity were dark brown, a stark contrast to the pale golden-blond hair on her head. He'd wanted to know, and now he did.

He skimmed his hands over her slender hips, his thumbs softly brushing the sides of her pubis and she gasped again and reached for his belt.

"C'mon, Billy." She said it as a plea.

Not one to argue at a time like this, he let go of her long enough to flick his tooled leather belt open, unzip his jeans and yank them down. Then he ran into the problem of boots. Damn, cowboy boots could be a pain, and these were tight. He sat down near Claudia's feet and started to tug, but she came to his rescue, jumping up and cupping his heel in her hand. She watched him with passion-glazed eyes and a naughty smile as she gave a mighty yank, nearly pulling him off the couch. The boot came off—and his spare gun spilled out onto the carpet.

"Oh, my." Claudia reached for it.

"Leave it," he all but growled.

For the second boot, she turned around and put his foot between her thighs, giving him a breathtaking view of her shapely bottom. Another tug, and the boot let go.

"That is the most fun I've ever had taking my boots off." His voice was rough.

She turned back around, her lips parted slightly. He didn't need to be an expert face reader to see that hers reflected blatant appreciation for the scenery.

"The best is yet to come," he said with a wink, unable to stop his cocky side from asserting itself, though he wasn't half as sure of himself with Claudia as he normally was with a woman.

She helped him take off his jeans and shorts, then sat on his lap and wrapped her naked body around him like a clinging vine. "Bring it on."

Enough of this play. He pulled Claudia close until they couldn't have slid a piece of paper between them. Her skin felt incredible, like she must lotion it ten times a day. The mental image of her slathering oils over every inch of her body inflamed him even more. Though he didn't want to rush her, he was hard as a steel pipe, half-afraid he would explode if she even touched him.

They stretched out on the couch, and then she did touch him, wrapping her surprisingly strong hand around him, testing his length and width, pausing to cup his balls for a few moments, then returning her attention to his shaft.

He liked watching her stroke him, liked the image of her pale, delicate hand with its manicured nails gripping his darker erection.

"I'm not gonna last long if you keep that up, *cielito.*" He gently pulled her hand away and pushed her back onto the sofa. From there he could reach his jeans and the protection he'd stashed there.

"I'm already protected," she said when she saw what he was up to. "But I like it that you're prepared for any situation, Mr. Boy Scout."

"And I'm no Boy Scout." He opened the condom packet despite her assertion. "You should insist on this no matter what. From me or anybody else." Although he had no reason to believe he would be a risk for her, because he was always careful, she didn't know that.

"You're right, of course. I should know better." She took the packet from him and pulled out the condom. "No reason this can't be part of the fun."

She made it fun, smoothing the latex over him slowly, carefully, as if it were the most important, serious task in the world and she had to get it just right.

"Oh, *querida.* You about done there?"

She grinned. "I'm nowhere near done with you." She shifted slightly, parting her legs so he rested between them.

As much as he wanted to just bury himself in her, he was still half-afraid of hurting her. Though she'd proved she wasn't quite the pampered, sheltered flower of a woman that she showed to the rest of the world, she was small. She had the slimmest hips of any woman he'd ever been with, which meant she might be small elsewhere, too. And not that he would brag, but he was a realist and he wasn't exactly a pencil.

He lifted himself up and rearranged them so he could caress her thighs, then the soft folds between her legs.

"Mmm. I'm ready, you know. You don't have to—"

"I know I don't have to do anything. I want to."

"Thought you were in a hurry."

"I'm on the edge," he admitted. "But I do have control." With that he dipped one finger inside her.

She was warm and wet, and almost humming with pleasure, sighing and closing her eyes. As he delved deeper, he imagined his shaft sliding where his finger was and he had to bite his lip to distract himself. If the imagined pleasure was that good, what would it be like for real?

Fingers wet with her juices, he lightly grazed her nub and earned a sharp gasp and an uncharacteristic giggle. He wasn't sure he'd ever heard Claudia giggle before.

"Billy! Don't you dare end this early. I want you inside me when I…when I…oh." She grabbed his hand and physically dragged it away from her body. "Now, Billy. No more messing around."

He loved his name on her lips. He would never tire of hearing her beg him to do her.

"No more messin' around." He shifted into the cradle of her legs and poised himself at her entrance, taking a deep breath to prepare himself for the onslaught of sensation.

Claudia grabbed on to both of his butt cheeks with those delicate but strong and capable hands, urging him closer. She would have enveloped him in one strong thrust if he'd allowed it. But he forced himself to take it slow, pushing inside her inch by inch, reveling in each new sensory impression. If this was going to be their only time together—and he had to recognize that possibility—he would make it count.

She took him deep, all the way. They were a perfect fit. He paused and looked at her eyes, really seeing the color for the first time. The bright grass-green with flecks of gold reminded him of precious gems, fathomless and reflecting both determination and vulnerability.

They remained that way for several long, deep breaths, locked together but not moving, staring into each other's eyes. He couldn't recall any other time he had joined with a woman this way, claiming not only her body, but her full, emotional attention.

Hell, he couldn't remember the last time he'd made love anywhere but a dark bedroom, where seeing anyone's eyes was impossible.

Claudia wrapped her incredibly long legs around his hips, changing their angle of contact as she hooked her ankles together.

He groaned in response as her muscles tightened on his shaft, and he hadn't even started moving yet.

But he did, slowly at first. She was warm and wet and tight around him, the slick friction of her womanhood a bold caress against his erection. He'd never felt anything like it. Which seemed crazy, but everything about this coupling was crazy, larger than life, the stuff of fantasy.

She was his fantasy, that cool blonde type he'd always yearned for, though God knew why. Yet she wasn't cool now. Her flesh burned hot beneath his hands where he gently squeezed her breasts and explored the intriguing angles and curves of her shoulder, her neck, her little pink ears with their understated gold hoop earrings.

He needed to kiss her some more. Her lips were already swollen and rosy-pink from his earlier kisses, reminding him of her *other* lips. He claimed them again, a voracious, hard kiss that involved teeth and tongue. She gave as good as she got, proving her hunger was every bit as sharp as his. With each thrust of his hips, she raised up to greet him, tilting her pelvis to take him deeper still and making quiet mewling sounds in the back of her throat, as if she couldn't quite contain her pleasure.

When his climax came, it was explosive. He buried his face in the curve of her neck, stifling his triumphant cry as he came. Surge after surge of ecstasy moved through his body like an electric current. As the pleasure slowly subsided, he actually checked to make sure he was still breathing, that his heart was still beating.

Men had been known to die in situations like this, but fortunately he had a strong constitution.

He was embarrassed to realize he had no idea if she'd found her own release. The words *Was it good for you?* trembled on the tip of his tongue, but he resisted saying them aloud. He wasn't some green kid bedding his first woman. He was savvy enough to pick up her thoughts on this episode without an interrogation.

Billy angled himself to one side, suddenly conscious of his hundred and ninety pounds sprawled across her delicate frame. "Am I hurting you?"

"Huh." She said it like a laugh. "Are you kidding me?"

He smiled, then blew on her chest to cool her. She was as damp with perspiration as he was. Though he was utterly spent, he still enjoyed watching her nipples pucker at the touch of his breath.

"Well," he said.

"Exactly," she said.

He didn't want to play games with Claudia. So though it might not be hip to be so straightforward, he told her exactly what was on his mind.

"That was one for the history books."

She smiled, and even gave a little chuckle. "Yup."

"You're incredible."

"Thank you. I've definitely had worse than you."

Now that they'd caught their breath, Billy became more aware of their surroundings—the hum of the air conditioner, the muffled traffic outside, a siren in the distance.

This was the trickiest moment of sex—how to end it. This was usually the time a woman would express her emotions, wanting to nail down the exact nature of their relationship, the exact degree of his commitment, which, he admitted, was usually zero.

Under ordinary circumstances, Billy was keen to escape the minefield of postcoital conversation. He usually invented some place he needed to be.

Claudia knew his schedule. She knew he wanted to meet with the Project Justice team and regroup, find a new angle for proving Mary-Francis's innocence to the district attorney. It would be perfectly natural for him to look at his watch, spring to his feet and declare he had to get going because a woman's life was at stake.

But he didn't move. It felt amazing to lie there with Claudia in his arms, relaxed and open like he'd never seen her.

"How soon before Kimmy checks on us?" Billy asked.

"A few more minutes."

"Good." Oddly, he was the one who felt like talking. "Um, Claudia…I take it bringing men into your office on your lunch hour isn't the norm for you."

"Nooo. There are only so many 'suicidal' emergency appointments I can claim before Kimmy would get suspicious."

"You could just tell her the truth."

"If this ever got to be a regular option for me, I guess I'd have to. But I'll cross that bridge when I come to it, if I ever do."

She sure didn't sound as though she was pressing for a commitment. He should be delighted, but for some reason he wasn't. Maybe because she didn't sound as though she was pressing for a repeat performance, either.

"I haven't had a regular man in my life in a very long time," she mused. "College, in fact."

That seemed off. A woman like Claudia could wink and crook her little finger and have just about any man she wanted. "Why not?"

"I told you before. Most men, I can tell exactly what they're thinking, and it's not pretty. But there was one man who fooled me."

*More than one, now,* he wanted to add. They had already proved she couldn't read him. He knew he was supposed to encourage her to elaborate. But this was one of the tricky parts. She would trust him with some intimate secret, then he was expected to reciprocate.

That was how it worked in the undercover world, as well. And he was a much better player at this game than she realized.

"This man appeared to be exactly the sort of guy I was looking for."

"And it turned out he had a string of girlfriends, I bet," Billy said. "Was he one of those chameleon types, who could be whatever a woman wanted him to be?"

"Exactly. But that string of girlfriends? They were all dead."

"Wh—what?" Suddenly the conversation had become more demanding than the standard after-sex banter.

"My last boyfriend was a serial killer. He locked his victims in a warehouse and hunted them with a bow and arrow. I was next on his list, and he would have carried out his plans for me, if one of his victims hadn't escaped and summoned help."

"Your last boyfriend was Raymond Bass?" Everybody knew about that case. It had generated worldwide publicity. "Oh, my God, now I know why your real name sounded familiar to me. You identified him. You testified."

"Yup. Pretty funny, me a wannabe psychologist and I couldn't spot the deadly sociopath I was dating. Having sex with."

Billy didn't want to think about Claudia having sex with anyone but him. He squeezed his eyes closed, willing the mental image away. "Some guys are just really, really good at what they do." It was the only comforting sentiment he could come up with.

"I've come to realize that."

Suddenly her choice of a lover's tryst made a lot of sense. She didn't trust him. She couldn't read him, therefore he might be a psycho killer.

"I need to know, Billy," she said with aching sincerity. "You're hiding something from me, something about your past, and until I know what it is, I won't feel safe. I *can't* feel safe."

Now came the part where he reassured her that he wasn't some crazy killer, that she should trust him. That she was welcome to know anything about him.

That wasn't going to happen.

He felt a keen sense of disappointment that he couldn't make her happy in this respect. But no matter how compelling her need to get inside his head—and it did go beyond mere curiosity, he had to admit—he couldn't oblige her.

"I'm not a serial killer." He could at least go that far. "Daniel had me investigated six ways to Sunday before I could be a part of Project Justice."

His argument failed to convince her. He could see it in the pleading way she looked at him.

"I'm not going to confess all my sins to you, Claudia. I don't need a therapist. If I feel a need to confess something, I'll see a priest."

She nodded, quietly accepting his decision. "If you change your mind, I'm always here. I won't judge."

Yeah, she would. He'd been a macho cop determined to bring down a bad guy, and he'd made a foolhardy decision that had cost an innocent woman her life.

She wouldn't be human if she didn't judge him based on that. It was hideous.

Time for him to leave. He sat up with one final caress to her hair, then began searching for his clothes.

"I have a private bathroom through that door," she said, pointing.

"Thanks, but I think I'll swing by home, grab a shower."

She froze, very briefly, but he could tell his impending abandonment took her by surprise. However, she quickly covered her reaction. "Okay. I'll just freshen up, then." She grabbed a throw from the back of the sofa and wrapped herself in it, sari style, knotting it just above her breasts. "Keep me posted on the case, and let me know if you need me."

"I will." He stood, unselfconscious about his nudity, and gathered up his clothes. She nodded and disappeared through a carved oak door with a brass plaque marked Private.

Billy blew out a breath. He felt like a complete shit. But hadn't he known Claudia would ultimately want something he wasn't prepared to give?

## *CHAPTER NINE*

CLAUDIA TURNED THE water as hot as she could stand it and stood under the spray, scrubbing herself vigorously with her bath puff and green-tea-scented shower gel until her skin was pink. She washed her hair, too, wanting to make sure no remnant of Billy's scent remained on her.

Not only would it be hard to explain to Kimmy, who was far too bright and curious for her own good, but any remaining eau de Billy would remind Claudia of him.

She didn't want to be reminded of her idiocy in having midday office sex with Billy.

As she rinsed the shampoo, she hummed a song from an old musical about washing a man out of her hair, only she was washing him out of her life, too. She was done.

If she had to see him professionally, that was one thing. She could handle that. But no more intimate meals, no more confessions and definitely no more sex.

She had told Billy things no one knew about her, not even her best girlfriends. These were things she'd sworn to herself she would never reveal. If anyone found out she had unwittingly dated a serial killer, it could destroy her credibility. It could end her career.

Claudia had been on the news when Raymond was arrested. She'd been the one to go to the police with her suspicions when she'd seen a sketch of the suspected serial killer on the news, and the media had found out. She had testified in court.

When it was all over, she'd had her name legally changed, attended grad school in a different state and radically altered her appearance.

Daniel knew. She'd had to explain the name change, which Mitch had ferreted out when he'd done a background check on her. Neither Daniel nor Mitch would ever reveal her secret, of that she was pretty sure.

But a lover—soon to be officially an ex-lover, she supposed—was a different matter altogether.

Why had she been so stupid as to put herself in such a vulnerable position? But she knew that answer. She'd hoped that by revealing more of herself, Billy would feel comfortable opening up to her. Instead, he'd closed himself off even more tightly.

She didn't know Billy, not really. He had one secret that she knew of, and if he had one, he could have a hundred. Some people were very good at compartmentalizing their lives. A man could be a regular churchgoer, loving to his wife and kids, a pillar of the community, and on the side he could be stalking underage girls.

She didn't want to believe anything bad about Billy. But if he did engage in some deviant behavior, how would she know? She was pretty good at spotting when people were off-kilter. They often gave themselves away with odd quirks, or by being almost too perfect in other ways.

But she couldn't always ferret out the truth. No one could. Especially when people possessed that weird ability to hide their feelings, the ability that both Billy and Raymond displayed.

Billy had caused someone's death. She knew that. Not knowing the whole story simply wasn't an acceptable option for her, not if she was going to get involved with him.

So she wouldn't get involved. Period. Let those secrets remain between him and his priest—if he even had a…

*Oh, my God.*

She turned off the water and quickly dried off, then climbed back into her suit. The pale turquoise skirt and jacket weren't as crisp as when she'd started out this morning, but they would have to do.

Still barefoot, she padded across her office to her desk and picked up the phone, dialing Billy's number from memory. "C'mon, pick up."

The call rolled over to voice mail. Had he intentionally refused to take her call because he was afraid she would try to turn their tryst into more than he wanted it to be? Or maybe he was driving or still in the shower. She had to stop overthinking this and do what she'd set out to do.

"Billy, it's Claudia. I thought of something, another avenue to investigate. Give me a call when you can and I'll explain." After she hung up, she realized she should have just told his voice mail of the epiphany she'd had in the shower. Now he would have to call her back.

Had she subconsciously withheld the information so he would *have* to call her back? Because he would. He might want to keep his distance from her, but when it came to the case, if he thought she had helpful information, he wouldn't hesitate just because their brief experimentation had ended in stalemate.

Claudia had appointments all afternoon, people she'd been shuffling around for days since she got involved in the quest to prove Mary-Francis's innocence. She did her best to concentrate on her patients' problems, to give them the very best she could. But it was hard to focus on the angst of a colleague's teenage daughter over a breakup with her boyfriend when Mary-Francis was headed for a lethal injection and the man she supposedly murdered was out there somewhere.

Between appointments, she checked her cell phone, and also checked with Kimmy in case Billy had called her office number. But she didn't hear from him.

It wasn't until she was straightening up her office at the end of the day that she discovered why. His cell phone was wedged between two sofa cushions. He must have silenced the ringer, because she hadn't heard it ringing when she'd called it earlier.

She didn't have a home number for him, and the Project Justice offices would be closed by now. But she did have an address.

Her mind made up, she stuck his phone in her purse, locked up her office—Kimmy had already gone home for the day—and headed for the parking garage. She should have been feeling dread over the coming meeting with Billy, which was sure to be awkward. But her steps practically floated over the concrete.

Her relationship with Billy was over before it really started, yet she still felt giddy as a schoolgirl as she headed for her car. Preoccupied with thoughts of what she would say when she saw him, she didn't realize someone had fallen in step behind her until he grabbed her from behind.

A gloved hand was over her mouth before she could get a good scream out. His other hand had her by one arm, which he wrenched painfully behind her back.

She had one free arm, and every survival instinct she possessed told her to grab, kick, struggle. *Don't let him get me into a car!*

Against the male's sheer power, her struggles were pathetic and ineffective. He whisked her off her feet, hauled her a few steps, then abruptly dropped her and pushed her face into the hood of her own car, slamming her head into the steel hard enough that she heard bells ringing.

Was he going to rape her?

He leaned over her, one hand pushing her face into the car, the other pressing down on the small of her back. She tried kicking back but found only empty air. He slapped away her leg, avoiding her feeble strikes with contemptuous ease.

"Stay away from the Torres family," he growled into her ear, his face so close she could smell his stinking breath. "That bitch Mary-Francis is where she needs to be."

Claudia tried to get one hand free so she could press the button on her personal-safety alarm, but she was completely immobilized.

Her assailant tossed her to the concrete garage floor as easily as he would a rag doll.

The fall knocked the wind out of her. As she struggled to draw in a breath, pain radiated from her wrist. Even in her physical anguish, she tried to see her assailant, but he was running away. She heard what sounded like work boots thudding against concrete—two sets of footsteps—but she saw nothing, and in a few moments even the sound was gone.

All that remained was the quickly fading scent from someone smoking a cigarette.

She sat up, taking in sharp sips of air, and took stock

of her injuries. Her wrist was blowing up like a balloon and hurt like a son of a bitch; she'd probably broken it. Her left hip hurt, too, and her shoulder, and her face. She didn't realize her nose was bleeding until she saw bright red droplets landing on her skirt.

Should she call the cops? Of course she should… but the Houston cops weren't involved in the Torres case. They wouldn't get the significance of the threat. She could call Hudson Vale, but Montgomery County was a long way away, and she wasn't going to sit here on the parking garage floor forever.

In the end she found her purse, which she'd dropped when her assailant had grabbed her, pulled out her phone and dialed 9-1-1. She stated her situation calmly, in as few words as possible, then hung up despite the operator's plea that Claudia stay on the line. Next, she dialed Daniel's number.

"Daniel. Claudia Ellison. I need for you to get in touch with Billy. He's without his cell phone—"

"Hold on, Claudia. He's right here."

Claudia's heart pounded in her ears. She'd just survived a violent assault, but she trembled at the thought of talking to him again. After the way they'd left things, so…awkward.

"Yo, Claudia. What's up?"

"Billy…" She crumbled. "Something h-happened. I was a-a-attacked—"

He swore viciously. "Where are you?"

She became aware of approaching sirens and knew she didn't have much time to get her message across. Her stomach roiled with nausea, and she was too dizzy to stand or think very clearly. "I think I'm on my way to the hospital."

BILLY HAD NEVER DRIVEN this fast on city streets before.

"Slow down, you're going to get us killed," complained Jamie, Daniel's wife, who had elected to go with Billy to the hospital. They didn't know the extent of Claudia's injuries, and no one had said out loud the word *rape.* Still, Daniel had insisted Claudia might want a woman present, and now Billy feared the worst. Jamie wasn't a close friend of Claudia's, but they at least knew each other.

"The emergency entrance is one block down," Jamie said. "I know, I've been to it twice in the past year."

Jamie had been shot by a crazy French lady, the mother of Daniel's private chef, when Daniel had involved her too closely in a mystery he was trying to solve. That was what happened when persons untrained in law enforcement got too near dangerous, desperate people.

"Damn, I should have known she might be in danger," Billy lamented as he whipped his truck into the E.R. driveway. He didn't even find a proper parking space in the tiny visitor lot; he parked at the end of a row and called it good.

"You're gonna get a ticket," Jamie said.

"So, you'll fix it for me." Jamie had recently been elected as Houston district attorney.

"Her injuries aren't life threatening," Jamie tried again. "The cops said she was just a little banged up."

"She lost consciousness while she was talking to me." Billy was halfway to the large, sliding doors that led into the emergency room. Jamie struggled to keep up. "That's more than 'a little banged up.'"

He didn't stop until he reached the E.R. front desk. Before he grabbed the nurse there and shook her by the stethoscope around her neck, he took a deep breath in an effort to calm himself. If he was hysterical, they wouldn't tell him anything. He'd been around emergency rooms—as a cop, a patient and a civilian—enough to know that.

"I'm here to see Claudia Ellison," he said. "Where is she?"

A uniformed cop was loitering around the double doors that led to the treatment rooms. When he heard Claudia's name, his ears pricked and he sauntered over.

"Can I see some ID, please?"

"Billy, get a grip," Jamie cautioned.

"Oh," the cop said. "You're Billy? The one she's been asking for?"

"She's asking for me?" Amazing how that knowledge made him feel good all of a sudden. If a woman was lying bleeding in the E.R. and she asked for you, that meant something.

"If you'll just show me an ID, you can go back and see… Ms. McNair?"

"Damn straight," Billy said. He had the freaking district attorney to vouch for him.

The cop forgot about checking any ID. "Y'all can go back. She's in Room 4."

"Power has its privileges," Jamie said under her breath as they made their way back to the treatment rooms.

He found number 4 and barged in, then skidded to a halt and almost lost his dinner.

"Claudia. Holy shit." He'd imagined bad, but the reality was much worse. Her face was puffy and bruised on the right side, that eye swelled almost shut. Any skin that wasn't blue and purple was as pale as the sheet on which she lay.

"Billy. I—I'm sorry I made you come out. I was a little panicked when—"

"Don't apologize." He was at her bedside in two strides. Her left arm was wrapped in a bandage with an ice pack, resting across her waist, but he thought nothing of taking her right hand and pressing it gently between his palms. "You look awful. How badly are you hurt?"

"Not as bad as it looks. I tore some ligaments in my wrist, but nothing's broken."

"You must have a concussion, though. You went unconscious on me."

She smiled, looking embarrassed. "I fainted. There's a difference. The doctor said the combination of adrenaline and fear and relief made me, um, I think the technical term is *swoon*... Oh, hi, Jamie."

Jamie hovered uncertainly near the door. "Daniel asked me to come," she said. "To make sure you're okay, that you have everything you need."

"They're treating me like a princess. Come on in, sit down."

On one hand, Billy wanted to be alone with Claudia. He wanted to take her in his arms and hold her close so nothing could hurt her ever again. The fierceness of his protective instincts shocked him.

But he didn't want to advertise to Jamie or anyone else that he and Claudia had become more than just colleagues—especially when he was so unsure of how it would turn out. This afternoon he'd been thinking *No way.* He might be all for physical intimacy, but not the sort of emotional closeness Claudia would expect in a relationship.

Now, he didn't know what he wanted. When he'd found out she'd been assaulted, he'd nearly come unglued. She meant something to him, and he couldn't just walk away from that.

Though he couldn't be completely frank with Claudia while Jamie was here, the D.A.'s presence eased some of the awkwardness that might otherwise plague them.

Jamie pulled up a plastic chair and sat near the gurney, her eyes welled with compassion. Still in her work clothes—a red power suit, her dark hair pulled back in a no-nonsense twist—she radiated honest compassion, which was one of the reasons she'd won the election by a landslide. "Can you tell us what happened, Claudia?"

"I was heading to my car in the garage. Not being as careful as I should have been—"

"Don't blame yourself," Billy interrupted.

"Well, it's true," she said gruffly. "Normally I am hyperaware of my surroundings. Some of my patients are pretty disturbed, and, well, you never know when one of them will turn on you."

"So it was a patient?"

Claudia shook her head, then seemed to think better of it as she winced with pain. "No. Not a patient. He grabbed me from behind and threw me facedown on the hood of my car."

The mental image her words gave him made him want to punch the wall in. Or better yet, someone's face.

Claudia must have seen something in Billy's expression, because she squeezed his hand. "He wasn't trying to rape me. His sole reason for being there was to scare me. He told me to stay away from the Torres family."

"Damn." Billy let go of her hand because he needed to move, to release his anger and frustration somehow. But the room was tiny; there was no place to go. He pinched the bridge of his nose. "I was hoping this wasn't connected to our investigation. I can't believe I didn't realize the danger. We've stirred up a hornet's nest."

"Someone doesn't want Mary-Francis exonerated?" Jamie asked.

Billy forced his brain to focus on something beyond his horror at Claudia's injuries, which he could have prevented if he'd rubbed two brain cells together. Unfortunately all of his blood had been circulating elsewhere in his body.

"I think it's more likely that Eduardo Torres doesn't want to be discovered alive. He was already facing a possible murder charge. If you add faking his own death, and possibly the assault to Theresa, the guy is in some pretty serious manure."

"There are also the coins," Claudia reminded him. "What if Angie told her father we were nosing around?"

"That's how we'll find Torres," Billy said. "We'll follow Angie, maybe tap her phone."

"That's an excellent idea," Claudia said. "Since the local cops aren't interested, maybe we can get the feds involved if we—"

"Whoa, whoa. There's no 'we.' I misspoke. You are officially out of the sleuthing business. I'm going to ask Daniel if he'll put a twenty-four-hour guard on you."

Claudia snorted. "Don't be ridiculous. We must be getting close, or Eduardo wouldn't be taking such drastic action. I'm not backing down from this cowardly bastard."

"The hell you aren't."

"You can't order me—"

Jamie halted the argument with one gesture of her hand. Though she was slender and not very tall, she had a commanding presence that everyone responded to.

"Let's focus on the assault for a moment. That's our best lead right now. Claudia, did you get a good look at the man who attacked you?"

"Unfortunately, no. He was behind me almost the entire time. But I can tell you a few things. He was big—taller than you, Billy, but strong and muscular like you. His body was hard—no fat around his middle. He was Hispanic—that much I could tell from his accent. And he had terrible breath—" She stopped short, looking as if she wanted to gag.

Billy's own gut churned at the thought of this animal getting close enough to Claudia that she could smell his breath or his clothing.

"Anything else?" Jamie prompted.

"There were two people there. I heard two sets of footsteps running away, and I smelled menthol cigarette smoke in the vicinity."

"Animals travel in packs," Billy said in disgust. *"Hijo de puta."*

"I'm sorry I don't remember more," Claudia said.

Jamie patted her hand. "You did good. Most assault victims don't have the presence of mind to notice details."

"They were both wearing boots, I think. Shoes with a hard sole, anyway. I remember hearing those shoes clunking on the concrete as they ran off."

Jamie had a notebook on her knee, in which she jotted the information. "Did you tell all this to the police?"

"Yes…well, most of it. I left out the threat. I let them believe it was a mugging gone bad, that I screamed and made such a fuss that I scared away my attacker. I didn't want to muddy the waters, getting the Houston police involved in the Torres matter. I figure we can tell Hudson Vale."

"Vale is the Montgomery County detective investigating the assault on Theresa Esteve," Billy explained to Jamie, who was frowning. She probably didn't like leaving her city's police force out of the loop. "He's familiar with the supposed Eduardo Torres murder, too."

"I think the more law enforcement we have on our side, the better," Jamie said.

"You know what happens when cops get involved," Billy argued. "They start closing ranks against *us*. They don't like it that we get people out of prison, people who have been convicted based on *their* investigations. They'll order us to stay out of it. Then they'll make a mess of things, and if we try to help, they'll threaten us with obstruction of justice."

Jamie smiled. "You have a pretty low opinion of cops, considering you used to be one."

"I'm okay with some cops. But I like to pick and choose who to work with."

Jamie nodded. "It's your case. Since I'm not here in any official capacity, you can call the shots. But keep me informed, okay? As a courtesy?"

"You bet, Jamie."

Jamie stood and stretched. “I’m going to get some air.” She gave them a knowing look, then left the room.

“Does she know something?” Claudia asked. “About us?”

“I promise you, I haven’t said a word to anyone. But she’s a pretty smart cookie.”

Claudia sighed.

“Why didn’t you call me?” He tried not to sound as hurt as he felt. “Why was your first call to Daniel?”

She rolled her eyes. “Because you lost your phone, jackass.”

“What?” He reached for his pocket, found it empty.

“I found it between the cushions of my office couch. It’s in my purse.” She pointed to a corner, where she’d stacked her personal belongings. Her white leather Coach bag sat atop a folded pile of clothes. “It’s tucked into the outside pocket.”

Rather than dig around in her purse, something his first high-school girlfriend had dumped him for, he brought the purse to her and set it in her lap. She dipped her uninjured hand into the pocket and handed him his phone.

“I wondered why no one had called me all afternoon.” He quickly scrolled through his missed calls. “Nothing urgent. Except…you did call me.” Several minutes before she was attacked.

“Oh, right…that’s why I was distracted walking to my car. I thought of something while I was taking a shower.”

Immediately he pictured her naked, under a water spray, her body slick with soap… *Don’t go there.*

“You said something about going to confession,” Claudia continued, unaware of the turmoil her words and the image she’d painted caused in his body. “And that got me thinking. Mary-Francis trusts no one. If she hid some valuable coins in a statue, as an insurance policy in case Eduardo divorced her, perhaps, she didn't tell anyone. I suspect not even her sister knew—she could have stashed the coins in the statue without Theresa seeing. And she certainly didn't trust us with the information. But she might tell..."

"Her priest."

## *CHAPTER TEN*

"RIGHT." CLAUDIA WAS RELIEVED Billy had caught on right away.

"She was contemplating divorce. And she hid assets from Eduardo. Both of those would be considered serious sins."

"So she might have confessed to the priest, or gone to him for counseling."

"A definite possibility. But how does that help? We already have a strong suspicion she hid the coins in the statue. The statue was moved *after* Theresa was assaulted. After Mary-Francis was incarcerated. So anything she might have confessed to a priest would be out of date by now. Not to mention, confessions to a priest are legally protected. No way could we get him to—"

"But the priest knew! He knew the coins were in a Virgin Mary statue. And when he came to Theresa's house for the memorial service, he spotted the statue. That's why he kept looking at the fireplace."

"You're saying the priest stole the statue?" Billy shook his head. "He's a priest, for cryin' out loud."

"And priests are immune to temptation? He spotted the statue at the memorial service, checked it out—"

"Then waited several months before actually removing it from the house. Remember, the statue wasn't stolen until a couple of weeks ago."

She folded her arms and stared at him.

"Claudia, this is pretty wild speculation."

"Not to me. I keep going back to what I saw on that video. Something was out of kilter with the priest's demeanor. Something distracted him. His body language wasn't congruent with his words or the situation."

"So what do you suggest?"

"Why don't we just pay him a visit?"

"Didn't you hear me earlier? You are done investigating. I want whoever hurt you to be confident he achieved his goal—scaring you away. Man, it just burns me that he's such a chicken-shit he wouldn't confront me."

"It makes sense, trying to get to you through me. If he threatened you directly, knowing you, you'd just laugh."

"Good point. But what does he think I'll do now, give up?" He looked at her and softened his stance. "I mean, I won't knowingly put you in danger again, that was stupid. But no one is safe until we find Eduardo."

"I wonder about Angie," Claudia mused. "She must know he's alive. Someone had to tell her about the coins, and it wasn't Mary-Francis."

"Mary-Francis hasn't exactly been a font of honesty."

"I know. But she's scared. Imagine being married to that ruthless bastard. She had to lie to protect herself, and now it's a habit for her."

"You're an amazing woman, to see the good in her." He wanted to kiss her again. Even in her current bruised and battered condition she was beautiful. She had an inner light shining through her eyes, her smile. But he had no right to kiss her. He'd blown her off earlier today, snubbed her attempts to know him better.

A doctor tapped on the door, then entered, smiling broadly. "How are you doing, Ms. Ellison?"

He should have called her *Dr.* Ellison, but Claudia didn't correct him. "Feeling better."

"I'll write you a scrip for some pain medication, but other than that, you should be fine. Keep that wrist immobilized for a few weeks, and you'll want to see a physical therapist so you can regain your full strength and range of motion."

"I can go home?"

"No reason to keep you here."

"I don't need the pain meds," she said. "It's not that bad."

"You might change your mind tomorrow." He thrust the prescription at her, and she stuck it in her purse. "Do you want some help getting dressed?" He glanced uneasily at Billy.

"I can manage," she said.

BILLY WAITED WITH JAMIE while Claudia put her clothes on. He'd offered to help, but that had gone over like a dud firecracker. Then they waited some more while Claudia completed the mountain of red tape. Since it was her left wrist that was injured, she could still sign papers.

"Claudia shouldn't go home by herself," Jamie said, watching Billy carefully.

Did she know? He was very good at hiding his true feelings, but where Claudia was concerned, his normal controls weren't as firm as they should be. She'd given him quite a scare tonight.

"I agree," he replied. "Whoever attacked her is still out there."

"She's welcome to stay with Daniel and me."

Claudia would certainly be safe behind the walls of Daniel's home. The billionaire had better security than the Pentagon—surveillance cameras, night watchmen, stone walls and iron gates.

But Billy would still worry about her. Unless he could see her with his own eyes, hear her breathing, he would feel uneasy.

Part of that was guilt. He'd taken unnecessary chances with Claudia. Although she viewed this case as *hers,* because she had brought it to the attention of Project Justice and pled for Mary-Francis's life, he was point man. Claudia's continued involvement had been his decision, and look what had happened.

With Claudia safely tucked away at Daniel's estate, Billy would be free to go after whoever had hurt her, no holds barred. But how long would she stay put? Overnight, probably. And by morning, she would be champing at the bit to get back in the game. She wouldn't let anything stop her from doing her bit to free Mary-Francis.

She had her own guilt to deal with.

"What do you think?" Jamie asked.

"What?" He'd lost track of the conversation.

"About Claudia staying with us."

"I was thinking I'd take her home with me. Next to your house, my apartment is the safest in the city." Because Daniel also owned Billy's downtown building, and it featured not only a secure entry, but a twenty-four-hour doorman. All four of the doormen who shared that post had paramilitary training.

After a sniper had damn near taken out two Project Justice employees last year, Daniel had installed bulletproof glass in every street-facing window.

Jamie gave him a knowing look. "I thought you

might say that. I ordered a car to pick me up, and it's probably here by now. I'll leave you two alone."

"Ah, Jamie…it's not what you think. Claudia and I aren't, you know, together."

"Maybe not, but when the two of you are in the same room, the sparks are so palpable I start worrying about nearby flammable liquids."

Billy couldn't deny that.

Jamie tried again. "If you need someone to talk to—"

"Nope. I'm good." Why did women always feel the need to dig inside his brain? Wasn't a man allowed to keep his thoughts private anymore?

"Okay." Jamie didn't seem to take offense at his curt response. "Let us know if you need anything."

"Thanks. Really, Jamie, thanks for coming with me."

"You're welcome. Daniel would have come, you know, if you'd asked."

"I know how much he hates hospitals." Daniel had made great strides in overcoming a bad case of agoraphobia, but he still felt safest when behind the walls of his estate, and he didn't venture out without a good reason.

By the time Claudia appeared in the waiting room, Billy was alone. She looked more fragile than usual, and when she flashed him a tentative smile, all he could think about was scooping her into his arms and taking her someplace far away from here, where no one would ever hurt her again.

"Thanks for waiting," she said.

"Like I was going to leave you here? Would you have taken a taxi home?"

She shrugged, then winced. "I guess."

Billy rolled his eyes. "I know you're used to making your own way in the world and not depending on anyone but yourself, but for today, would you at least admit that you're hurt and a little scared, and let me do my macho-caveman-protector thing?" He held out one arm, inviting her closer.

Tentatively, she stepped toward him so he could put a protective arm around her. "I *am* hurt. And I *was* scared, but now I'm mostly mad that someone got the drop on me. I'm normally more careful, more aware of my surroundings."

"That makes two of us who are mad." But not for the same reasons. He was furious that anyone would use Claudia to get to him. "Let's go. I'm your wheels tonight."

"You aren't going to pull back the investigation because of this, are you?" Claudia asked as they walked to the parking lot. He kept his hand at her waist, ready to catch her if she faltered. But even in her heels, her gait was sure and steady.

"I don't let bullies stop me from doing my job," he said. "Project Justice has a policy about threats. We take them very, very seriously, and Daniel will do anything in his power to protect his people, including anyone working with us."

"Meaning me."

"Yeah. If you'd feel safer, you can stay at his estate. Nothing short of a Sherman tank assault could get to you there."

She laughed. "Don't be ridiculous. I don't need that kind of protection. Eduardo, or whoever is behind the attack on me, made his point. I doubt anyone will try to hurt me again."

Billy wasn't so sure. "I'm not pulling back," he said.

"Because that's the other part of our policy. We don't let bullies tell us what to do. Since we aren't following orders, whoever hurt you could make a stronger statement next time."

"Hmm. I hadn't thought of it that way."

"Which is why you're staying with me. Or, you can stay at Daniel's. He offered. It's your choice. But you're not going home alone."

She stiffened her spine at the ultimatum, as he'd known she would. Claudia didn't like taking orders. But after a few moments to mull it over, she acquiesced. "I suppose if I insist on going home, Daniel will plant an armed guard at my door."

"Wouldn't be surprised."

"And that would be a waste of resources. Okay, I'll go home with you. For tonight. Tomorrow, we can reassess."

"Fair enough."

When they reached his truck, Claudia couldn't use her left hand to grab on to haul herself into the high cab. Rather than watch her try to figure out how to manage the maneuver, Billy scooped her up and deposited her into the passenger seat.

"Now that's service."

Was it his imagination, or did she hold on to his arm a tad longer than necessary? He wouldn't be human if he didn't fantasize, at least a little, that he and Claudia could be together, but without all the touchy-feely soul-baring that she was after.

"You know what?" he said after climbing behind the wheel. "We make a good team."

"You think so? What brought on that observation?"

"I mean, we work well together. We spark ideas off

each other. We can spend time together without irritating each other."

"Billy, we argue all the time."

"But it's the good kind of arguing. What I'm trying to say is, I like working with you. I like being with you."

"I like being with you, too, Billy," she said softly.

"So isn't that enough?"

"I'm not following. Enough for what?"

"For us to be together," he said flatly.

"What about the sex?"

He almost drove into a barricade. Claudia could certainly be direct when she put her mind to it. "What about it? It's about as good as it gets. Kinda goes without saying."

"So what you're saying is...we work well together. We like being together, even when we argue. We're great in the sack, if we can judge from one sexual experience."

"Do you have to talk like a scientist all the time?"

"What you're suggesting is that we be friends with benefits."

He had to think about that one. Was that all he wanted from Claudia? To be buddies, with sex on the side? "Is that a horrible idea?"

He expected her to say yes. Without hesitation. It would have been easier if she had. What she said was, "Works for some people. So long as both parties know where to draw the line, it's the sort of arrangement that can serve a purpose."

"That's Claudia the psychologist talking. What about for you, personally?"

"Are you actually proposing that we be sex buddies? Or is this a theoretical discussion?"

There was a sharpness to her tone that didn't bode well. "I shouldn't have even brought it up. The way you describe it…it's not what I want. All I know is, I'm not happy with how we left things."

"The way I remember, you're the one who left."

She had him there. "Whatever. I'm not happy."

"I'm not, either."

That was good, at least. He hoped.

They stopped at Walgreens to fill Claudia's prescription and buy a few necessities she would need for the night. When they reached Billy's apartment building downtown, he pulled in to the garage, protected by a passkey as well as a human guard who eyeballed Billy, then waved a greeting when he was recognized.

"This building really is secure," Claudia said. "I'd heard about it, but I've never been inside before. How many Project Justice people live here?

"Raleigh and Griffin, Jillian…"

"Daniel's assistant? I thought she lived on the estate."

"She's an intern at the foundation now. Daniel has a new assistant, Elena. Ford Hyatt used to live here."

"I helped with one of his cases two years ago."

"He moved out when he and his wife got married. She has a son, and they wanted a yard and a dog and a swing set."

"Who else lives here, then?"

"Anyone who wants hypersecurity—celebrities, politicians. The chief of police lives here. Also—and don't go telling anyone this—but the U.S. Marshals maintain a safe house here."

"Witness protection?"

"Uh-huh. Short-term, high-profile stuff."

"Well, I guess if it's good enough for them, it's good enough for me."

BILLY'S APARTMENT WAS a research gold mine, as far as Claudia was concerned. She was achy and exhausted, but not too tired to inspect every inch of the place that was visible to her to try to learn as much as she could about him. Though he wasn't comfortable enough to share certain elements of his past with her, the fact that he had opened his home to her indicated a certain amount of trust.

The roomy apartment wasn't a typical messy bachelor pad. But neither was it a museum. The living room featured a couple of vintage brown leather sofas with a square pine coffee table between them. The larger of the sofas was situated for optimum viewing of the gigantic flat-screen TV. The floors were covered in off-white Berber carpet with a couple of Navajo-style throw rugs. A corner bookshelf overflowed with books stacked and wedged in every which way. This was not a bookshelf for show, but one well used.

That was a slight surprise. She hadn't thought of Billy as the literary type.

The walls were painted a rich cream color with an adobe-style texture. And while the room didn't look like a set from *Bonanza,* there was a definite Western feel to the place that went well with Billy's boots.

"You're a cowboy at heart," she said with a smile.

"Huh? Oh, you mean the 'decor.'" He made finger-quotes in the air. "Blame my mother and my two sisters. They follow me around wherever I go and decorate, because otherwise I just wouldn't bother."

Her heart warmed at the thought of having a family

to care about where you lived. “Your family is from here?”

“They all live within five miles of here. Which can be a blessing and a curse. Originally I was glad that Dallas was the first department to accept my application. I thought I needed distance. But…” He shrugged. “I missed ’em.” He stood indecisively in the middle of the room, holding the bag from Walgreens. “Claudia, I’m going to be honest here. I don’t have a guest room—my extra bedroom is set up with a weight bench and some other junk I never use. I’m going to put you in my bedroom. And don’t worry, I have no intention of trying anything, not when you’re all scraped and bruised.”

“Oh. Um, thanks for not dancing around the issue.” She hesitated, her mouth working as she formulated her next words.

“So you’ll…sleep on the couch?”

“I think it would be better. You’re gonna be sore enough as it is. You can at least sleep in a proper bed with no one else trying to hog the covers. Why don’t you sit down? Relax, put your feet up, turn on the TV. I’m gonna change the sheets and get you fresh towels.”

“You don’t have to—”

But he didn’t stay to hear her objection. He proceeded down a hallway and disappeared into what was presumably the master suite.

Claudia decided to take Billy’s advice. She sat down on the surprisingly comfy sofa, grabbed the remote and hit the power button.

Billy had every channel available on the planet. At her house she had only basic cable—she seldom watched TV. But tonight seemed like a good time to find something mindless and put all disturbing and scary thoughts out of her mind, at least for a while.

She found a really stupid reality show where idiots were engaging in frightful and dangerous activities for cash, but she found it too scary. So was the replay of a Harry Potter movie.

She finally settled on a *Brady Bunch* rerun. The only thing scary about that show was the clothes.

After grabbing a fuzzy maroon throw from the back of the sofa and wrapping herself in it like a moth in a cocoon, she settled back and let her mind empty.

When next she became aware, the news was on and she was no longer alone on the sofa. She was snuggled up against Billy's chest like a contented cat. He had his arm around her and a paperback on his knee.

She stirred, and he stroked her arm. "You awake?"

"Mmm. Kind of."

"Hope you don't mind me sharing the sofa with you."

Did she look like she minded? "Did they give me something for pain at the hospital? I honestly don't remember."

"I don't know. You want a pain pill?"

"No, I'm okay." She did hurt, but it wasn't more than she could handle, and she hated the way pain medication made her feel, as if she was swimming through Karo syrup.

"You must be hungry. I got you a snack."

As her eyes focused on the plate of fruit, a bag of tortilla chips and a tub of hummus, she realized she was famished. She hadn't eaten since breakfast, and it was after midnight.

"Thanks, I'm starved." She pulled away self-consciously from Billy, already missing the warmth of his body and the scent of his soap and freshly washed T-shirt. He'd showered and changed while she'd been snoozing.

After five minutes of concentrated noshing, Claudia's hunger beast was tamed for the moment. "Sorry I fell asleep on you."

"I'm glad you felt comfortable enough to do that. Your body needs rest to heal."

Actually, she was a bit surprised she could so utterly relax in a strange place, with a man she knew but still didn't know well, that she could fall asleep inside of five minutes. They *must* have given her something at the hospital.

"I should go to bed."

"Okay. Your toothbrush is in the bathroom. I also put one of my T-shirts on the bed for you to sleep in, if you want. It should fit you like a nightshirt."

Sleeping with Billy's shirt next to her naked skin sounded appealing. But not half as delicious as Billy himself would be.

With some effort, she scraped that thought out of her brain. This wasn't the time to be thinking sexy thoughts. She wouldn't even be here if she hadn't needed a safe haven.

Claudia stood and wobbled a little before finding her footing.

"You sure you're okay?"

"I'm fine. Thanks again for everything."

"*Mi casa es tu casa.* Until we get to the bottom of this investigation. Okay?"

"That's generous of you."

He laughed. "Generous has nothing to do with it." He stood and surprised her with a quick but gentle hug. "I'm really glad you're okay. You scared me half to death."

"Not as bad as I scared myself. Good night."

She got as far as the bedroom door. It was a nice room with a king-size bed covered with an old white chenille spread. The furnishings were older and made of dark-stained oak. Basic but sturdy, well loved. She imagined they'd belonged to some older relative before Billy got them. A cross hung over the bed, a garish plaster thing painted in bright colors that had faded with age. It might have come from Mexico.

Claudia clumsily undressed with her one hand and climbed into Billy's T-shirt. She caught a glimpse of herself in the dresser mirror and thought for a moment she'd regressed to being a little girl, playing dress-up. With bruises.

She quickly averted her eyes and made her way to the bathroom. After brushing her teeth, she returned to the bedroom and stared at the big, soft-looking bed with its half-dozen feather pillows covered in a mixed bag of old cotton cases. And suddenly she couldn't bear the thought of sleeping there alone.

When she peeked back into the living room, she saw Billy had stretched out on the sofa in just his boxers and a T-shirt, the fuzzy throw wrapped haphazardly around his legs.

Though she was sure she made no noise, he sensed her presence anyway and looked up. His brow immediately creased with concern. "Is everything okay?"

"No. Would you maybe want to sleep with me? I mean, really sleep-sleep," she clarified.

He was on his feet in an instant. "Of course I will. Of course."

"I guess I'm afraid to be alone."

"It's okay, you don't have to explain. You've been through a lot today."

He was being so nice to her, and every bone in her body believed he was genuine. But Raymond had been nice, too. A chameleon, Billy had called him. A consummate actor who could be anything the current woman in his life wanted him to be.

And she hadn't spotted it.

She aggressively swept all thoughts of Raymond aside. She was safe. She had to believe she was safe or she would never sleep.

Claudia climbed into the bed first, sinking into the feather mattress topper as if it were a cloud. Billy got in after her. "Are you okay on that side, or do you want to switch places?"

"No, this is good."

He snapped off the lamp, but a glow of silver light from the city drifted in through the half-open blinds. At first he didn't touch her. But then he reached a tentative hand out and brushed it against her bare arm, producing shivers through her whole body.

"Could you hold me till I fall asleep?" she asked.

"I thought you'd never ask."

Careful of her injuries, he drew her against his chest until they were nestled together spoon-fashion. "Comfortable?"

"Like you wouldn't believe."

She had almost fallen asleep again when a sudden thought occurred to her and her eyes snapped open. "Billy."

"What? Huh?" He'd already been asleep.

"The priest. I want to go see him tomorrow."

Billy sighed. "Claudia, even if he knows something,

he can't tell us. Ever heard of the seal of the confessional?"

"I know he can't tell us Mary-Francis's sins. But I'm more interested in finding out what *his* sins might be."

# *CHAPTER ELEVEN*

BILLY HAD BEEN HOPING Claudia would forget the priest. He didn't want to think of that sweet, elderly man as a suspect; it went against his grain. He'd been raised Catholic, and though the priesthood had suffered some credibility blows in the past few years, his experience with Catholic school and priests had been nothing but positive. If not for some firm guidance from Father Miguel and Father Pat, Billy would have ended up on the other side of the law.

But the last thing he wanted to do when Claudia was in his arms was to start an argument. She had reached out to him tonight. This afternoon, she had hinted that she couldn't trust him if he didn't come clean about every sordid detail of his past. But tonight, her actions said something different.

She did trust him, enough that she could fall asleep next to him when she was at her most vulnerable, when contact with any man was most likely to be frightening. That realization filled him with hope that they could move forward somehow.

"We'll talk about this tomorrow, okay?" he said.

"Okay, but don't let me forget about it. My brains feel like mush."

"That's totally normal after you get beat up. Now sleep. I promise we'll talk about the priest in the morning."

Amazingly, she did sleep. And amazingly, Billy managed to limit his handholds to relatively innocuous parts of Claudia, like her knee or her waist.

He couldn't do anything about certain other parts of his own anatomy, which had gone rock hard at the mere thought of climbing into bed with Claudia. She probably couldn't miss the fact that he was jabbing her just below her enticing little bottom. But it didn't seem to bother her, because she was breathing the soft, untroubled breath of dreamless sleep.

It was a long time before Billy could drop off. Questions about this case kept chasing their tails in his head. Why hadn't Mary-Francis told them where she'd hidden the coins? Was it because Eduardo had stolen them, and she didn't want authorities to find and seize them?

Was Eduardo still alive? It sounded as though he was. Eduardo was a prime suspect for not only the assault on Claudia, but the one on Theresa, as well. He might have sent henchmen to do the job, or he might even be personally involved. His organization was falling apart. With his authority deteriorating and his money running out, he might have gotten desperate enough to come out of hiding.

And what was Angie's role? Did she have criminal involvement, or was she merely her father's pawn?

He finally fell asleep at about two in the morning.

When he woke, he and Claudia had switched positions. He was on his back, and she was draped over him like a blanket. Her head was tucked under his chin so that her soft hair tickled the sensitive flesh of his neck. She'd flung her left arm over him so that her splinted wrist rested on the mattress next to him. Her soft breasts pressed against his chest and his inadvertent look down the neckline of his repurposed T-shirt had him instantly hard. Her knee was between his legs, resting dangerously close to his family jewels. All she had to do was bend her knee suddenly and raise her leg a few inches higher…

But it felt nice, having her nestled there. In fact, he could get used to this real fast. He'd always had a firm rule about women not spending the night. He usually managed to have sex at the girl's place, so he could leave when he wanted to. So waking up with a warm, pliant woman…that was a novelty.

Not that Claudia was pliant. When she woke up, she would probably be embarrassed by their position, even if they had enjoyed sex just yesterday. She was kinda prim in some ways.

It was still early, but Billy had a full slate of plans today. Before Claudia's call, he'd been brainstorming with Daniel on new ways to attack his case. Daniel, always good at thinking outside the box, had come up with some excellent ideas.

Claudia stirred and murmured something in her sleep. He played with her hair because it was soft and silky and one of the few places he could touch her without the temptation to stray into trouble.

"That feels nice," she said softly.

"Good. How'd you sleep?"

"Like a baby." Probably realizing how intimately they were wrapped together, she started pulling back, coming more fully awake.

Now he could look into her eyes, which were relaxed and sleepy still. "I'm glad."

"I hope I didn't keep you awake. I've been told that I thrash around in my sleep."

"No thrashing."

"What time is it?"

"A little after eight."

"What?" She jerked herself upright, then winced. "Oh, hell, they weren't kidding about hurting worse today. I don't want to take whatever drugs the doc prescribed. Got any plain ol' aspirin?"

"I'll see what I can find." He couldn't resist leaning in and kissing her on the forehead.

She gave him a perplexed look, which he definitely couldn't decipher. Now is when he wished he had her training.

Funny, a week ago he'd thought Claudia's face-reading skills were phony, a gimmick. But he was starting to believe they were real. He had learned to shield his true feelings out of necessity, and through trial and error, but any cop working undercover—any cop at all—could benefit from formal training on body language, both reading others and being read.

He was going to recommend that Claudia teach a class for Project Justice. At least she'd be hanging around where he could see her. Right now, he had no idea what would happen once they concluded work on this case.

If they ever did. Leads were slim and Mary-Francis's execution date drew closer.

Billy found a bottle of Advil. Back in the bedroom, he discovered Claudia out of bed, looking damn fetching in his T-shirt, which barely covered her panties.

"I need a shower—bad."

"You need help?" he asked hopefully.

She rolled her eyes. "If we could just bottle men's libido, we'd put an end to our dependence on fossil fuel." She softened her comment with a smile, took the bottle of drugs from him and sashayed into the bathroom.

When she found her way to the kitchen forty-five minutes later, he was amazed at the transformation. She'd managed to get the blood stains out of yesterday's skirt, which she'd paired with a five-dollar tank top from the drugstore. Instead of wearing her hair loose and curled under, which was her usual style, she'd slicked it back into a braid and fastened it with a scrunchie. She'd even made up her face, softening the bruises to the side of her cheekbone and around her eye. She must have had some cosmetics in her purse.

In short, with very few resources, she'd managed to transform herself from assault victim to high-fashion model.

"Wow, you look great." His uncooperative mind conjured up all kinds of X-rated images. He could take her right here. On the kitchen table—

"Is something burning?"

He yanked the frying pan off the burner and quickly salvaged the bacon. "Hope you like it crispy." This was the reason he didn't do much cooking. His mother had tried to teach him, but he invariably got distracted and let something burn.

"You didn't have to fix breakfast for me...but that's very sweet of you."

"Nothing sweet about it," he corrected her. "You need fuel—and rest—so you can heal."

She brushed away his concern with a wave of her splinted hand. "I'm fine. So how do we find out this priest's name? Can we just ask at the Torres' parish church?"

He'd been hoping to distract her from the notion of the priest being a player in their drama. But she'd apparently gotten the bone in her mouth and she wasn't going to let go of it.

"Sit down, we'll eat breakfast, and we'll talk about the priest." He'd made enough bacon, scrambled eggs and toast to feed a family of ten, and for a while, the meal was enough to distract Claudia.

But she wouldn't let it go. "So how do we find what parish Mary-Francis belonged to?"

Billy pulled out his phone. "The priest introduced himself at the beginning of the memorial service. Father Benito." Billy did a quick Google search. "There's only one Father Benito in the whole metroplex. And…" With a few more clicks, he called up the website for an urban church less than two miles from Billy's apartment. "Voilà."

He turned the phone so Claudia could see it. "That's him!" she said with a smile of wonder. "Church of Our Lady of Perpetual Hope?"

"Located right downtown. It's so close, we could walk." Billy took a long sip of coffee, wishing the caffeine would hurry up and kick his brain into gear. He felt slow from the lack of sleep.

"I guess that's why you're the investigator, and I'm not. I'd have taken all day to find the guy."

"I'm still not sure he can help," Billy argued, momentarily entranced by the way Claudia's long, pale neck moved when she swallowed. "Priests take the seal of the confessional seriously. No law can force them to reveal anything they've learned from penitents within the confines of the Sacrament of Penance. Priest-penitent privilege is protected under the law."

"Yes, but suppose the priest *does* something as a result of what he learned from someone. *That's* not protected."

Billy ate a few more forkfuls of egg, mulling over Claudia's words.

Suddenly he noticed something about Claudia's hands. He'd never known her to have anything but a perfect manicure. Now, though, two of her fingernails were broken. "Did you scratch him?" he asked abruptly.

"The priest?"

"The guy who attacked you. I just noticed your broken fingernails."

She examined her right hand briefly. "Maybe I broke them when I fell…"

"You fell on your left hand. Do you remember anyone taking scrapings from your nails at the hospital?"

She closed her eyes, probably thinking back to last night. "I don't think so. Oh, but I scrubbed my hands really hard this morning. If there was any evidence, I washed it away."

"But you broke two nails. Were the police treating the garage like a crime scene? Did they put up yellow tape, or bring in any crime scene investigators?"

She shook her head. "Not that I remember."

He pulled his phone out of his pocket and dialed work.

"Project Justice," came Celeste's no-nonsense greeting. "Where can I direct your call?" The question came out like an order.

"Celeste, it's me, Billy. Is Beth in yet?"

"Of course. All the *prompt* employees are here already. It's nearly nine o'clock."

"Can I speak with her, please?"

"Hold, please."

A few moments later, Beth picked up. "Billy. What's up?"

"Can you meet me at Claudia's office building, in the parking garage? I need to find some possibly overlooked evidence."

"How is Claudia? Daniel told everyone about the assault this morning."

Interesting that Beth knew Claudia was with him. "She's good."

"I'd be happy to meet you at the garage. What are we looking for? Should I bring any special equipment?"

"Fingernails. And really, all we need are flashlights and sharp eyes. Oh, and you might wear a crawl suit. In case we have to wiggle under parked cars."

"Ah. You need me to do the dirty work."

"Two sets of eyes are better than one. See you around ten?"

"Sure. I'm anxious to get out of this place. I'm afraid to walk down the hall."

"What?" Billy sat up straighter, his breakfast forgotten. "Is there some kind of threat at the office?"

"Oh, since you haven't been back here, you probably don't know. There's a wild pig loose in the office."

Billy couldn't help laughing. "Celeste's javelina, you mean?"

"Whatever. It looks like a pig to me. When it got away from her, it hid somewhere and no one's been able to find it. Last night it got into the break room and wolfed down an entire bowl of mini chocolate bars. Chocolate and wrappers everywhere. Chewed the leg off a chair. Uprooted every potted palm tree in the place. Finally, it pooped in the conference room."

"How could an animal that size hide and not get caught?" Billy asked, and Claudia smiled as she listened to the one-sided conversation.

"I have no idea. But don't tell Daniel. He doesn't know yet, and Celeste is afraid she'll get fired. She insists she can catch it."

Shoot it, more likely. And Billy was willing to bet Daniel *did* know. He always knew everything.

"So, you think we might find DNA under my broken fingernails?" Claudia asked when Billy had finished his call.

"Exactly." He grabbed his dishes and took them to the sink, eager to get going now that he had something to investigate. "If it wasn't Eduardo himself who grabbed you, it might be one of his henchmen, who might be in the CODIS database. If we can find him, he might lead us to Eduardo." Not to mention that Billy intended to kick the ass of whoever had assaulted Claudia. Nobody terrorized his woman and got away with—

*His* woman? Where had that come from? Claudia wasn't anywhere close to his.

But whose fault was that? If he came clean, if he cracked open his heart and bled all his secrets to her, perhaps she would feel satisfied that he wasn't a serial killer.

He shook his head.

"What?" Claudia had risen, too, and had managed to stack her dishes and pick them up one-handed.

"Here, let me get that." He took the plates and set them in the sink with his.

"Don't you need to rinse those?"

"Cleaning lady comes today. That reminds me, I

should call her and let her know you'll be here. Unless you'd rather I reschedule her—"

"I won't be here. I'm coming with you."

He shook his head. "Claudia, be reasonable. Someone tried to kill you."

"He didn't try to kill me. If he'd wanted me dead, that would have been easy enough."

"You should lay low anyway."

"I'm not going to cower in a cave just because there's a bad man out there. Anyway, if I don't come with you, how will you know where the attack took place? It's a big parking garage."

"You could tell me."

"Let me get my purse. Oh, c'mon, Billy, don't look at me like that. I'll be with you. Are you saying you can't protect me?"

"Oh, sure, attack my male vanity." His first instinct was to say, *of course* he could protect her. But the best bodyguards in the world—even the Secret Service—could be foiled by a smart and skillful person determined to do harm.

"What about Father Benito?" she asked in the elevator on the way down.

"I feel very uncomfortable investigating a priest," he said. "Besides, what are the odds that an older guy like that is caught up in a mess like this? Stolen coins, fake death, assault…I don't see it."

"We're just going to have a friendly chat," she reasoned. "It's not like we'll drag him to an interrogation room and break out the rubber hoses and cattle prods. If he can help us, fine. If not, what have we lost?"

"Claudia. So what if we find the coins. How does it help us clear Mary-Francis?"

"We know Eduardo is looking for the coins. If he

finds them, he's lost to us. He runs back to Mexico or wherever, sells the coins, creates a new identity, maybe gets plastic surgery…and Mary-Francis dies. But if *we* find them first, Eduardo is still close, still looking. Still catchable."

Damn. She had a good point. "All right. We talk to the priest. But let me do the talking. I grew up around priests. I understand how the system operates."

"Okay, but we should work out a signal I can give if I spot possible deception."

He grinned. "We don't have to work out anything. When you spot a lie, you give this tiny shake of your head."

"I do?" She sounded genuinely surprised.

"I noticed it that first day, when we were interviewing Mary-Francis. And again when we were talking to Angie."

"Huh."

He loved that he'd surprised her. "Now who's the body language expert?"

"If I'm doing that, I need to stop it. How about if I just touch my ear?"

"You think that's more subtle?" he asked dubiously.

"Never mind. We'll stick with what's working."

BY THE TIME THEY REACHED Claudia's office parking garage, Beth was already there, dressed neck-to-foot in a baggy, white Tyvek jumpsuit. She even had a white shower-cap-type headgear covering her curly brown hair.

A man who had just exited his car gave her a curious look as he walked past.

"About time you two got here," she said good-naturedly. "I was afraid someone would call the cops on the whack job hanging out in your garage. Claudia, how are you doing?" She raised a hand to her mouth. "Did you break your arm? Oh, and look at your poor black eye."

Claudia appreciated Beth's concern. "I'm okay. I tore some ligaments. Not too bad, all things considered."

Billy looked nervous. He gave the parking garage a thorough going-over to make sure no one was lurking, waiting for a chance to attack, though logic told them her assailant wouldn't be hanging around the scene of the crime.

"So we're looking for fingernails?" Beth snapped a pair of needle-nose tweezers in the air, obviously anxious to get to work. She had a big case at her feet, like a tackle box on steroids, in which she carried all the tools for evidence collection.

"That's it." Billy said. "Claudia, where did it happen?"

"I'm parked right over here." She led them to the general area where she always parked. And there was her Roadster, right where she'd left it. She paused and closed her eyes as a wave of nausea washed over her.

"Claudia?" Billy was at her side in an instant, his hand at her waist, ready to catch her if she should topple.

"I'm sorry, I just need to..." She was shocked at the sudden onslaught of feelings, almost as if the assault were only now occurring. All of the terror and the fierce, violent anger she'd felt toward her attacker bloomed in her chest and tears sprang to her eyes.

Was this what post-traumatic stress felt like? She'd seen it in her patients, read descriptions, but she'd had no idea it could happen to her.

"I've got a bottle of water right here." Beth sounded worried.

Claudia held out her good hand in a halt gesture. "Just give me a minute." Billy's hand at her waist felt nice, reassuring. She took several slow, deep breaths, silently reminding herself that she was safe, she was with friends. Billy would protect her.

The tears receded, her throat relaxed. She opened her eyes to find Billy and Beth staring at her as if they expected her to start screaming or foaming at the mouth.

She managed a smile. "I'm okay now. Sorry. That was weird. I guess I haven't fully processed—" She stopped herself. Billy and Beth didn't want to hear her psychological justification for her minor freak-out. They just wanted her to be okay.

Claudia deliberately stepped away from Billy's light, protective embrace so he would know she was better now. She walked between her car and the one next to it, trying to remember if this was the right place. "I think it happened right here. The struggle, I mean." She tried to recall exactly what she'd done when he grabbed her, when she'd scratched him, when she might have lost the fingernails, but she drew a blank.

"He was probably hiding behind a parked car near yours," Billy theorized.

"Let's start with this area, right around Claudia's car," Beth said. "If we don't find anything, we'll expand outward. In a struggle, sometimes evidence can get flung much farther than you'd guess."

Claudia felt superfluous, just watching Beth and Billy do all the hard work, but she was hardly in any shape to crawl around on concrete. She perched on the hood of her car—right where her attacker had banged her head, she realized grimly—and watched as the two of them shone their enormous flashlights over the ground inch by inch.

Twenty minutes later, they'd found four pennies and a dime, an earring, a few minute drops of blood—probably Claudia's—and a Kool cigarette butt, which Beth dutifully collected and bagged.

No fingernails.

"They probably ended up on the bottom of someone's shoe," Claudia said glumly. "Or wedged in someone's tire."

Beth's face brightened. "The tires. That's one place we didn't look."

They searched the treads of nearby cars, extracting every pebble hiding there in case it was a fingernail in disguise. Just when they were about to give up, Billy called out.

"I think I found one!"

Beth rushed over, across the aisle and into the next row, where Billy was stooped over the front tire of a Jeep Cherokee. Claudia followed at a more sedate pace, but she was no less excited. If she had Eduardo's DNA under her nails, that annoying district attorney in Montgomery County couldn't continue to pretend the man was dead. They would *have* to overturn Mary-Francis's conviction.

Beth first examined the object Billy had found with a magnifying glass, then took pictures of it as well as the Jeep, widening her field of vision until she took in the vehicle's location within the garage. Only then did she use her trusty needle-nose tweezers to extract the foreign object.

"This is definitely a fingernail. Claudia, let me see your hand."

Claudia held out her right hand, including the two fingers with their ragged, partial nails, which she purposely hadn't filed down. Beth held up the specimen close to Claudia's pinky finger, then grinned. "I think we have a match."

## *CHAPTER TWELVE*

"GREAT." CLAUDIA TURNED to Billy. "Please let me know when you find out anything." She lowered her voice, glancing nervously at Beth, who seemed to be engrossed in properly storing and tagging the fingernail. "I really appreciate how you took care of me last night. You were very understanding. You'll let me know when you go to see the priest? I'd really like to be in on that interview." She'd figured out that it was useless to push Billy into questioning Father Benito. This was his investigation, and he would proceed in his own way.

She also knew that sooner or later, he would reach the same conclusion she had—that the priest was up to something. She only hoped no one else figured out he might be involved.

She leaned in to give Billy a chaste kiss on the cheek, though she longed to do more, and turned toward the door that led into her office building.

"Wait a minute. Where are you going?"

"I have work to do. Patients to see?"

"Claudia..."

"What? My office is secure. Everyone who visits the building has to check in, you saw that. And I can have a security guard walk me to my car when I'm ready to go home." The thought of retracing yesterday's steps made her slightly queasy, but if she didn't immediately face her fears, she risked developing a phobia about parking garages or walking anywhere alone. She'd treated enough patients with phobias to know that an irrational fear could spring from any traumatic event, even a minor one.

Billy widened his stance and folded his arms. "Someone. Tried. To. Kill. You."

"Scare me," she corrected. "If he'd meant to kill me, why would he have bothered to warn me away from the Torres family?"

"Let me put it another way. If you stay here, *I* stay here. And if I stay here, I can't do any more investigating."

She wouldn't mind Billy hanging around, but not if he was going to watch her as though she was a five-year-old with a penchant for walking off cliffs. She folded her arms, mirroring him, and leaned against the cinder block wall of the parking structure. "What investigating do you have to do?"

"First, I'm going to see what Angie and Jimmy are up to. We can't legally tap their phones or plant listening devices, but Aaron Ziglar, one of the Project Justice techies, has a listening device that picks up voices through walls. Since the houses are so close, I'm going to see if a sympathetic neighbor will let me set up surveillance in their house, at a window that faces the Torres house."

"That's brilliant. Is it legal?"

Billy shrugged. "If it leads us to Eduardo, that won't matter. Once we prove he's alive, the prosecution can't unprove it."

"Good luck, then." She turned away again, intending to make a clean getaway this time. She needed some time away from Billy to get her head on straight.

Spending the night half-naked in bed with him, even if they'd mostly just slept, had played havoc with her good judgment.

"Wait."

She tried to hide her impatient sigh. "Yes?"

"I want you to go back to my apartment and stay put. Rest. Recuperate. You're injured. You're traumatized."

"I'm fine. No one is trying to kill me. I will take necessary precautions."

Billy's phone rang, interrupting their argument. He yanked it out of his jeans pocket and frowned at the screen. "Cantu."

She could have used the distraction to escape his eagle eye; he couldn't *force* her to hide in his apartment. Not even Daniel could do that. He wasn't her boss. But she was curious about the phone call. She couldn't tell who was on the other end of the conversation because Billy did more listening than talking. But judging from the serious, intensely interested expression on his face, the caller had important news.

When he ended the call, she looked at him expectantly. "Well?"

"I don't suppose you'd believe that was my mother."

"C'mon, Billy, don't shut me out."

"Okay. It's good news, for a change. That was Hudson Vale. Theresa has roused from her coma."

Beth, done with her evidence collecting, joined them, having overheard Billy's announcement. "That's great news! Is she okay? Talking? Does she have brain damage?"

"Apparently she's talking, but only a few words that don't make a lot of sense. But her doctor is hopeful she'll continue to improve. Hudson thought we'd like to know."

"We have to talk to her—before anyone taints her memories or plants ideas into her head. People with head injuries and possible memory loss have to be treated very gently if you want to get accurate information from them."

"Good to know." Billy seemed uneasy all of a sudden.

"Billy, you have to let me talk to her."

Billy looked away and blew out a frustrated breath. "This time, you'll get your wish. Hudson specifically asked for you to interview Theresa. He's read up on you and would be honored if you'd 'help out.'"

Claudia saw that the admission had cost Billy. He could have pretended that part of the conversation had never happened. He could have told Hudson that Claudia was unavailable. But he'd opted for the truth, even though it didn't jibe with the way he wanted things to go.

"Let me get my recorder from my office, and we can go."

ST. CECELIA'S MEDICAL CENTER was the largest Catholic hospital in the city as well as one of the oldest and most prestigious teaching hospitals in the Southwest. It was situated in the medical corridor on Fannin Street, just south of the Southwest Freeway and only a few minutes from Claudia's office building.

Hudson Vale met them in the lobby, wearing a different Hawaiian shirt, this one featuring garish ukulele-playing hula dancers, along with a pair of faded jeans. Claudia wondered if the story about working undercover was legitimate; maybe he dressed like this every day. He certainly looked right at home attired like a beach bum, albeit a very good-looking one.

"So glad you guys could make it." He shook their hands enthusiastically. "Oh, man, I'm so jazzed she woke up and I'm terrified she'll drop back into a coma. Her doctor said she wasn't out of the woods yet, and it could be several days before he can give a reliable prognosis."

Claudia appreciated Hudson's compassion, which obviously went beyond just concern over solving his case. He cared about his crime victim, too. He hadn't been working at the job long enough to treat life-or-death situations with a blasé attitude.

He might even care a little *too* much; cops who didn't learn to detach emotionally from their work tended to burn out faster. But she was still charmed by his passion, though not in any way that should make Billy jealous.

Billy seemed okay today around Hudson. Maybe her reassurances had actually convinced him. With some men, jealousy was a way of life; those were the kind to steer clear of.

Raymond Bass hadn't acted jealous. He'd been respectful of Claudia's career aspirations, accepting of the fact that she had male friends and study partners. He'd passed himself off as enlightened, as if he'd viewed her as a true equal because he'd known, somehow, that was what she was looking for in a man.

Raymond hadn't been enlightened, of course. In reality he'd viewed women as playthings to be hunted and butchered like deer.

She shivered and forced the memory out of her mind. Billy wasn't a murderer or an abuser. But his experience as an undercover cop had taught him to reflect whatever persona or attitudes would get him what he wanted, and he sometimes used that ability in his work. She'd seen him do it with Theresa's neighbor, Patty.

He *seemed* more genuine with her, but she wasn't a hundred percent sure she could take him at face value.

"Theresa is still in intensive care," Hudson was explaining. "That means one visitor for ten minutes each hour."

"Does she have family members who also want to visit?" Claudia asked as they all stepped onto an elevator. She hated the idea of monopolizing Theresa's limited visiting times she could be spending with loved ones.

"The son from Arizona is on his way but not here yet. We have her to ourselves for now. I haven't said very much to her, other than explaining she was involved in a crime I was investigating."

"That's good," Claudia said. "That you haven't influenced her memories, I mean."

"Claudia," Hudson said, "I want you to talk to Theresa first. She seems fearful, and I'm afraid if she opens her eyes and sees Billy straightaway, she'll be so scared she'll clamp her mouth shut and never open it again."

"Hey," Billy objected. "Maybe I'm not a pretty boy like you, but I've never frightened animals or small children."

"He didn't mean it that way," Claudia said. "He means you can be pretty intimidating when you're questioning someone."

"Me?" Billy said innocently.

He probably didn't like giving over control to her. This was his case, his baby. He'd made the decision to pursue it, committed all kinds of resources to it—surveillance teams, equipment, his time. Successfully closing cases at Project Justice was the way employees there achieved status, position and pay raises.

But in her heart she knew Hudson was right. Theresa would feel more comfortable with a woman than a man she didn't know.

"All right. But you get one crack at her. If she doesn't spill, next hour it's my turn." Billy ran his fingers through his short hair, something he did when he was unsure of himself. It didn't happen very often. "Is her doctor okay with this?"

"Dr. Kim. He wants to catch the bastard, too. So long as we follow the rules and don't upset her, he's cool. He said she's still emerging from the coma, but she's started to speak purposefully—she hears and understands some, at least."

They had to cool their heels a few minutes in the ICU waiting room. A group of medical students were observing Theresa so they could learn about a patient emerging from a coma.

Claudia spent her time formulating how she would approach Theresa, depending on her condition. And when she felt sufficiently prepared, she jotted some notes on her phone as to how she would question Father Benito.

Whether Billy agreed or not, she intended to talk to the priest.

After a few minutes, a nurse poked her head in the doorway and announced that Theresa was ready for her visitor. Claudia nodded, stood and smiled as Billy and Hudson gave her two encouraging thumbs-up.

Theresa Esteve looked ghastly—there was no other word for it. She was hooked up to all kinds of machines—a heart monitor, a machine that analyzed the carbon dioxide content of her breath to see if she was getting enough oxygen into her lungs, another machine that measured the actual oxygen absorbed into her bloodstream. There were so many machines, tubes and wires that Theresa nearly disappeared.

There was only one place to sit, the rolling stool used by the doctor. Claudia claimed it and sat down, reaching for Theresa's emaciated hand.

*There but for the grace of God go I.*

If nothing else, Theresa's gaunt face, hollow eyes and labored breathing reminded Claudia how very lucky she'd been to escape her assault with only minor scrapes and scratches.

"Theresa? Hello, my name is Claudia," she began. "I know you're probably not feeling up for a conversation, but if you can understand me, would you squeeze my hand?"

At first there was no response, and Claudia feared the patient had dropped back to sleep. But after a few seconds she felt a squeeze to her hand, very weak but definite.

"Good, good," Claudia said soothingly. Then, for the benefit of the recording she was making of the conversation, "Thank you for squeezing my hand. Do you mind if I record our conversation? Squeeze my hand if it's okay to record."

Theresa squeezed.

"Thank you. That was another squeeze." Claudia pulled her tiny digital recorder—which was already turned on—out of her pocket and placed it on the tray table next to the bed. It was very sensitive and would pick up everything, even a whisper, if the whir and hum of the medical equipment didn't drown out the sounds they wanted to record. "You're in the hospital. You're injured, but you're getting better and the doctors think you'll make a full recovery." Claudia didn't know if this was true, but she figured giving the patient positive expectations couldn't hurt. "Do you understand what I'm saying?"

Again, a barely discernible tightening of Theresa's hand.

"That was another yes. Good. Some men came into your home and attacked you. Do you remember that night?"

Another squeeze.

"Again, yes. I'm working with the police to try to catch the men who hurt you. Did you know them? Just squeeze my hand if you knew the men who hurt you."

Theresa's eyes opened briefly, reflecting naked fear. Maybe the woman was recalling emotions from the night she was attacked. Or maybe she was afraid to name her assailant.

Claudia soldiered on with the interview. She'd been hoping for a miracle, that Theresa would open her eyes and clearly speak the names of the men who tried to kill her.

No such luck.

"Okay. No squeeze that time. Very good, Theresa. You're doing great. Were the men looking for something?"

No hesitation this time; Theresa squeezed Claudia's hand hard. She seemed to be gaining strength. Maybe she felt encouraged that the police were working to solve the crime that had been perpetrated upon her.

"Another yes," Claudia said.

This was where it got tricky. Claudia couldn't simply ask, "Were they looking for coins?" Because

Theresa might very well be answering yes to most of the questions just for the novelty of being able to communicate, or because she wanted to please Claudia. Claudia's patients tended to want to make her happy.

"Can you tell me what they were looking for?"

This time, Theresa didn't squeeze Claudia's hand. Instead, the muscles of her face tensed and she worked her mouth, as if trying to persuade it to function properly.

Claudia stood and leaned over the bed, placing her ear close to Theresa's mouth. She brought the recorder close to Theresa's mouth, as well. "You don't have to speak very loudly," Claudia said. "Or very clearly. Just try."

Theresa made a noise like a snake. *Sssss.* It was a start.

"Can you try again?" Claudia asked. "I got the *sssss* part.

Next, Theresa whispered something that sounded like *liver.*

*Sssss* plus *liver.*

"Silver?"

"Mmm." Theresa squeezed Claudia's hand.

Claudia felt disappointed. Maybe the home invasion wasn't connected to Eduardo's disappearance after all.

"Yes to the word *silver.* Good. Did they take the silver?"

"No." That was the first clear word Theresa had spoken. "Dint have…dint know."

Every word was a supreme effort, but Claudia got the gist of what the woman was saying. "So you didn't have any silver to give them, and they got mad and hurt you?"

No hand squeeze. And Theresa was becoming agitated. Her heart rate went up slightly; the steady *blip-blip-blip* of her monitor had accelerated.

"Theresa, please relax. Whatever it is you need to tell me, I'll keep coming back until I understand, okay?"

That seemed to reassure her. "Silver," Theresa said, getting the word right this time. "Gold. Money."

Silver, gold, money. Claudia inhaled sharply. Could be coins. But it also could be the standard stuff burglars stole.

Finally, Theresa said something unambiguous. "Eddy."

Now it was Claudia whose heart rate accelerated. "Do you mean Eduardo, your brother-in-law?"

Theresa's hand trembled.

"What about Eddy? You don't have to be afraid. He can't hurt you here."

*"Fantasma."* Her eyes opened wide. *"Espíritu. Muerto."*

Claudia hesitated to ask for a translation. She had the words on her digital recorder; she sort of knew what they meant, but Billy would be able to translate for sure, and her time was running short.

"It's okay, Theresa. You don't have to be afraid. You're safe here." She hoped so, anyway. "I just have one more question. Before your sister, Mary-Francis, was arrested, did she give you anything? Something to keep safe?"

Theresa thought for a moment, then squeezed Claudia's hand so hard the bones were in danger of cracking. Theresa opened her eyes again and opened her mouth, but no sound came out.

"What was it, Theresa? What did your sister give you?"

*"Tesoro español. Ocultado en la estatua."*

That was when the nurse came in. "You'll have to leave now. You shouldn't have gotten her all riled up."

"I'm sorry," Claudia said. "I didn't mean to. But she had something important to tell me."

"Her? She's talking?" The nurse sounded skeptical. Maybe she hadn't gotten the memo that Theresa was awake.

"In two languages." Claudia collected her recorder. "I think I understand, Theresa. I'll be back, and we'll talk some more, okay?" She thought Theresa might have smiled, but it was hard to tell.

Both Billy and Hudson jumped to their feet when Claudia returned to the waiting room.

"Did you get anything?" Billy asked.

"Did she talk?" Hudson asked at the same time.

"She did. But some of what she said was in Spanish, which I don't speak very well, especially when it's slurred."

"I'll figure it out," Billy said.

Since they were the only ones in the waiting room, they all listened to the short recording Claudia had made. She set it on a table, and the three of them leaned their heads in to hear every word.

"Holy crap," Hudson said under his breath when Theresa mentioned Eddy.

"Wait, it gets better."

Billy listened, nodding, then quickly translated. "She said 'Ghost.' Then, 'spirit' and 'dead.'" He paused, then laughed and turned to hug Claudia. "You did it. *Cielito,* you did it!"

"What did she say?"

"She said, 'Spanish treasure hidden in statue.' You

were right all along. Mary-Francis hid the coins in the statue, and someone stole it."

"More important," Hudson said, "she identified Eduardo. She might have thought he was a ghost, but she recognized him as one of the men who attacked her."

"And he was looking for the coins," Billy said. "When Angie turned the Torres house upside down and couldn't find them, he must have figured out that Mary-Francis gave them to her sister for safekeeping."

"Theresa knew where they were," Claudia murmured. "But she didn't tell. Even when they beat her nearly to death. That is one brave woman. Unfortunately, so long as those coins are still out there somewhere, she'll be in danger."

# *CHAPTER THIRTEEN*

"SO IS THE CASE CLOSED?" Claudia asked as they headed back to Billy's truck. "I mean, once Fitz is back from his cruise, Theresa should be strong enough to tell him herself… Ah, hell."

Billy was shaking his head. It was the same old problem. Theresa presumably would say anything to free her sister; her statement about seeing Eduardo's ghost wouldn't convince Fitz of anything.

"Father Benito," she reminded him.

"Claudia, you don't really want to browbeat a priest, do you?"

"I just want to talk to him."

"Even if he knows something about these coins, it's not going to help free Mary-Francis," Billy reasoned.

"Yes, it could," she argued. "Eduardo obviously wants the coins—badly. We find them, maybe we find Eduardo. Boom. Mary-Francis goes free."

"Sure, and maybe we dig one of those pits with the pointy sticks at the bottom, cover it with grass and lure Eduardo into it."

"I think you're making fun of me."

"It's just that my job is to prove innocence, not catch crooks, not solve crimes, though sometimes solving a murder is a side effect of what we do."

They had reached the truck, but Claudia didn't get in. She leaned back against the door, folded her arms and met Billy's brown-eyed stare, her own gaze steady, unwavering. "I'll go by myself if I have to."

He maintained eye contact a few more heartbeats, testing her resolve, perhaps. Finally he looked away. "If we go see the priest, will you lay low afterward? Hang out in my apartment so I can get some work done without worrying about you?"

Though his bossiness rankled her, she knew she wasn't going to get a better offer. "Deal." She let Billy help her into the truck.

Billy seemed to relax slightly as he got behind the wheel. "I guess going to church isn't such a bad idea. This case could use a little divine intervention. Maybe while we're there, we can light a candle and pray to the patron saint of DNA that we get a hit."

"*Is* there a patron saint of DNA?"

Billy laughed. "You're kidding, right?"

"Only a little. According to the Catholic girls I went to school with in seventh grade, there's a patron saint of almost everything."

"Well, we have the patron saint of scientists, Saint Albert the Great. That's about as close to DNA as I can get. Then there's Father Raymond Nonnatus, patron saint of those falsely accused."

"We should take all the help we can get."

THE CHURCH OF OUR LADY of Perpetual Hope was a small, squat redbrick structure in a downtrodden section of downtown Houston. It was the third-oldest continually operating church in the city, dating back almost a century.

"I never even knew this place was here," Claudia commented as she approached Billy, who fed quarters into a meter.

"My fourth-grade class went on a field trip here," Billy said. "I hadn't thought about it for a long time." Now, though, the images of elderly Sister Ruth, shuffling lines of uniformed kids around the Stations of the Cross, flitted through his mind.

Claudia had been champing at the bit to take a crack at Father Benito, but now that they were here, she lingered on the sidewalk, gazing at the humble church. Only a few of its original stained glass windows remained, covered now with burglar bars and a protective layer of yellowing Plexiglas. The roof was missing a few shingles, and a rain gutter was hanging off the roof edge, ready to crash to the ground any second. A couple of lush pecan trees offered shade from the brutal south Texas summer sun, but that was the only thing that resembled landscaping.

"How do you think we should approach him?" Claudia asked.

Billy shrugged. "This was your idea, remember?"

"Are you really uncomfortable questioning a priest?"

"Twelve years of Catholic school can't just be swept aside."

"So your Catholic school experience was good? You liked the priests and the nuns?"

"Sure. If not for a couple of priests who were constantly on my case—and one old nun with a ruler who makes Celeste look like a Girl Scout—no telling where I'd have ended up. Illiterate and in jail, probably." He started to launch into what he thought was a funny story, then paused when he saw the frown on Claudia's face. "I'm guessing you had a not-so-nice Catholic school experience."

"I was told repeatedly that I was going to hell because not only was I not baptized, I didn't go to any church. Once during recess, Judy McGill got her friends to hold me down while she baptized me. But I never felt that I was quite saved."

Billy struggled not to grin. The way she told it, it was kind of funny, but he suspected at the time it had been terrifying.

"Not all Catholics are like that."

"I know. I can't picture you forcing baptism on anyone."

"No, I was more the type to steal communion wine and try to get drunk. Which was impossible because it was just grape juice."

"I was going to ask if you'd put in a good word for me when you die, but it sounds like you'll be busy trying to get your own sorry self through the pearly gates."

Billy didn't laugh. His sins weighed heavy on his conscience. An image of Sheila's face, grinning and full of life, slammed into his mind, followed by how she looked thirty seconds after she'd been shot through the heart.

"I didn't mean that," Claudia said quickly. "I don't mean to make light of your faith. I'm sure you'll be a shoo-in."

"Doubtful." He adjusted his Stetson and headed for the church's faded wooden doors.

Inside the church it was surprisingly cool and hushed. Though Billy couldn't detect the whir of an air conditioner, the thick brick walls and the shade trees shielded the building from the worst of the heat.

The church was better maintained inside than out. The tile floor, though chipped and cracked in places, was immaculate and the battered wooden pews bore the sheen of recent waxing. The scent of candles, incense and old hymn books assailed him, and immediately he was awash with memories of other churches, other times.

On the tidal wave of nostalgia, he walked over to a bank of candles, put a couple of folded bills through the slot of a locked brass box and lit a candle for Sheila.

He used to do it once a week, but as his churchgoing had slacked off, so had this ritual. He knelt on a worn velvet kneeler nearby and said a quick prayer for his old partner—his lover—but he imagined she was already in that joyful place good people ended up.

After a few moments, he realized Claudia was watching him intently—not in the respectful way that most people he knew observed Catholic rituals they weren't familiar with, but like a scientist observing a subject.

She was still trying to decipher him, pull every last secret from his soul, and he chafed at her intrusion.

They were alone in the nave of the church, but Billy figured there was someone here or the building wouldn't be open. In this part of town, an open, unattended door was an invitation for anything not nailed down to disappear.

Or worse.

Just as Billy was wondering where someone in charge might be lurking, Father Benito himself strolled into the nave, easily recognizable from the video. He wore the traditional cleric's clothing of black pants, black shirt and white-tabbed collar. A brass ring with several keys dangled from his belt.

"Hello," he said with a pleasant smile. "I'm Father Benito, and welcome to Our Lady of Perpetual Hope. Would you like to take a tour? It doesn't take long." He had a slight Spanish accent, but it sounded as if many years in the States had blunted it.

Billy strode toward the priest with his hand outstretched. "Hi, Father, I'm Billy Cantu. This is my associate, Claudia Ellison. I'd love to learn more about the church."

The priest assessed them shrewdly. "But you're not tourists."

His reading of nonverbal hints must have impressed Claudia, because her eyebrows shot up.

"That's true," she said. "We want to talk to you about one of your parishioners, Mary-Francis Torres."

Father Benito's face immediately clouded up. "Ah, Mary-Francis. That is a very sad case. She's actually not my parishioner. This little church doesn't have a regular congregation anymore. They all go to the bigger, newer churches now. The diocese maintains the church mostly for its historical significance, though I still say an occasional Mass here and administer other sacraments. Weddings are popular."

"But you're a friend of the Torres family," Claudia said. "You presided over the memorial service for Eduardo Torres."

"I've known the family for many, many years. In fact, Mary-Francis and her sister came from the same small village in Mexico as I did, Rio Verde."

The door opened and an elderly nun wearing a traditional black habit hobbled in, leaning heavily on a cane. Father Benito nodded to her, and she nodded back, then worked her way to a front pew and levered herself to her knees to pray.

"Sister Marguerite," he whispered. "She comes here every day to pray but never says much." He resumed speaking in a normal tone. "Perhaps you'd like to go into the vestry? It's quiet there, and more private."

Billy would actually have preferred to conduct their interview right in the church. Surely a priest would have a hard time lying in a place so filled with the presence of God. But Claudia had already agreed to the change of location, and soon they were all three squeezing into the small room that housed priestly vestments and other liturgical objects, as well as a small desk and an old-fashioned computer shoved against one wall. Father Benito invited them to sit at a tiny table in the center of the room, with two chairs. He dragged in a third chair from another room for himself.

"Can I offer you some cold water? I'm afraid that's all I have in the way of drinks."

"No, thanks," Billy said. "We just have a few questions, and we'll get out of your hair."

"Are you two with the police?" He didn't seem upset at the idea, just wanting to know.

"I'm Mary-Francis's counselor," Claudia said smoothly. "We're looking into some matters at the behest of Mary-Francis herself. There are many things she would like to set right before her execution date comes around."

Father Benito bowed his head. "Yes, of course."

Billy didn't explain his presence, and the priest didn't ask. Apparently Claudia's credentials were good enough to cover the both of them. He admired how she had soft-pedaled their real reasons for being here, all without lying. Since her approach seemed to be working, he remained silent, letting her take the lead if she wanted it.

"We believe Mary-Francis is innocent," Claudia said, jumping right in with both feet.

The priest's eyes lit up. "I do, too! I've known her since she was a child. Although she is not without sin, she simply is not capable of purposefully taking another human being's life."

"Even that of a husband who was abusive?" Billy asked.

Father Benito jumped at the abrupt question. "I knew of the violence in the Torres family."

"And you counseled Mary-Francis to…to what, endure?" Billy asked. "To stick to those marriage vows no matter what? Maybe try praying?"

The priest looked horrified. "No, of course not. In another time, that would have been the thing to do, but the church has modernized its views. While the specifics of what I counseled Mary-Francis to do are private, protected within the walls of the confessional, I can assure you I did not advise her to remain in the house with a man who thought nothing of harming her."

"Of course you wouldn't," Claudia said.

The priest turned toward her, pretending Billy wasn't there. He folded his hands and steepled his index fingers. "I can tell you in general terms what I would normally advise a wife in such a situation. I would tell her to first seek physical safety for herself and her children. Then I would advise that she seek an annulment."

"But she still would have had to get a civil divorce," Billy pointed out.

"True enough," Father Benito said curtly to Billy, then smiled at Claudia. "My feeling is that Mary-Francis announced her intention to dissolve the marriage, and Eduardo Torres—a brutal man, by the way—

didn't take the news well. In defending herself, Mary-Francis killed her husband, then was frightened and did her best to cover it up."

"Did she tell you that's what happened?" Claudia asked, and Billy just sighed quietly. The good priest wasn't going to tell her that.

Predictably, Father Benito shook his head. "If she had told me such a thing, it would be within the seal of the—"

"—the confessional, yeah, we get it," Billy said.

Claudia shot him a warning look, then returned her attention to the priest. "Father, would it surprise you if I told you that I believe Eduardo is alive?"

Billy knew he should be observing the priest, but he was busy watching Claudia watch him, like a lioness on the hunt. If the priest already knew Eduardo was alive, Claudia would spot it.

Father Benito merely looked confused. "The blood…"

"The test results can't be trusted," Claudia said without going into details. "Just believe us when we say there's good reason to believe Eduardo's murder, if it happened at all, didn't happen the way the police thought it did."

After considering this a few moments, the priest smiled benignly. "I'm but a simple man of the cloth." His statement was almost a joke, it was so clichéd, and maybe he meant it that way. "I don't pretend to understand the ins and outs of this complicated case, but I'm all in favor of anything that could help Mary-Francis. But tell me, what does any of this have to do with me?"

"We were hoping you might have some insight into the family dynamics," Claudia said smoothly. "Without violating the seal of the confessional, of course… but you must know some things about the family that are general knowledge to anyone who's observed them. For instance, Mary-Francis's daughter, Angie."

Father Benito's reaction to Angie's name was immediate and undeniable. He flinched. "Angie is...well, I won't pretend to know what's between her and her maker. But she refused to go to church from an early age, turned away from God before her first communion. I've had little contact with her over the years, even after her father's supposed death. While Mary-Francis welcomed my comfort, Angie steered clear of me. She didn't even come to the memorial service for her father."

"And what about Mary-Francis's sister, Theresa? You are close to her, as well?" Billy asked.

At the mention of Theresa, he smiled sadly. "A lovely woman. I assume you know what happened to her?"

They both nodded.

"I pray daily for her recovery. And while I'm not a vengeful person, I do hope the police catch the terrible men who did this to her."

"Men?" Billy repeated. "As in, more than one?" Claudia might be quick to catch nonverbal cues, but the verbal ones were all Billy's. How would the priest know there were two assailants? Billy didn't think that fact had been reported in the press.

The priest shrugged. "Living and working in this neighborhood, I've unfortunately been privy to many sad stories about violent crimes. A home invasion almost always involves more than one man. These kids, these gang members, egg each other on. They are cowards, and they stack the deck in their favor. One man could probably overpower a middle-aged woman living alone, but why take chances? Bring along a buddy."

He was overexplaining, perhaps, but what he said made sense. Statistics bore him out.

"One more question, Father," Claudia said. "Mary-Francis and Eduardo had a coin collection, supposedly quite valuable. In the confusion of Eduardo's disappearance and Mary-Francis's arrest, the coins have gone missing. You wouldn't happen to know anything about that, would you?"

"I can't tell you anything about any coins," he said quickly.

"Look, Father, I know you're not supposed to betray certain confidences, but we're talking about Mary-Francis's life here. Already, Theresa has been assaulted by someone—possibly Eduardo or his friends—looking for the coins. If he succeeds in finding them, he will disappear forever, and Mary-Francis will be put to death. So if there's anything...anything at all, even if it doesn't seem relevant—"

The priest shrugged and folded his arms. "That's out of my hands. I will pray that you find them. Perhaps Saint Anthony will intercede. Lighting a candle to the patron saint of lost items might not be a bad idea."

Billy had been the one who felt queasy over accusing a priest of a crime, but Father Benito's answer struck him as smug and uncooperative. Maybe he just didn't like being asked to betray his vows, or maybe he was covering something up. Either way, Billy couldn't stop himself from pulling one more interrogation card out of his sleeve—preying on a witness's fear.

"We'll do that," Billy said. "But one woman has already been gravely injured, and Claudia here was attacked and beaten. We have reason to believe the men who assaulted Theresa did not find what they were looking for. They won't stop. You might consider who could be next on the list—Mary-Francis's daughter? Eduardo's elderly mother? Or even you?"

"I don't fear hoodlums," the priest said firmly. "I also don't fear dying, so long as my conscience is clear. How about you?"

"I think we're done here," Claudia said, standing and half dragging Billy out of his chair. "Thank you, Father, for visiting with us."

Once they'd cleared the office, Claudia slowed down and took a few deep breaths. "Wow," she said in a hushed voice. "I thought you didn't want to play hardball with the priest."

"I didn't—until I realized he was lying."

"I thought so, too." Claudia's voice had dropped to a whisper. "Let's go."

"No candle for Saint Anthony?" He was only half kidding. How many times, as a child, had he chanted the familiar verse: *Dear Saint Anthony, please come around. Something is lost and must be found?*

"This place gives me the willies," Claudia said. "How did Father Benito even know we were here? We didn't make any noise when we entered. He must have a hidden camera or a remote doorbell or something."

They were halfway to the door when Billy paused to take a closer look at the church. All around the nave, in between the stained glass windows, were wall niches in which statues of various saints were enshrined. On the far wall, partially hidden by an old pipe organ, was a statue of the Virgin Mary.

"Hey, Claudia, check it out." He made a quick detour to take a closer look at the statue. A rack of candles had been placed in front of it; almost every candle was lit, many more than any of the other statues had.

"This looks a lot like the one we saw in the video and the crime scene photos," Claudia said. "But these statues are common, right?"

Billy examined the statue base. A line of dirt was visible on the stucco floor of the niche. It didn't match the size or shape of this statue. He pointed it out to Claudia.

"You think another statue was moved to make room for this one?" she asked.

"Maybe. And look." He pointed to a spot at the edge of Mary's sleeve that had been broken and clumsily patched. He didn't have the fragment from Theresa's house with him, but the color looked about right.

## *CHAPTER FOURTEEN*

"I AGREE WITH BILLY," Daniel said. "We can't just go accusing a priest—especially a priest with the sterling reputation of Father Benito—of stealing valuable coins from one of his flock. Right now, due to the high-profile cases we've tackled in recent months, we're all living in a fishbowl. And, realistically, a burglary has nothing to do with proving Mary-Francis's innocence."

They were gathered in the conference room at Project Justice—Billy, Claudia, Raleigh, Beth and Mitch, with Daniel again on the video screen and the pig wandering somewhere in the building.

Although Billy wanted to take Claudia back to his apartment and make her stay there, per their agreement, he had felt a need to touch base with some of his Project Justice colleagues. The foundation was on his way home, and no bad guy would try anything in this building, not with so many ex-police officers wandering around.

This case was a mass of loose threads. He felt they ought to be focusing on finding Eduardo, not a statue full of coins. And yet Claudia made a persuasive case that Eduardo might be looking for the coins, as well.

The physical evidence was laid out on the table where everyone could see it—the blue ceramic chip, the video camera and the photo Billy had taken with his phone at the church, which had been blown up on the video screen for everyone to ponder.

"It sure looks like the same statue," Claudia said.

"But it might not be." Beth, who'd been tapping away on her laptop, swiveled the screen around so the others could see. "It's an extremely common chalk statue, sold at thrift stores and flea markets all over Mexico and the Southwest." Her screen revealed several photos of the same Virgin Mary statue—or rather, copies—she'd found with a simple Google search. "If you could actually get me the statue, I could compare the repair to the chip and know for sure."

"Even if you prove it's the exact same statue," Mitch said, "what will that get us? So, a priest stole a statue."

"But *why* would he steal it?" Claudia asked. "It's not worth anything on its own. He was showing definite signs of deception."

"You think the good Father Benito is in cahoots with Eduardo?" Daniel asked. "A priest and a gangster?"

"It wouldn't be the first time," Claudia pointed out.

"Unfortunately," Raleigh said, "we can't just haul a priest in for questioning. We're not the police."

"Could we involve the police?" Claudia asked.

"First, there would have to be a crime," Daniel said. "No one has reported the theft of a statue, and since the statue was still at Theresa's house after the assault, it can't be connected to the home invasion."

Everyone seemed to collectively slump at the table.

"Billy," Daniel said decisively. "Put a tail on Angie. If she knows about the coins, she must be in contact with her father. Put another tail on the priest."

"Okay. What else?" Billy asked. It seemed as if

Daniel had taken over his case, which no doubt didn't sit well with him. Billy liked to be in control.

"Go with Beth back to the church. Distract the priest while she takes the chalk chip from Theresa's house and compares it to the statue in situ."

"I'll need to take a sample," Beth said. "Compare them microscopically."

"Which is why Billy will keep the priest busy. Once we know for sure the statue in the church was stolen from Theresa's house, we can lean on him a little harder."

Billy checked his watch. "The church is closed now."

"In the morning, then."

"What about me?" Claudia asked. It seemed as if everyone else had a job to do.

"How do you feel about party planning?" Daniel asked. "I've invited two hundred of my closest friends over for the Fourth of July—that's tomorrow."

"Nice try, Daniel, but I'm no good at planning parties. You want me to just keep out of the way?"

"I want you to keep yourself safe," he amended. "Stay at Billy's, or stay with Jamie and me. You'll attend the party as a guest, at least. That goes for everyone." He made it sound like a command performance, not an invitation. "Elena has worked really hard to make it a memorable holiday."

Billy gave Claudia a hard look. "Your choice. My place or Daniel's. You did say you'd lay low if I took you to see the priest."

"You're right. I did." Damn it. She thought about going back on her word, but would anyone at the foundation want to work with her again if she couldn't be trusted?

The meeting broke up. Claudia and Billy headed toward the bull pen and Billy's cubicle. "I just have to make a few calls and get that surveillance set up."

"Sure, no problem." Claudia's mind was awhirl with all the pieces of this case. It was so close to fitting together. Those coins…those stupid coins. Where could they—

Suddenly something small and furry dashed down the hall straight for Claudia. She screamed and plastered herself against the wall as the creature clattered by, snorting noisily and sliding on the polished wood floor on tiny hooves. It took her a moment to realize it was Buster, Celeste's javelina. Moments later, Celeste herself burst through a doorway and ran for them, looking not so different from her quarry as she clattered by on high heels, on two feet instead of four but huffing and puffing, a huge net gripped in both hands. Today she wore a dress that looked as though it had been made of silk scarves sewn together, and it billowed out behind her like a half-dozen fairy wings.

"Which way did it go?"

Claudia and Billy both pointed, and Celeste was off, moving a lot faster than a woman her age normally did.

"Has it been loose in the office this whole time?" Claudia asked.

"Apparently so. It's a destructive little critter. Not housebroken, either."

"I thought I smelled something odd in the conference room."

BILLY ARRANGED FOR SURVEILLANCE on both Angie Torres and Father Benito, as Daniel had suggested. Project Justice had a pool of carefully vetted police officers who were willing to moonlight for such projects, given that the pay was a helluva lot better than the usual overtime gigs available to them, such as concert security or neighborhood patrol.

He wanted to keep digging. There were still leads to follow, phone calls to make, cages to rattle. But he also saw the fatigue in Claudia's eyes and knew it was time to take her home and let her rest.

Billy stopped at Foodi's, a place that specialized in gourmet take-out meals, and ordered pretty much one of everything on the menu at the drive-through.

"We'll never eat all this food," Claudia said as he piled the white bags into her lap and onto the passenger-side floorboards of his truck.

"What we don't eat will keep."

"It sure smells good. Um, Billy, are you going to insist I stay at your place?"

"*Insist* is too weak of a word. I'll handcuff you to a doorknob if I have to. I wouldn't be able to sleep, or think, or breathe for that matter, if I had to worry about whether some crazy was shooting at you through the windows of your condo. I don't even like being out in the open right now, although at least we're a moving target."

Claudia bristled. "You can't bully me. I won't stand for it."

A muscle twitched near Billy's mouth, and he made no response for a long time, just focused on the traffic. "Okay." He took a deep breath. "Okay, you're right. But the thought of something happening…" He stopped again, clamping his mouth shut. "If you were just anybody, I'd worry. I'm a guy, you're a girl, and I'm supposed to protect you. It's in my DNA."

"Actually, from a scientific—"

"Don't start. You know what I mean. It's what I'm

programmed to do. *Socialized* to do. There, like that better?"

"I don't like being thought of as the weaker sex."

"You're not weak. Believe me, I don't think of you that way. But you're also not trained in law enforcement. Yeah, you're tough, you've faced down some bad dudes, I get that. You could be the freaking Terminator, and I'd still twist up inside at the thought..." Again, he clamped his mouth closed.

"You don't have to censor yourself around me."

"The hell I don't. There are things I can't—I don't want—" He clammed up again, and Claudia sighed in frustration.

"Why can't you just be open with me? Is it a matter of trust? We've spent a lot of time together the last few days. You know me pretty well by now. Do you not trust me?"

"Of course I trust you."

"Then why—"

"There are things about me I don't want you to know. Is that so hard to understand?"

"Frankly, yes." She was used to people opening up to her, trusting her with everything. From childhood, she'd been a good listener, a keen observer of human nature, which made her understanding and nonthreatening. It was what made her a good counselor, especially with people who were deeply troubled.

Of course, for all that she was easy to be around, she hadn't cultivated many close friends or lovers. That had been deliberate on her part; she usually didn't open up enough herself to let people get really, really close.

With Billy, she had. She'd trusted him with secrets she hadn't revealed to anyone else, secrets that could damage her if her trust was misplaced, secrets that she would never have told anyone she didn't have special feelings toward. That he wouldn't do the same for her had to mean that he didn't share those feelings, and that hurt.

Billy banged the heel of his hand on the steering wheel when someone cut him off in traffic. "I don't want to drive you away, okay? Some things about me, you aren't ready to hear. You'll have to take my word for it."

Okay. She turned his argument over and over in her head. It made sense; he cared for her enough that he didn't want to reveal parts of himself that he thought Claudia might find unpalatable.

A small ember of hope glowed inside her. If she was patient, if she gave him space, in time he would realize that there was very little he could reveal—short of confessing he was an ax murderer—that would drive her away. Surely his secrets couldn't be that bad… could they?

"I can accept that."

He flashed a sideways glance at her. "Really?"

"I think so. I mean, for all the letters after my name, I'm not really that great at relationships. I can tell other people how to do it, but my track record isn't something I brag about. I'm fumbling a bit."

He nodded. "Okay, then."

Okay? Had she just agreed to something? Were they entering into a relationship, or were they still negotiating? Or were they back to the friends-with-benefits idea? She'd better figure it out quickly, because Billy was turning in to his apartment building's garage. They had food to keep their hands and mouths occupied for the next little while, but when that was gone, she was afraid other, more pressing biological urges would take over.

Ten minutes later, Claudia sat across from Billy at the kitchen table, an amazing array of food as well as a bottle of Cabernet Sauvignon between them. He'd probably bought the wine for her; she'd observed that his alcoholic beverage of choice was beer. She appreciated his thoughtfulness, but she wasn't sure that dulling her normal caution with alcohol was the smartest decision.

Still, as stressful as today had been, she would never be able to sleep if she didn't do something to unwind. So, one glass. That wouldn't hurt.

Their breakfast dishes had been washed and put away in their absence; the housekeeper must have been here.

"This food is amazing." She was so overwhelmed by the choices she didn't know where to start—with the spinach and artichoke dip, the Vietnamese pot stickers or the sushi? There was also a small tub of fresh, cut fruit, some gourmet cheeses and crackers bristling with sesame seeds. "How come I never heard of Foodi's before?"

"I wouldn't know about it if I didn't pass it every day on my way home." He popped the cork on the wine and poured her glass almost to the brim. "Tried it one day when I decided I couldn't stomach one more take-out hamburger, and I was hooked." He popped a wedge of chicken quesadilla into his mouth.

"I may never cook again." Oh, crab Rangoon, she hadn't seen that before. She took a bite of the tasty, crunchy morsel and closed her eyes in ecstasy. Maybe it was her recent brush with danger, but it seemed as if since she'd left the hospital, her senses had expanded to take in more. Colors were brighter, music was more complex, she registered smells she'd never noticed before, and food tasted great.

Or maybe it was the effect of endorphins. She'd studied enough about "love" to know that all the neurotransmitters swimming through the blood of a person who was in a deep state of attraction could alter the physical senses.

She'd never really thought she would fall prey to what people called love, and she wasn't sure yet that she had. But something was making her feel different, as if her own skin was no longer big enough for her.

Or maybe she ought to stop eating so much. She resisted gobbling down just one more bite-size quiche.

"I think I'm finally full." Her wineglass was empty, too. That wasn't good. She didn't even remember drinking it. "Let's clean up this mess." It looked as if a barbarian horde had been through Billy's kitchen.

They closed various plastic containers and stashed them in Billy's immaculate side-by-side fridge. "Your housekeeper does a nice job on the fridge."

"The fridge is easy. I pretty much only use it for beer and an occasional box of leftovers. You should see her getting the spots out of my Berber carpeting—now that's true artistry. She's a miracle worker. I never had a maid before I lived here, but these apartments come with weekly housekeeping service. Now I'm spoiled."

"Nice." Although she could easily afford maid service, some deeply ingrained part of her hesitated to give herself that small bit of luxury. She well remembered those snotty rich kids whose dorm rooms she'd cleaned as part of her work-study program, kids who deliberately left a disgusting mess on the days they knew she was coming. Maybe a part of her was afraid of being like them. The luxury car she could do, but not the maid. Funny how she somehow justified the distinction, when logically it made no sense.

When she went to the sink and picked up a sponge, intending to wipe off the table, Billy came up behind her and took the sponge away. "Enough. You're my guest, you don't have to clean."

The heat of his body radiated through her clothes, and for a moment she fantasized about simply leaning back against him and going limp, falling into his embrace as easily as she might step into a shower.

She wanted him. She craved his touch, his scent and the lovely mental vacation she could take while they made love. Their interlude at her office was the only time since receiving Mary-Francis's email—other than when she'd been asleep—that she'd put the woman's dilemma out of her mind. She'd put everything out of her mind except how good she felt.

He didn't move away, but neither did he touch her. His breath tickled the back of her neck, and she knew he was waiting for a signal from her.

"Do it," she whispered.

"Do what?" he asked innocently.

How dare he tease her! Did she have to spell it out? "Touch me."

"Is that what you want?"

"Would I ask if I didn't want it?"

He lifted the hair off the back of her neck and planted the softest of kisses there. "I need to take a shower. Want to join me?"

Her knees actually buckled, and she had to support herself on the edge of the counter with her one good hand. Was she really going to do this?

A sudden rush of cool air wafted over her back, and

she realized Billy had pulled away. He was walking out of the kitchen without a backward glance, putting the decision squarely in her court.

She saw what he was doing. He didn't want her to be able to say, later, that he'd seduced her or caught her in a weak moment. If they had sex again, it was going to be a conscious decision on her part. If she followed him to the bedroom, to the bathroom, took off her clothes and hopped under the spray with him, she was fully consenting, no reservations, to sex and, she was afraid, a whole lot more.

But that was exactly what she did. No more analysis, no more second-guessing. If it was a mistake, it probably wouldn't kill her. She'd either be really happy, at least for a while until the half-crazy love-haze faded, or she would learn something from her folly. The experience would help her better understand the illogical actions her patients sometimes took in the name of love...right?

She followed the hallway to Billy's bedroom, where she could hear running water beckoning from the bathroom. With one flick of her arm, her tank top was over her head and gone. She kicked off her heels and wiggled out of her skirt and her Walgreens bra and panties, then gingerly removed the splint from her arm. She entered the bathroom.

Billy was already buck naked, and he was a sight to behold. He was golden tan all over except for the parts covered by shorts or trunks outdoors, and his muscular glutes gleamed pale in contrast. As he leaned into the shower to adjust the spray, Claudia's breath caught in her throat.

Why on God's green earth had she hesitated?

## *CHAPTER FIFTEEN*

BILLY TURNED TO FACE the warm spray and caught movement from the corner of his eye. For a split second his old reflexes surfaced, and he reached for a gun that wasn't there. Then sanity returned, followed quickly by excitement and arousal. Claudia was here, standing not four feet away, wearing nothing but a smile.

The glass door was still open a crack. He pushed it open farther, beckoning her into the warm steam cocoon.

Once they came together, they were in a private world where nothing else could intrude—not doubts or dangers, unhappy memories, guilt or insecurities. There was only Claudia, more beautiful than he'd ever seen her. As she wrapped her good arm around his neck and let the other rest on his shoulder, he realized with a pang why she looked so beautiful.

Her eyes were open and filled with love—or at least something he interpreted as love. The wariness, the caution, were absent for the first time since he'd known her. Not even the bruises on her cheekbone and around her eye could detract from the ethereal beauty.

The trust she'd begun to build had matured until it was almost complete.

He wished it was a two-way street, but even that uncomfortable thought drifted away as he claimed her mouth with his.

As they kissed, he maneuvered her around until the gentle spray was on her shoulders, wetting her hair and slicking her back. Feeling his way to the niche in the tile where he kept soap and shampoo, he grabbed his trusty bar of Ivory and ran it up and down her back until a layer of slick bubbles coated her smooth skin. He moved her again so the shower wouldn't wash it all away, then worked the suds up and down, to her neck and then to her hips, giving her a firm massage.

Claudia groaned, which he took to mean she liked what he was doing. Her muscles were probably still sore from the beating she'd taken. He lightened his touch when he encountered the purple bruises and tried not to think about the animal who'd done this to her.

Later. He would get his revenge before this was all over. But for now, there was only Claudia.

Before he'd realized what was happening, she'd gotten possession of the soap. Even without the use of her left hand she was incredibly clever, running the creamy white soap all over him, and for a while they were content to kiss and squish those delightful bubbles all over each other's torso and arms, neck, face.

"You want your hair shampooed?" His voice was hoarse.

"Mmm. You'd do that for me?"

"I'd do just about anything to make you feel good, *mi amor.* Besides, I figure it takes two good hands to shampoo a head of hair." He grabbed his shampoo bottle. It was nothing special; he tended to buy whatever bottle he saw first, so long as it didn't smell like flowers. This one was almond extract and green tea, and though he'd never paid much attention to the smell, as he worked the liquid into Claudia's pale blond hair, he noticed it smelled slightly sweet, a little bit tangy.

He swiveled her around so she faced away from him, then worked the lather all through her hair, gently massaging her scalp, being extra gentle near the discoloration at her right temple. He massaged the back and sides of her neck, feeling the tension there melt away.

Eventually, playing the role of masseur wasn't enough. His hands strayed down, splashing lather on her breasts as he cupped and caressed them. Her nipples, large and rosy, were hard as nail heads.

She grabbed one of his hands and guided it down to between her legs. Standing there with the warm water tumbling over them, he slipped into her silky warmth and slowly stroked the pebble-hard nub he found there, pausing to circle, slowing things down, speeding them up until she was begging him to finish her off.

When he did, her cries echoed against the white tile of his shower. He wrapped one arm around her waist, holding her in place as he drew every last cry of ecstasy from her.

Gasping for breath, she turned to face him, her eyes glazed with pleasure, water dripping from her blond hair, kiss-swollen lips parted, and he thought she was the sexiest, most beautiful creature he'd ever seen. He could easily have lifted her up and impaled her on his erection, and the temptation to do so was fierce. With his need driving him so strongly, though, he feared he would be too rough—Claudia was brave but she had been badly injured and those bruises on her hip looked painful.

Besides, he wasn't looking for a quickie in the shower. He wanted to take his time.

Billy switched off the water and opened the door. Claudia didn't protest. He grabbed a fluffy white towel and blotted her dry, sopped the worst of the moisture from her hair, then quickly ran the towel over himself. Finding another dry towel, he wrapped it around Claudia and lifted her into his arms.

She squeaked in surprise, then grinned up at him. "What have you got in mind?"

"Just a bed, that's all. You, me, a bed and all night long, how does that sound?"

"Bring it on."

He made love to her slowly, kindling her desire once again like rubbing sticks together to start a fire. He made sure she took as much pleasure from each step as he did.

When he entered her, her breath caught in her throat, and then she sighed; when he lengthened his stroke, she grasped him, pulled him hard into her. And when he finally unleashed himself and peaked, buried deep inside her warmth, he let loose with something that sounded like a war whoop, and Claudia climaxed, too, laughing and crying at the same time.

Afterward, he held her for a long time and they were quiet, each lost in their own thoughts.

*This is it,* he realized. This was what his sisters had meant when they told him that someday he'd find someone to love, someone whose soul meshed with his seamlessly.

And yet…he still wasn't sure he was ready. His thoughts lingered way too often on Sheila and her horrible fate. He hadn't been in love with her; hadn't felt the way he felt about Claudia. But he'd liked her a helluva lot. Respected her. Depended on her. Desired her. Spent more hours with her than anyone else.

They wouldn't have stayed together in the long run. They clashed too much, what with both of them being bossy and territorial. Still, her death had left a hole in his heart that a herd of cattle could stampede through.

He could see himself long-term with Claudia. Until recently, he'd thought no woman would tempt him to give up his independence. This woman, though, was certainly in the running.

She couldn't fill the hole in his heart. It was there to stay. But somehow, she made his heart feel bigger, as if for the first time he had enough room in there to love someone.

Claudia slid out of bed to brush her teeth and put her splint back on her arm, but when she came back she happily cuddled up against him and sighed contentedly.

He allowed her that contentment. He could give her that, at least for a while. But a nagging voice inside him warned him that this moment of perfection was temporary. They'd reached an agreement that covered here and now. But the future was one big question mark.

CLAUDIA SNUGGLED MORE DEEPLY under the lightweight chenille spread, drowsy and content and so darn comfortable. She didn't know if it was Billy's bed, or the fact that he was in it next to her, but for the second night in a row, despite her aches and pains, she slept like a contented puppy.

She woke up once, at about two in the morning according to the bedside clock, but hearing Billy's steady breathing next to her, feeling his warmth and the arm thrown possessively across her body, even in sleep, reassured her and she immediately drifted back to sleep.

That all changed when she awoke suddenly to Billy thrashing around in the bed next to her. He'd kicked the covers off; one of his pillows was at the foot of the bed, the other on the floor, and he was in the midst of a terrible nightmare.

He shouted out angry, unintelligible words, whipping his head from side to side and obviously in severe emotional pain.

Claudia's adrenaline surged, and her first, very human instinct was to reach out and shake him awake, to hold him and soothe him and tell him it was okay.

The professional side of her urged her not to do anything foolhardy. Adult nightmares were often the result of post-traumatic stress syndrome. In his dream state Billy was mostly paralyzed, prevented from acting out whatever violent actions were taking place inside his head. In that split second between waking and sleeping, his mind would still be in the dream but he could move his body, and she might wind up having two black eyes instead of just one.

She grabbed a pillow and scooted off the bed. "Billy! Billy, wake up, you're dreaming."

"No!" he shouted, still in his dreamworld. Then, a long, agonized, "Nooo! Sheila, oh, God, Sheila!"

She couldn't stand this. Holding the pillow in front of her like a shield, she closed the distance between them and reached for his shoulder, shaking him hard.

"Billy!" she said again. "Wake up!"

When he moved, he moved fast. He came out of the bed swinging, and the only thing that saved her from getting hit, aside from the pillow, was that he pushed her off balance and she fell to the floor, landing painfully on the same hip she'd injured in the parking garage.

He took two more steps, lashing out with his fists.

He ran into the dresser and knocked off an old ashtray full of change.

Coins exploded everywhere and scattered across the carpeting. The dish slammed into the wall and shattered into hundreds of glass shards.

Billy stopped moving, breathing as if he'd just run three blocks to catch a bus. Dawn light seeped through the blinds enough that she could see his eyes were open. He looked slightly confused, but completely sane again.

He looked around, spotted her crouched on the floor. "What just happened?"

"You were having a nightmare."

"Oh, yeah…I guess I was." His face tensed with remembered pain; then he seemed to swat it away like a troublesome mosquito. He returned to the bed and sank to the edge, then offered her a hand. "I didn't hurt you, did I? Please tell me I didn't hurt you."

"No, I got out of the way." She pulled herself up, then sat down next to him, pulling the covers over her legs and hips in a sudden fit of modesty.

"I guess I should have warned you not to try to wake me if I had a nightmare."

"You have a lot of these dreams, huh?"

He gave her a wary look. "Not so often anymore, but yeah, every once in a while."

"I did a rotation in a sleep clinic, so I know about this kind of dream. I know it's dangerous to wake someone…like you…having a violent dream, but you sounded like you were in agony so I had to do something." She was careful not to use any jargon that he might interpret as a diagnosis, knowing how he felt about her head-shrinking ways.

He reached up and lightly caressed her cheek with two fingers. "Thanks. Sorry I scared you."

"I wasn't scared. I knew what was happening." She *was* concerned, because she knew what was going on. He had suffered some kind of physical or emotional trauma.

But Billy was definitely not the kind of man to comfortably wear a label like post-traumatic stress disorder.

"Do you want to talk about it?" she continued.

"No. It was just a dream."

"I promise, I can listen without judging or offering advice. Just as a friend, not a therapist."

"You might be able to keep quiet, but that wouldn't stop you from thinking all kinds of things I don't want you thinking about me."

"I won't think you're crazy. I would already know if you were in need of a padded room." Maybe if she kept it light, he would feel comfortable enough to open up.

Billy rubbed his knee. "Maybe I do need a padded room. I hit that dresser pretty hard."

"Come on, let's go back to bed," she said soothingly. "I could kiss that knee and make it all better."

He smiled, but it looked a bit forced to her. "I won't be able to go back to sleep," he said. "I know enough not to try. Why don't you try to catch a couple more hours of sleep? I'm gonna get up."

She hadn't actually suggested that they *sleep.* She was frankly surprised he hadn't jumped at her blatant invitation for more sex. The dream must have upset him a lot more than he was letting on.

She hated that he wouldn't trust her with his true feelings, that he felt he had to shield her from his real self. He wasn't evil like Raymond, but he was a man who hadn't come to terms with himself and until he did, he was a danger to himself and those who loved him.

He patted her knee and stood up, the incident over as far as he was concerned. But she wasn't ready to let it go.

"Billy, I *need* for you to come back to bed. I need holding, if nothing else. Just for a few minutes, then you can get up. Okay?"

"Of course, *cielito,* of course. I guess it's pretty upsetting, waking up and finding your bed partner acting like a raving lunatic."

"A little unnerving, if you're not expecting it," she agreed, crawling back to her side of the bed and wiggling under the sheet and beadspread. She held up the covers, inviting him to slide in beside her.

He opened his arms, and she snuggled up next to him.

Her ear was against his chest, and she was shocked by how rapid his heart rate was. He might be pretending normalcy, but his vital signs gave him away.

"Comfy?" he asked.

"Yes," she lied. "Thank you."

"I might have been a little hasty, wanting to get up. I'm not used to having a woman hanging at my place, in my bed."

"Well, I'll be out of your hair soon."

"I wasn't complaining."

"Billy?"

"What?" he asked warily.

"You've called me by a nickname several times now, and I don't know what it means. *Cielito?*"

"Oh." He sounded embarrassed. "Literally translated, it means 'little sky.' What it really means is 'my little slice of heaven.'"

Tears sprang into Claudia's eyes. "That's so sweet."

It was tempting just to lie there and fall asleep. It felt so good, having him hug her and protect her with those muscular arms. But she wasn't really the one who needed comforting, despite what she'd said.

"Billy?"

"Mmm?"

"Sheila. She was your partner back in Dallas, right?"

He immediately tensed. "Yes."

"Was she more than your partner?"

"Would it matter if she was?"

So, the answer was yes. "I know you've had lovers. That's not a problem. I've had a few myself. So I'm not asking out of idle curiosity. It's just that...you called out her name."

"When we were making love?" He sounded horrified.

"No. When you were having that nightmare."

"It was just a dream," he said impatiently. "Forget about it."

She sighed. "I can't."

"It doesn't concern you. She's way in the past and she has nothing to do with you and me."

"I disagree." She sat up, wanting to see his face. Then she wished she hadn't. He was angry with her. But she couldn't let this pass without at least making sure he understood how she felt. "Past relationships I can deal with. But if you're going to shout out another woman's name while I'm sleeping with you, just hours after we made love...that tells me you have unfinished business with her. And that makes it my concern."

"Could you just let it alone?"

"Only if I don't want any true intimacy. If you're wanting a friend with bedroom privileges, that's fine, but it's not going to be me. I'm sorry, I can't do that. I can't do casual relationships without collateral damage."

"You were willing to have an hour of smutty sex with no strings," he reminded her. "The first time. At your office."

She grimaced. "Sometimes I manage to lie to myself, too. But on some level, I'd hoped making love with you would open the door to other things. Anyway, we weren't talking about me."

"We weren't talking about me, either, and I'd like to keep it that way."

"Why are you being so stubborn about this?"

"Why are you?" he countered.

"I care about you," she said softly. "Maybe I even love you a little. I know it's only been a week, and that's kind of crazy on my part." She chanced a peek at him. He didn't seem shocked by her admission. That was good. Wasn't it?

"I care about you, too, *mi coshita linda.* Which is exactly why you shouldn't know everything about me."

"There's nothing you could tell me that would frighten me so badly I'd run. Please, tell me what happened with Sheila. Do you still have feelings for her?"

"Yes."

Her heart sank. Maybe he was right; maybe it was better if she didn't know.

"But not the kind of feelings you're talking about." He pulled away from her, climbed out of bed and went to the dresser, rummaging around for underwear and a T-shirt. "Sheila was my partner, my friend, and yes, my lover. She's also dead, shot through the heart, and I killed her.

"There, now, aren't you glad you asked?"

He stomped into the bathroom and slammed the door. Moments later, she heard the shower running.

She was so stunned, she couldn't move. He'd *killed* her? Claudia hugged her pillow as memories swamped her. She thought of that awful moment when she'd seen the police artist sketch of a suspected serial killer and had realized with stunning clarity that it was the man she'd just slept with.

But this was different. Billy wasn't a killer, that was preposterous. Maybe he'd shot his partner in self-defense. No, she couldn't picture that at all. He had to mean he was responsible somehow, not that he'd pulled the trigger.

He'd already as much as admitted he'd been responsible for someone's death. But his partner? His lover? Something like that would brand a man for life. It was the sort of trauma you never got over. You might learn to function, rejoin society, you might even take a lover or marry and have kids.

But you didn't forget. It was likely Billy thought about Sheila's death, whatever the circumstances, every day of his life. And if he'd never gotten help, professional help, it might be worse than that.

What sort of Pandora's box had she opened?

She should have left well enough alone. What right did she have to push and prod him like she had? Yes, she'd been trying to help, but she'd also been looking after her own interests. *She* was the one who couldn't feel safe with a man unless she knew every nook and cranny of his psyche.

Sound relationships were built on trust, and she

wouldn't back away from that truth. But did she have the right to expect Billy to trust her completely with his deepest, darkest secrets when their relationship was only a few days old?

Really, she'd asked too much, pushed too hard until she'd broken what she'd hoped to build.

It was a moot point now. She'd probably blown any chance they had of making this relationship work. The only thing she'd accomplished was convincing Billy she was an inflexible, nosy, interfering harpy.

BY THE TIME BILLY WANDERED into the kitchen, Claudia was already dressed and making coffee. She stood over the coffeemaker now, staring at it as if that would make it brew faster.

He started to smile, then remembered he was mad at her.

And a little mad at himself for losing his temper. Shortly after the incident that had cost Sheila her life, he'd had a hair-trigger temper. Anything could set him off. But he'd worked on that, and now he almost never lost his cool.

He knew Claudia was just trying to be helpful, but he'd made his feelings clear on this subject matter, and she kept pushing and pushing. Finally she'd pushed him beyond his capacity to be understanding about it.

"You want breakfast?" he asked. "I think I have more eggs. Or cereal, if you'd rather."

She glanced at her watch, as if she was worried about the time. Which was utterly ridiculous. The sun was just nudging its way over the horizon, peeking through the kitchen window. It was still early, not even six o'clock.

"I need to get home, do a few things there."

"Just because we had an argument doesn't mean I'm going to wash my hands of you," he said. "I promised Daniel I'd keep you safe."

"That's…noble of you." She came out of the shadows, and he realized she'd been crying. Damn it. He'd made her cry. But he couldn't change that, and he couldn't go backward. She knew, now. Maybe she didn't know all the details, but she could find those out easily enough. A simple Google search would bring up numerous articles about the bust that had netted some pretty big drug kingpins for the Dallas Police Department—and cost one detective her life.

"Regardless of what happens with us," he said evenly, "we still have a case to work on. A woman's life to save."

"You still want to work with me?" she asked, sounding surprised.

"I might ask you the same thing. Last woman I worked with didn't fare so well."

He expected her to jump on that, maybe demand, once again, that he tell her what happened.

"I'm not worried about that," she said dismissively. "I'm still committed to finding Eduardo and freeing Mary-Francis. That hasn't changed. But I really need to go home. I have plants to water, my mailbox is probably overflowing, I need clothes, I left a bowl of fresh fruit on my dining room table that must be turning to mush as we speak."

"Fair enough."

"Afterward…maybe I should take up Daniel and Jamie's offer. Go to the party, then stay at their place until this mess is resolved. Even if we never find who assaulted me, if we find Eduardo, no one will have any reason to try to scare me again."

Claudia moved to stare out the window, and Billy took up her vigil over the coffeepot. "You can stay here, you know."

"No, I've inconvenienced you enough."

Billy's heart sank into his stomach. She was leaving. In the back of his mind, he'd been hoping there was some way to smooth over what he'd done, first scaring her with his violent nightmare and then blurting out the harsh truth. He hadn't wanted to tell her at all, but he certainly shouldn't have told her like that.

She'd already dated one guy who'd killed people. After hearing his unvarnished confession, she must doubt her ability to pick boyfriends.

"Claudia, about what I said earlier—"

She held up one hand, stopping him. "Please, there's no need to explain or apologize. I should never have pressured you like that. You have a right to your privacy."

And she had the right to walk away.

"I shouldn't have lost my temper."

She shrugged. "It happens. What time are you meeting Beth at the church?"

"Not until eight o'clock."

"Plenty of time to get to Daniel's and back. It's a holiday, so the traffic won't be bad."

If she wanted to get away from him that bad, he'd oblige her. He gulped down his hot coffee, burning his mouth and strangely welcoming the pain. His penance for hurting her. No, that wasn't right. His penance was far worse than a sore mouth. It was a lifetime knowing that he'd pushed away the best chance he'd ever have at happiness.

## *CHAPTER SIXTEEN*

AS BILLY DROVE THROUGH the massive gates of the Logan Estate, he was impressed all over again by the almost ridiculous opulence in the tony River Oaks area, smack in the middle of Houston. Daniel's father, who'd made millions, then billions, in Texas petroleum and natural gas, had built the house brick by brick using building materials reclaimed from an English castle. Even the driveway was made from old cobblestones, and if Billy hadn't known better, he would think he had been transported to some English manor house.

Inside, however, everything was up-to-date. The decor might be traditional, at least in some rooms, but the whole house was computerized with surveillance, sensors on all of the valuable paintings, a climate control system that sensed when rooms were occupied and acted accordingly, and a kitchen that would dazzle any professional chef in the world.

Daniel had promised that today's party would be understated. No one wanted to be reminded of the Christmas party, when the house had been tricked out like a holiday fantasy land with ice sculptures and fake snowfall, and Daniel's future wife had nearly died from an attempted murder.

But as a valet took possession of Billy's car keys, Billy couldn't help noticing that a truck was delivering cartons of fireworks, which were being stored in the five-car garage.

The party was well underway as Elena, Daniel's personal assistant, greeted Billy at the door in a festive red, white and blue shorts outfit and high heels. She reminded Billy of a 1940s pinup girl, and maybe that was the intention.

"So glad you could make it," she said. "Did you bring your bathing suit? We have loads of extras in all sizes if you need something."

"I'm good."

Had Claudia brought a swimsuit? He'd dropped her off here early this morning, but they'd stopped by her condo so she could pick up the mail, water the plants and pack a few things.

He wondered what kind of bathing suit she would wear. Bikini? Or conservative one-piece? Suddenly he wanted to know. Despite everything, he didn't want *other* people to see her in a swimsuit unless he was there to warn the wolves away.

He would bust the chops of the first man who made any kind of off-color comment about Claudia's hot bod, no matter who it was. Hell, he wasn't sure if he could tolerate any guy even *looking* at her. Maybe this wasn't such a good idea.

Elena flashed a thousand-watt smile. "There are all kinds of food and drink out on the patio. Just follow the stars."

Sure enough, someone had stuck red, white and blue glittered stars on the floor.

Billy followed the star path through the marble-floored foyer with its central fountain, into the airplane-hangar-size living room, through a solarium and a set of French doors onto the flagstone patio, where the party was already in full swing.

A live country band held sway under a canopy on the other side of the Olympic-size pool. Huge barbecue grills were set up at points all over the patio, with professionals in tall white hats prepping everything from sirloin tips to plain old hot dogs. The smell of grilling meats, popcorn and cotton candy filled the air. It was as though he'd stepped into a high-class carnival. A sign near the band read Pony Rides and pointed toward an oversize golf cart, where a couple of kids bounced up and down, anticipating the adventure that awaited them at the stables.

A passing waitress offered him a cold bottle of beer, but he declined. He wasn't in a drinking mood. His eyes scanned the crowd, looking for Claudia, but he didn't see her.

Daniel's golden retriever, Tucker, ran up and down the side of the pool, barking at some of the people from the foundation in the midst of a spirited game of pool volleyball.

"Hey, Cantu," shouted Griffin Benedict, one of the other investigators and also Raleigh's husband. "Come join our side, we're hurtin'."

"What are you talking about?" said senior investigator Ford Hyatt from the other side of the net. "You guys are one point ahead."

"Yeah, but we got one less player."

"But half our team is girls!"

"And we suck," Raleigh said good-naturedly.

"Sure, I'll play," Billy said. "Give me a couple of minutes." He made a quick circuit around the patio area, again looking for Claudia. Now that he was in the habit of worrying about her, it was hard to stop.

Not that anything could happen to her here; Daniel had enough security to host a United Nations summit.

But he'd had security at the Christmas party, too, and look what had happened there.

Finally Billy spotted Claudia, sitting under a striped umbrella talking to Jillian, the intern and also his neighbor, who cradled a tiny infant. Claudia looked elegant in a pale green sundress and blue metallic sandals, a wide-brimmed hat shading her from the sun. He willed her to look up, but she seemed totally entranced by the baby, who must have belonged to one of the Logan Oil people. No one he knew at Project Justice had a new baby.

Shaking off his black mood, he peeled off his T-shirt and jumped into the pool with a splash big enough to make the women complain about getting their hair wet.

Billy paid just enough attention to the game that he could hit the ball every once in a while and carry his weight. But his gaze continually strayed to Claudia, tracking her movements around the patio as she held the baby, got herself a hot dog and a glass of wine—funny combination—and applied some sunscreen to her pale arms and legs. At one point she took the hat off and fanned herself with it. She looked like a magazine ad.

She was so beautiful. It was just too damn bad he couldn't be the man she wanted, The One, that sensitive guy who wrote her poetry and watched Lifetime movies and shared his feelings. But that wasn't him, and it would never be him.

The volleyball game broke up as the players drifted off to find food, drink and other amusements. A gang of teenagers invaded the pool. Billy recognized one kid as Arturo, Ford's son, but the rest were strangers—probably more Logan Oil family members. Lots of them had been invited to the party. Some of those oil people were rich, good-looking executives who wore suits and drove Beemers.

The kind who would be drawn straight to Claudia. The kind who were probably right for her.

As Billy sat on the edge of the pool, letting the hot sun dry him off a little, he saw Claudia talking to some guy with a crew cut and Brooks Brothers casual clothes.

That fast? She could just flirt with some random guy five minutes after they'd called it quits? Was he that easy to replace?

He was about to push to his feet and go tell Mr. Brooks Brothers where to put his money clip when he realized someone had sat down beside him and stuck his feet in the pool.

If it hadn't been his boss, Billy wouldn't have let himself be delayed.

"Daniel. Nice party."

"Thanks. Elena did most of the planning. She went a little overboard."

"That's what happens when you give someone an unlimited budget."

"You think that's my mistake?"

Daniel wasn't really asking for Billy's opinion. He was just making conversation, being a good party host.

"I think women like to spend money," Billy said with a shrug.

"Everybody likes to spend money, Mr. Shiny New Ford F-1 Pickup with all the bells and whistles. Not to mention those custom-made Tony Lama ostrich skins you wear."

"Point taken."

Daniel sobered. "So how'd it go at the church this morning with Beth?"

Billy grimaced. "We couldn't get in. The place was locked up tighter than a nun's new shoes. But a sign on the door said it would be open this afternoon at three for confession. We thought we'd try again then."

"And how is Claudia?"

"She's got one of your Logan Oil starched shirts eating out of her hand."

Daniel glanced over his shoulder where Billy was looking, then laughed. "I meant, how is she doing physically? And you don't have to worry about Brent. He plays for the other team."

"I think she'll make a full recovery, and I'm not worried," Billy said quickly, kicking out a rooster tail of water at a teenage boy who'd ventured too close.

Daniel snorted. "Please. Claudia might be a nationally recognized body language expert, but you guys are so easy to read a child could do it."

This day just got better and better. So now everyone would know that not only had he and Claudia hooked up, but she'd dumped him before they'd even gotten off the ground.

"Not something you want to talk about, I take it," Daniel said. "My mistake. Just so you know, I have no problems with office romance. If I did, I'd lose half my staff."

Wasn't that the truth.

Just then a whooping sound caught their attention, coming from the cabana. A tall, thin figure emerged with a huge, dragon-shaped pool toy wrapped around its middle. The figure had a mane of silver curls, and it—she—was wearing a lime-green bikini. She streaked toward the pool with another war whoop and did a cannonball, splashing everyone in the vicinity, including Daniel and Billy.

Billy shielded his eyes with his hand. "Oh, wow, that was way more of Celeste than I needed to see."

"No kidding," Daniel said. "Although you have to admit, she's in amazing shape for a seventy-something-year-old woman."

"I didn't look that close."

The teenagers were laughing, and a dark-haired boy of about sixteen approached and hugged her. "Hey, Aunty Celeste. Nice entrance. Did you catch the—"

"Shh!" Celeste glanced nervously in Daniel's direction. "I've got traps set all over. I promise you'll have Buster by next week."

Daniel just shook his head. "She still hasn't caught the javelina? I can't imagine what it's doing to the office."

"You don't want to know."

Daniel seemed much more concerned about work. "So, have there been any more breaks in the case?"

"It's pretty well stalled." This, at least, was an area of conversation he was comfortable with, though he wished he had better news to report. "We can't get a lead on Eduardo, we can't find the missing coins, the district attorney is being a horse's ass, our client's daughter is spending all her mom's money and we can't stop her."

"Something will break. Keep hammering away."

"I don't know, Daniel. I'm not sure I'm cut out for this. I'm doing my best, but what if that's not good enough? What if we can't stop them from putting Mary-Francis to death? I'm not sure I can handle having that on my conscience."

"Well, aren't you a bright ray of sunshine today."

"It's hard to be optimistic, under the circumstances. It's just…maybe you should assign someone else to this case."

Daniel got very serious. "All you can do is your best, Billy. I know that's a cliché, but it's true. It's all any of us can do. But circumstances can change in a heartbeat. Case in point…" He nodded toward the house. Two new party guests had arrived—Mitch and Beth. But Mitch had his laptop case in hand, and Beth was clutching a sheaf of papers. They didn't look as though they were ready to dive headfirst into frozen margaritas and barbecued bratwurst.

Mitch's gaze focused on Billy. "Hey, Cantu. Boss man." He motioned for Billy and Daniel to come over.

"What's going on?"

"I don't know," Daniel said, "but it looks like Mitch and Beth have been working overtime."

Billy and Daniel both pulled their feet out of the pool and stood. Beth waved to Claudia, who now sat under the umbrella clutching the baby, and beckoned her to join them.

Seeing Claudia looking so naturally maternal, Billy's heart almost stopped. He'd never thought of her that way, but for a split second he wondered what kind of mother she would be. To his kids. Their kids.

He squinched his eyes closed and banished the thought. When he opened them again, Claudia was looking around for someone to pass the baby off to, and when she came up empty, she brought him with her. "Hey, you guys, what's up?"

Beth waved the stack of papers in front of Claudia and opened her mouth to explain, then caught sight of the baby. "Oh, my God, look at that baby, how cute."

"Isn't he adorable? His name's Scotty. I told his mother I'd watch him while she plays tennis."

"He looks fast asleep," Mitch said. "Just bring him with you. This can't wait."

That sounded ominous, Billy thought. But at least there was movement on the case. They had to solve this thing. He couldn't keep working so closely with Claudia and not go insane, and Daniel wasn't going to let him back out.

"Can we go inside, somewhere quiet," Beth said, "and talk?"

They went into the library. Daniel's dog followed them into the cool haven. Tucker liked to keep his master in sight.

Daniel's library, unlike the rest of the house, was a casual, manly room with a massive stone fireplace, rustic wood floors, and an oak bar that stretched across one entire wall. Various cushy sofas and chairs were scattered about, along with a couple of card tables and one long library table, which was where they chose to sit.

Billy pulled out Claudia's chair—she was holding a sleeping baby, after all. She murmured her thanks, and Billy chose a chair as far away from her as he could reasonably get without it looking odd.

"So, I got nothing off the cigarette butt," Beth began. "But I did get a DNA profile from the fingernail. And I had my friend at the Houston P.D. run it through the national database. You won't believe who came up."

Billy pressed his palms together. "Please tell me it was Eduardo."

"Not Eduardo," Beth said, "but something just as intriguing. The guy's name is Pedro Madrazo." She turned to Claudia. "Does that name mean anything to you?"

"No," Claudia replied. "Pretty sure I've never heard it."

"So he hasn't been one of your patients?"

"I'll double-check my records, but no. I tend to remember names." The baby stirred, and she absently rubbed his tummy to soothe him. "Who is he?"

Mitch took over the explanations from there. He'd already opened his laptop and fired it up. "Pedro Madrazo is a big-time felon. He used to be a so-called manager at Eduardo Torres's import-export company."

"Yessss!" Billy made a fist in the air.

"He wouldn't normally involve himself in something like petty assault. He's a little higher up the food chain. At least, he used to be."

Something about Mitch's tone of voice alerted Billy that the other shoe was about to drop. "Is he in custody?" Billy asked hopefully.

"Unfortunately, no," Mitch said. "In fact, no one has any clue where this guy is because he's supposed to be dead."

For a few moments, everyone in the room went silent. The only noise was Mitch's fingers busily tapping at the speed of light on his computer.

"It can't be a coincidence," Daniel said. "Now we have two men, former associates, who are supposed to be dead who probably aren't."

"Pedro Madrazo was supposedly gunned down in a drive-by shooting seven years ago," Mitch said, reading from his computer screen, "shot in the face. He had Rio Grande Mafia connections. The case is officially unsolved. His body was identified by his wife, based on his clothing. He was carrying a wallet with his ID."

"So they might not have done a DNA test to establish the victim's identity." Beth shook her head and clicked her tongue. "Sloppy, sloppy."

"Madrazo was facing some pretty hefty criminal charges at the time," Mitch continued. "Human trafficking, drug smuggling and so on."

"Sounds way too familiar," Daniel said.

"Madrazo undoubtedly faked his own death," Beth concluded. "Probably found some poor homeless guy of about his build and coloring, dressed him up in his clothes, shot him in the face, then got his wife to swear it was him. The wife and kids moved back to Mexico shortly afterward and seem to have dropped out of sight."

"Eduardo was also facing criminal charges," Billy concluded, "and he decided to take a page out of his buddy Pedro's book."

"The ties between Pedro and Eduardo are undeniable," Daniel said. "We can take this to the police and get them to reopen the Madrazo murder. Once they confirm Pedro isn't dead…" He paused, thinking it through.

"That's all good and fine," Billy said, "but it won't be strong enough to get the Montgomery County D.A. to reopen the Torres murder case. We have to find Eduardo, 'walking and talking.' His words.

"The priest knows something," Billy said. "He for sure knows something."

"I'll talk to Jamie," Daniel said. "The Eduardo Torres murder might not be in her jurisdiction, but the Pedro Madrazo case is. Maybe she can convince her investigators to connect the dots and put some resources into finding both of these supposedly dead guys. Also, I've got some contacts in Mexican law enforcement, such as it is. I'll try to pull in a few favors."

Billy's cell phone rang, and he checked the screen, figuring it was one of his sisters or his mom, wanting him to come to the family picnic. But the caller was blocked.

He stepped away from the table to a quieter corner, leaving the others to debate how best to trap Eduardo.

"Cantu," he said into the phone.

"This is David Blaire—I'm on the surveillance team watching Angie Torres?"

"Oh, yeah, David. What's going on?"

"She drove to a house in Conroe. On Baxter Avenue."

"That's her aunt's house." Billy's skin tingled, the way it did before a case broke open big.

"She waited for the boyfriend to leave before she went over there, like maybe she didn't want him to know what she was up to. She's inside now."

"Did she get in with a key?"

"No. The windows are boarded up, and she found a loose board and squeezed through."

This was good news. The police had a reason to arrest her and hold her, now. He wanted the little junkie in an interrogation room…damn, not that he would get to do the interrogating. Sometimes he missed being a cop.

"Do not let her leave. If she tries to leave, arrest her. Say you were driving by and saw her breaking in."

"Cool. You coming?"

"I'll be there as soon as I can."

When he hung up, everybody was looking at him. He quickly repeated what he'd just learned from the off-duty cop. "I need to get over there and question her, find out why she's there."

"I'll check and see who she's been talking to lately," Mitch said as his fingers blurred over his keyboard.

"You can check her phone records?" Claudia asked incredulously. "How do you do that? I thought you needed a warrant."

"Don't ask, don't tell," Mitch said with a grin, never looking up from his screen. "I did find one thing interesting about Angie Torres. Once a day, she receives a phone call at about 8:00 p.m. But it's never from the same number. So I checked to see what the numbers had in common—they're all throwaway prepaid cell phones."

"Eduardo," Billy and Claudia said at the same time.

"Take someone with you to confront Angie," Daniel said to Billy. "Take Ford, or Griffin."

"I want to come," Claudia said.

"Not this time, *cielito.*" The endearment had slipped out, and Billy could have kicked himself. "Last time we faced Angie she almost...well, you know what happened."

She sighed. "So you're going to get *your* head blown off instead?"

Daniel looked from Billy to Claudia and back again. "What happened last time you faced Angie Torres?"

"I stupidly put Claudia's life at risk," Billy confessed. Eventually Daniel would find out somehow; he always did. "I don't want to have to worry about any civilians this time."

"He's right," Beth said to Claudia. "Let the ex-cops handle this one, okay? Drug addicts can be very dangerous."

"I know," she said resignedly. "You guys be careful, huh?"

Billy's heart nearly melted. At least she cared what happened to him, even if he'd behaved like the bastard he was. "We will."

## *CHAPTER SEVENTEEN*

MITCH PACKED UP HIS LAPTOP and left the women in the library with the baby. Little Scotty was just about the cutest thing Claudia had ever seen, but even a warm, cuddly baby wasn't enough to distract her from worrying about Billy.

He knew what he was doing. He was a highly trained, decorated ex-police officer, and Ford Hyatt was Daniel's top investigator. Still, who knew how desperate Angie really was?

"Can I hold him?" Beth asked.

"Huh?" It took her a couple of seconds to realize she wasn't talking about Billy. "Oh, Scotty. Sure. My arm's getting a little tired." The splint did a good job keeping her wrist immobilized, and it didn't hurt much, except when she put pressure on it. Like holding a baby.

"Look at his little ears," Beth said as she settled the infant somewhat awkwardly into her lap. "They're so perfect. Just like big-people ears but, like, the size of a quarter."

"I like his little tiny eyelashes," Claudia said. Holding a baby made her hormones run amok. "So, do you want one?"

"Oh, yeah, definitely. I mean, not right this second. Mitch and I need to have some 'just us' time first. But eventually. What about you?"

"I used to think I didn't. So many things can go

wrong raising a kid, even with two loving parents who try their best. I've seen so many disturbed kids, abused, unloved, throwaways." *Like me.* "It's heartbreaking. But then you see one like this, so precious, so perfect…"

"And you wish you could just run to the store and buy one."

Claudia laughed. "Yes. Exactly. Or at least rent one by the hour. We're biologically predestined to want them. The hormones are there. We can't do anything about them."

"Those can get damned inconvenient, can't they?"

Claudia blew out a sigh. "You said it, sister."

"You and Billy…?"

Claudia nodded. "Yes, and no. It's not going to work out."

"Really? Does he still want to play the field?"

"No, that's not it. I mean, he seems like a real player, but I think he'd be loyal. It's just that we want different things. I want him to trust me enough to open up. He wants me to trust him despite that he won't open up. We tried to just let that be, go with the flow, but I couldn't do it. I pushed, and he got mad, and then I felt terrible for asking something he can't give."

Beth looked genuinely sad. "I'm sorry."

"It's for the better," Claudia said pragmatically.

"Being alone is not better. Trust me on that one."

ON THE WAY TO THERESA'S HOUSE, Billy filled Ford in on the highlights of the case. "On her own, I don't think Angie is dangerous," Billy said. "And supposedly she sneaked off while her boyfriend was gone, so I'm guessing he won't show up waving his gun again. But I'm not ruling anything out. You packing?"

"Can you think of any other reason I might wear a jacket in this heat?"

Billy nodded his understanding. Ford Hyatt was an all right guy. He'd been at Project Justice almost from the beginning. When Billy had first met him, he'd acted like his spine was forged of pure steel. Everything was by the book, and absolutely nothing was funny.

Since he'd met his wife a couple of years ago, though, he'd loosened up a lot.

"Do you think love can change people?" Billy asked suddenly. "Change their personality, I mean?"

"Um, I don't talk about stuff like that with other guys. Sorry." But the faint smile on his face said more than he intended. Maybe Claudia's face-reading abilities had rubbed off on Billy.

When they got to Theresa's block, David Blaire's unmarked car was parked a couple of houses down, but he wasn't in it.

"That's interesting," Billy said as they cruised slowly past.

They parked across the street, then approached cautiously on foot, taking cover behind the neighbor's bushes until they were right up to the weedy front yard.

Even from this distance, they could hear shouting from the backyard—female shouting, shrieking, even, and not the happy kind of shrieking.

A man who could only be Officer David Blaire was standing at the top of the driveway where the fence cordoned off the backyard, and he stared intently through the cracks. Like a good cop, he kept a lookout over his shoulder, and he saw Billy and Ford approaching. He motioned for them to hurry over.

"So far they haven't come to blows," Blaire said.

"But if the neighbor lifts that shovel any higher, I'm going to consider it brandishing a weapon and I'm going in."

Billy stepped up on the edge of the planter and peered over the fence. Angie Torres and the neighbor, Patty, were squared off in the middle of the yard.

Obviously someone had been digging—it looked like every square inch of that backyard had been turned over—and since Patty was the one wielding the shovel, he guessed she was the culprit.

"This is *not* gardening," Angie was saying. "You don't have to dig holes to China just to harvest a few potatoes."

"I wasn't just digging potatoes," Patty said. "I was taking out the weeds."

"Looks to me like you dug up all the tomato plants, as well."

"They were dead, anyway."

"Look, if you found so much as one penny in this yard, you better turn it over to me right now, or I'll call the cops."

"The cops! Oh, that's a rich one. You positively reek of pot. You probably got enough weed in your car to qualify as a felony."

"And you got enough fat on your rear end to qualify as toxic waste!"

"Whoa," Ford said under his breath. "That was uncalled for."

"You're just jealous because your rear end looks like the flat side of this shovel!"

Angie reached down and grabbed one of the dead tomato plants, which was about four feet tall, and began slapping at Patty with it like a whip.

"Ow! You can't do that! That's assault!"

"I can do anything I want in my own aunt's backyard in which you are *trespassing!*"

"Okay, that's it," Billy announced as he vaulted over the fence. Blaire and Hyatt were right behind him, but Billy dropped back and let Blaire, the only one of them who carried a real badge, take the lead.

"Excuse me, ladies," Blaire said. "Break it up now, okay?"

They both whirled around. Patty immediately dropped the shovel and took a step away from it, pretending it wasn't hers, but Angie continued to clutch her dead tomato plant.

"Who are you and what the hell do you want?" She glared at Billy, recognition dawning. "Not you again. I checked, and you are not a cop and I do not have to do anything you say."

"I'm not a cop, but he is," Billy said, nodding to Blaire, who already had his badge out, holding it stiff-armed in front of him.

"What's going on here?" Blaire demanded.

"Well, I'm taking care of Theresa's garden while she's in the hospital," Patty said self-righteously. "This little snipe is here to steal whatever's not nailed down and sell it for drugs."

"That's a lie!" Angie screamed, brandishing her tomato plants again.

"Whoa, whoa, let's just everybody calm down." Blaire came behind Angie and took her shoulders. He was merely attempting to move her back from Patty, put some distance between them, but Angie took that as her cue. She shook Blaire off and ran like a rabbit.

"Oh, hell." Blaire took off after her.

She didn't get far. He caught her before she could

get to the back gate, cuffed her and half dragged her back to where the rest of them were standing.

"She is nothing but trouble, that one," Patty said with a sniff.

"If you arrest me," Angie said, "you gotta arrest her, too. She's trespassing, looking for those coins."

"Your father's coin collection?" Billy asked innocently. "I thought it had only sentimental value. Are you looking for the coins, as well?"

Angie ignored the barb. "They weren't anywhere in Dad's house. I figure my mom musta given them to Aunt Theresa so my dad wouldn't find them. After what happened to Theresa, I wanted to find the coins and put them someplace safe. *Anybody* could break into this house and steal stuff." She gave Patty a pointed look.

It was a pretty good story. Angie actually sounded sane and reasonable.

"If I'd stolen the coins," Patty interjected, "would I be digging up the whole backyard—" She caught herself, but it was way too late. "Look, now, I figured it was my civic duty to stop those coins from getting into the hands of a drug user. Can you imagine how much dope she could buy with a million dollars' worth of—"

"Shut *up!*" Angie shouted.

"Guess your dad's gonna be pretty disappointed you couldn't find the hidden treasure," Billy said.

"My dad's deceased."

"Sure he is. That's why he keeps calling you from those throwaway cell phones. Eight o'clock every night."

"If he's alive, how do you explain the blood?" Angie said belligerently, but he could see the fear in her eyes.

"Give it up. The police already got your dad in custody."

Blaire and Hyatt raised their eyebrows at Billy's blatant lie, but they didn't give him away.

"Right now you're only looking at a breaking and entering charge," he continued. "Plus whatever narcotics charges get added based on what's in your car. But you're just a little fish. You testify against your father, and maybe all those other charges against you will go away. Otherwise…" Billy shrugged, as if it didn't make that much difference to him one way or the other "…you might be looking at conspiracy charges." Conspiracy to what, he wasn't sure, but plotting with your father to fake his murder and put your mother on death row had to carry some kind of stiff penalty.

Angie suddenly crumbled and burst into tears. "It was his idea."

Everyone else went very still, even Patty.

"Whose idea, Angie?" Billy asked softly.

"Dad's. He didn't want to give her half his money. So I got him the medical stuff and showed him how to draw his own blood, and he kept it in the fridge in the garage until he had enough that it would look like he couldn't survive. He said they wouldn't give Mom the death penalty since she was a woman. He just wanted to sell everything and hide the money. Then he was going to reveal that he was alive. But when we couldn't find the coin collection he got mad, said she'd stolen it and he wouldn't ever let her off the hook."

"You could have gotten her off the hook," Billy said. "I asked you if your dad was alive, and all you had to do was say yes. Which means you were conspiring with your father to have your mother killed by lethal injection. That's conspiracy to commit murder, huh, guys? Don't you think?"

Blaire nodded. "Sounds like it to me."

"Angie Torres, you are despicable!" Patty spat out.

"And you, neighbor-lady..." Billy pointed his finger at Patty. "Haven't you ever heard about people who live in glass houses?"

"Huh?"

"You were trespassing, and you admitted you were looking for the coins. What were you planning to do with them?"

"I told you, I wanted to keep them safe. Until Theresa recovered."

"And they wouldn't have been safe enough buried in the backyard?" the ever-logical Ford asked.

"Are they here?" Patty's eyes glittered with greed.

"Who the hell knows?" Angie said in disgust. "Wherever my mom hid those coins, she did a good job. And she's not talking."

"Actually, we know where she hid the coins," Billy said. "In a statue of the Virgin Mary. You wouldn't happen to know anything about that statue, would you?"

Angie's eyes widened, but she shook her head even as she glanced toward the house.

Billy had had enough. He was sweating like a mule and Officer Blaire's fair skin was starting to turn pink.

"Take 'em both in," Billy said, already thinking about returning to Daniel's swimming pool, maybe a cold beer and Claudia.

Claudia. He couldn't wait to tell her the good news. Angie had admitted her father was alive, in front of four people including an impartial Houston police officer. Surely *that* would be enough to sway Fitz and force him to get Mary-Francis's conviction overturned.

"Wait," Patty said as Billy attempted to cuff her. "I might know something about a statue."

"Yeah, what?" Finding the coins would only be the icing on the cake at this point, but it was still an important part of the puzzle.

"Take the cuffs off, and I'll tell you."

Billy didn't care one way or another if Patty went to jail, so he took off the cuffs. "This better be good or the cuffs go back on."

"Late at night, after Theresa was attacked, a priest came to the house. He let himself in—I think he had a key."

"Go on."

"He didn't stay long. When he came out, he had something big and heavy under his arm, about three feet long, covered in a blanket. It could have been a statue."

CLAUDIA'S STOMACH CHURNED as she sat in the shade on the patio, waiting for word from Billy. The party was still going strong as more and more people arrived.

Daniel was known for putting on an impressive fireworks display over his small private lake. He got a special permit from the city and imported the finest, latest and greatest Chinese fireworks and the pyrotechnics experts to coordinate the ignition, and he brought in a symphony orchestra to play "The Star-Spangled Banner," the *1812 Overture* and a bunch of Sousa marches suitable for the occasion.

Robyn, Ford Hyatt's wife, had been keeping close by, since it was her husband who'd gone with Billy to confront Angie Torres. Her year-old daughter, Annie, played with Tucker under their umbrella table.

"They'll be fine," Robyn kept saying. The tall, slender woman with long blond hair was an art teacher and one of the few in the Project Justice inner circle who had no law enforcement or professional connection to the foundation, other than being a former client. "It was hard for me to get used to at first, knowing Ford would sometimes put himself in dangerous situations. But you have to believe me when I tell you, these guys know how to handle themselves. They used to be cops."

"You obviously haven't been around Billy much," Claudia countered. They watched the pool hijinks from a safe distance as the World Champion of Cannonballs was being determined. So far, Celeste was winning. "He skirts the law. He really puts himself out there, confronting people he shouldn't, getting in their faces." Claudia gave a delicate shiver. "He scares the pants off me."

Robyn looked at her sympathetically. "You'll get used to it."

"I don't plan to get used to it."

"Oh? I thought you and Billy… Guess I got it wrong."

Claudia didn't know how her almost-relationship with Billy had become public knowledge so quickly. She didn't think Billy had bragged, that wasn't his style. Perhaps speculation had turned to certainty as people had seen them together. She'd done a poor job of disguising her feelings, and the way Billy had been so protective of her after the assault…well, she could see how people would draw conclusions.

"We're not a couple," Claudia said, feeling the weight of that statement, and also the wrongness of it.

"You want to talk about it?"

Claudia smiled at Robyn and squeezed her hand. "I already unloaded on Beth, and I don't want to become known around here as that dreary woman who's always whining."

Robyn laughed. "No one would ever say that about you. I mean, you're a psychologist. You spend all day listening to other people whine, and even when you're off the job, you're a very good listener."

"You learn more by listening than talking."

"I might be able to offer some insight. Ford and I had some rocky moments early in our relationship. I had a hard time adjusting to his cop mentality…you know, everything is black and white, everyone is good or bad, you're either with me or against me."

"How did you adjust?" Claudia was curious.

"We each gave a little. The usual. He tries not to be judgmental, to give people the benefit of the doubt. And I've realized that his job requires him to have a certain attitude, that being suspicious keeps him safe."

"I always recommend compromise when I do couples counseling," Claudia said. "But I'm not very good at it myself, apparently." She could tell herself all day and all night that pressuring Billy into revealing the most traumatic incident of his life had been wrong and unfair. But if he'd continued to stonewall her, she wouldn't have been able to tolerate it.

"I need for him to trust me," she said, giving her fears a concrete, tangible expression.

"That seems fair. Do you trust him?"

"Absolutely." Did she? "Well, mostly. I could trust him one hundred percent if he trusted me."

"Sounds like a chicken-and-egg problem. Maybe he can't trust you unless you trust him. Unconditionally."

Claudia's head hurt from thinking about it. "It doesn't matter. It's over. We missed our window of opportunity."

Robyn snorted. "Drink some more of that nice fruity drink. See if another window doesn't open."

When Claudia spotted Daniel approaching their table with a purposeful stride, she feared the worst—especially because Jamie was with him. By now, Billy and Ford had to have confronted Angie. Nearly two hours had passed.

Claudia jumped out of her chair and took a few steps to meet them. "Is there bad news?"

"On the contrary. Angie's in custody, everything's fine."

"Oh, thank God." Claudia hadn't realized how truly worried she'd been until her knees nearly buckled with relief. She managed to make it back to her chair without falling, and she took a long draw on her frozen strawberry daiquiri. She didn't normally indulge in such a sweet drink, but on this hot day, the icy, sugary concoction slid down easy.

"Billy says he has even better news, but he wants to tell you in person."

"Did he find Eduardo?" she asked, because that would be the best outcome possible.

Daniel winked mysteriously. "All I'm saying is, I've got champagne on ice, if it's needed."

Robyn punched her lightly on the arm. "That's good news. Daniel only breaks out the champagne when a case is closed."

Claudia was saved from pulling out Daniel's fingernails one at a time to get the answers she craved;

Billy and Ford had just exited the house through the French doors and were heading their way. Billy had changed into khaki shorts and a wild Hawaiian shirt with parrots and surfboards—something Hudson Vale would wear—looking much more in the party spirit than before. He'd even traded his cowboy boots for flip-flops.

Claudia didn't think through what she did next. She jumped out of her chair, put her arms around Billy and hugged him for all she was worth. "I'm so glad you're okay."

"Of course I'm okay," he murmured in her ear. "I've faced off with drug kingpins and mass murderers. I wasn't going to let one little strung-out junkie get the best of me. But thanks for worrying about me."

Claudia remembered herself and pulled away, straightening her clothes and getting a grip on herself. What must everyone think? Even Robyn hadn't greeted her husband with that much enthusiasm, preferring to give him a quick peck on the cheek and a smile full of intimacy, and Ford had been in just as much danger as Billy.

"Daniel says you have good news?" Claudia prompted.

He grinned. "Angie confessed. She blurted out that she and her father planned the whole thing from the beginning. There were four witnesses—me, Ford, a Houston police officer and the neighbor, Patty."

"That's fantastic!" She resisted the urge to hug him again. They'd done it. "So where is he?"

"Still at large." Billy didn't seem troubled by this fact. "But we'll find him soon. Angie said she would cooperate. And even if we still can't find him, I doubt Mr. Fitz can continue to argue that Eduardo Torres is dead."

Everyone in the group standing near the umbrella table was smiling and giving each other high fives, with one exception. Jamie McNair stood there like a stone. She clearly didn't want to share in the celebration. Of course she wouldn't want to see a fellow district attorney forced to eat crow for prosecuting a murder that didn't happen, but still…

"Jamie," Claudia said. "Is something wrong?"

All eyes turned to her. "I don't want to rain on your parade," she said carefully, "but I don't think we should break out the champagne just yet."

# *CHAPTER EIGHTEEN*

"YOU HAVE TO LOOK AT THIS from a D.A.'s point of view," Jamie continued.

Claudia had to admit, even though Jamie was wearing a bikini top and a grass skirt, she managed to *look* like a district attorney. Her commanding presence was one of the reasons she'd won the election despite her relative youth.

Daniel pinched the bridge of his nose, as if he knew what was coming.

"Angie is Mary-Francis's daughter. Her flesh and blood. Now that the date of her mother's execution is drawing near, all quarrels are forgotten, and she might be apt to say or do *anything* to save her mother's life."

Billy's expression changed abruptly from one of elation to a look of dawning horror. "She can't be making it up. She gave too many details."

"On video?" Jamie asked.

"No, it was a spontaneous confession. But we had witnesses."

Claudia groaned inwardly. "Most of them have already forgotten the particulars of Angie's confession. Her lawyer will urge her to recant. She'll claim she said whatever you wanted to hear because she was afraid."

"Damn." Billy scrubbed his face with his hands. "Damn! So we're back to square one? We have to find Eduardo and trot him before Fitz to save Mary-Francis's life?"

"I'm not saying you can't try, going with what you've got," Jamie said. "But a living, breathing Eduardo Torres is what you really need."

"Then we'll get him," Billy said, pounding one fist into his palm. "We'll set a trap. I'll get the cops to let Angie go. She'll get in touch with her father, tell him what she learned about the priest taking the statue full of coins."

"You're going to use an aging priest as bait?" Daniel asked.

"Hey, he stole the statue. Besides, it's the only way. We'll arrange for Angie to be released tomorrow morning. We'll stake out the church. Someone will show up, guaranteed, and whoever it is, if it's not Eduardo himself, will lead us to him."

"We can't just let Father Benito sit in his church, unaware," Claudia said. "We need to warn him that he now has a big, fat red target on his back."

Billy looked at Ford, who looked at Daniel, then back at Billy. This was his operation. They wanted him to make the call. The priest's life might be riding on his decision.

"We need to make sure Angie doesn't talk to her father until we're ready," Billy said. "I'll talk to the priest this afternoon. I'll send him someplace safe, then we'll get a team into place, *then* arrange for Angie's release."

"What if he won't cooperate?" Daniel asked.

"I'll talk to him," Claudia said. "Father Benito is afraid of Billy, but he likes me. I'll gain his cooperation."

Billy was shaking his head, but Daniel clearly liked

the idea, if she was correctly reading the slight shift in his weight and the quirk at the side of his mouth.

"I'll take care of Angie," Jamie said. "I'll keep her on ice until you say. But she might already have called her father. Arrestees are allowed their phone call, you know."

"Eduardo won't be that easy to contact. Remember, all the phone calls to Angie suspected to be from her father were incoming, each from a different number. I'm betting she doesn't know how to get in touch with him. He was too afraid she would give him away."

"Let's move," Daniel said quietly. "Billy, you and Claudia go now. It's imperative to get the priest and any other civilians out of that church. I'll put the surveillance team together. I won't be far behind you."

"Then I'll turn Angie loose," Jamie said. "I'll put one of my investigators on her."

It wasn't until Billy and Claudia were in a silver Jaguar borrowed from Daniel, a vehicle Eduardo wasn't likely to recognize, and heading for the church, that Billy spoke again. "I don't know how you managed this. You're supposed to be lying low, keeping yourself out of sight. Now you somehow have insinuated yourself right into the middle of things. Again."

"You need me," she said plainly. "I won't pretend there's no danger at all, but you guys risk your lives every day for causes you believe in. Well, this is something I believe in. I want to save Mary-Francis, and if that means a small amount of personal risk, that's okay with me."

"I don't like it."

"We all have to put up with things we don't like."

"I don't like it so much that I might have to stop the car and puke."

"Billy."

He did pull off the freeway, but he didn't get sick despite his threat. He parked on the shoulder, but left the engine and air-conditioning running, for which Claudia was grateful.

"I should tell you how Sheila died."

"What? Now?"

"Yes. I was running an undercover operation. I brought Sheila in because she was young and hot and a new face, not one my target would know. I needed her to elicit one small piece of information from him. Just one word, in fact, and we could make the arrest. They were supposed to trade information. She supposedly knew the location of a drug mule who'd gone missing with a large shipment of heroin, he was supposed to cut her in for a percentage of the recovered drugs. She had a wire and I was outside the meeting place, listening. I was waiting for the guy to say enough that we could get a conviction. But he kept dancing around the issue, playing dumb.

"Finally I realized he knew she was a cop, and he was playing her, but it was too late. He shot her through the heart."

"Oh, my God. Billy."

"Yeah. So you can understand why I'm nervous. She was a trained police officer, for God's sake. You're a pure civilian. You probably don't even know how to use a firearm."

"This situation is very different." Her heart went out to him. No wonder he'd been hesitant to return to field work. "We're just going to warn the priest. Maybe he has something to hide, but he's not violent. He's not packing, he's not going to hurt anyone."

"He took the coins. He has something to lose. Or *he* could get hurt."

"He won't. Eduardo doesn't know Father Benito took the statue, not yet. By the time he finds out, we'll be ready for him. *You'll* be ready," she amended. "I'll be far away. I promise."

"You know, it's a little scary, but you're starting to think like one of us."

"Don't worry, I have no aspirations to become a Project Justice investigator. If I did, this past week would have cured me of it, that's for sure."

Once they reached the church, Billy drove twice around the block, peering at every parked car, giving a couple of homeless guys a long, hard look before deciding neither one was Eduardo or Pedro, his buddy.

Finally he parked not far from the front door. The church looked quiet. From somewhere nearby, children shrieked happily as some firecrackers went off. Claudia hoped they were being careful.

Billy's phone rang just before they reached the front door. He checked the screen, then answered. "Yeah, Daniel."

Claudia watched his face closely. This time, he knew she was watching and gave nothing away. She waited patiently as he nodded, then disconnected.

"What?" Claudia asked.

"They released Angie. The moment she arrived at the station."

"Seriously?"

"Some joker at the city lockup said she had a get-out-of-jail-free card and just let her go. She's off the radar."

"And possibly talking to her father right this second.

She must have *some* way to get hold of him in an emergency."

Billy glanced back at the church. "Let's get this over with. I'm giving you ten minutes to convince Father Benito to cooperate with us. Then I'm transporting you, and the priest if he'll go, to the nearest hotel."

"What if Eduardo doesn't come?"

"He will. We might have to wait for him awhile, but he'll come."

The church's front door was unlocked. Billy instructed Claudia to stand aside as he entered alone, his hand resting on the grip of his gun, which was thrust in the back of his khaki shorts. He'd traded his flip-flops for a pair of running shoes, but hadn't wanted to take the time to change clothes.

Churches were supposed to be places of sanctuary, and it must have been hard for Billy to carry his weapon into a building he'd been trained since childhood to believe was sacred, hallowed ground.

But apparently his prime directive—to catch the bad guy—was stronger.

"Okay," he whispered, "no one here but the old nun."

Claudia gasped. "Billy, the nun. She'll have to be taken to safety, too."

"They'll all go with you. In fact, I'll stay here, you can take the car keys."

"First we have to talk to Father Benito."

They made their way through the nave along the side wall to the little door that led to the vestry and Father Benito's office, but the door was closed and locked.

"Excuse me, Sister," Billy said in a hushed voice.

"I apologize for disturbing your prayers, but we need to find Father Benito. Do you know where he is?"

She shrugged but said nothing. Maybe she'd taken a vow of silence.

Claudia tapped Billy's arm and pointed to the confessional on the other side of the church.

"Didn't you say something about the church opening for confession?" she whispered.

"Right." He started toward the confessional, but Claudia halted him.

"Let me."

The confessional consisted of two small closet-like rooms tucked into the corner behind the organ near the Virgin Mary statue. Mary looked as serene as ever, glowing in the light of the many candles lit in her name.

Small signs on the doors indicated that the priest's side was occupied, the penitent's side, available. Claudia opened the door and found herself in a space so small she could barely turn around. But she managed to contort herself onto the worn velvet kneeler and closed herself in, pushing the sign so it would read Occupied.

She wasn't Catholic, but she remembered the words to the Sacrament of Penance, taught to her by her fellow seventh graders when she asked what went on behind those mysterious closed doors in the church.

"Bless me, Father, for I have sinned…"

BILLY SAT WHERE HE HAD a good view of the confessional as well as the door leading to the priest's office and the main church entrance. It wasn't easy to keep his eye on all three, but he did. The clock had started running as soon as Claudia had closed the door.

After a couple of minutes, the nun made the sign of the cross and pushed her arthritic body to her feet. Clutching her rosary beads, her hands completely hidden by the long sleeves of her old-fashioned habit, her head bowed, she made her way to the locked door, creaking along, leaning heavily on her cane.

She had a brass key ring identical to the one Father Benito carried—and she tried first one, then another on the locked door, seeming to have no luck.

It was then that something odd about the nun registered in Billy's brain. When she'd made the sign of the cross, she'd done it backward. With her right hand, she'd touched forehead and heart, but then she'd touched her right shoulder first, rather than her left.

No real nun would make that kind of mistake.

He jumped out of the pew and made it to her in two strides. "Here, Sister, let me help you with that."

"No, I can get it." She sounded half-panicked, and not nearly as old as she should have. As she finally found the right key, the door opened and she attempted to slip inside and slam it in Billy's face, but he got his foot wedged inside. He pushed inside the hallway, and the nun was running—skirts hiked up, revealing a pair of rhinestone sandals that wouldn't be part of any nun's habit.

Billy was after her like a bolt of lightning and caught her arm just as she reached the back exit.

She turned and fought him like a wildcat, scratching and biting and screaming for him to let go.

He yanked the veil off; it was Angie Torres. He'd made another rookie mistake by not looking past the habit, the thick glasses and the supposed nun's arthritic gait.

"Let me go!" she screamed again, still struggling,

but Billy was sitting on her and had her arms pinned so she couldn't do him any more damage. She'd landed a good scratch on his face, and he could feel the blood trickling down his cheek.

"For your sake," he said, "I hope the nun this habit belongs to is alive and well. Where is she?"

Angie went stonily silent, looking up at him with a smart-ass expression, as if she was the one who had him pinned to the carpet rather than the other way around.

"Fine, we'll do it the hard way." He flipped her on her stomach and reached into his back pocket for a pair of handcuffs that weren't there. Damn it. He hated not being a cop.

That realization stunned him.

Improvising, he grabbed the discarded nun's veil, intending to tear a strip of fabric from it to use as a binding.

"Wait," Angie said. "Let me up, and I'll take you to my father."

"Where is he?" Billy cranked her arm a little harder behind her back—not hard enough to cause injury, but just enough to remind her he could deal out a whole lot of pain if he chose.

"Not here. He's meeting me here. If I don't call to give him the all clear, he won't come. You'll never catch him. If I take you to him, you'll say I cooperated, right?"

"If you cooperate, I'll tell the cops the truth."

"Then let me up."

Billy knew better than to give her her freedom. At the first opportunity, she'd bolt. But she was small and weak, no match for him physically. So long as he kept one hand on her, she couldn't get away.

He finished tying her hands behind her despite her protests. The fabric from the veil was old and fragile, but Billy wrapped it around several times and tied it in a square knot. He frisked Angie to make sure she didn't have any weapons, then finally let her up.

"Where's the nun?" Billy demanded.

"What nun?"

"The one who belongs to this habit. If you hurt an old nun, there is no prison bad enough for you."

"I didn't hurt her."

"Then where is she?"

"Do you want my dad or not?"

"Not until I make sure the nun is okay." Billy's hands were itching to get hold of Eduardo, and he hoped the guy resisted arrest. He wanted an excuse to beat the crap out of him.

Then he remembered that he couldn't officially arrest anybody.

Angie sighed. "She's in that room, you know, where the priest gets dressed."

"It's called a vestry." He dragged her to the small room in which they'd met with Father Benito yesterday. That door was locked, too.

"Keys, keys, where are they?"

"I dropped them when you assaulted me."

Billy saw the keys gleaming from the worn carpet near the doorway leading back into the church. He wasted precious seconds hauling a resisting Angie to the door, retrieving the keys, dragging her back to the other door, then painstakingly trying one key after another until he finally found the one that worked. He opened the door and turned on the light.

There was the nun, lying on the carpet in only her

shift, her hands and feet secured with zip ties. She blinked myopically at him, her eyes filled with terror.

"Good God Almighty," Billy swore. "How could you do this?" He threw Angie facedown into the carpet. "Do not move one muscle, you hear me?" Then he knelt beside the nun and gently peeled the duct tape from her mouth. "It's gonna be okay, Sister. Don't be afraid of me, I'm here to help you."

Once her mouth was free, she gulped in several breaths of air as Billy used his pocketknife to cut the zip ties from her hands and feet. He yanked his cell phone from his pocket and dialed 9-1-1.

"I'm gonna need an ambulance at the Church of Our Lady of Perpetual Hope." He rattled off the address.

"And what is your name, sir?" the operator asked.

"Sergeant… Scratch that. Billy Cantu. I'm with Project Justice." It wouldn't carry quite as much weight as if he were a police officer, but maybe it would help.

The nun was sitting up now, rubbing her hands together and weeping. Billy yanked the cloth off the small table where they'd sat the other day and draped it over her shoulders, figuring she was probably humiliated to be sitting there practically in her underwear in front of a strange man.

"I can't talk right now," Billy said to the operator. "But I'll leave the channel open. Oh, um, send cops, too. A nun's been assaulted."

The nun was trying to tell him something. She was pointing and mumbling, and it took her a few tries to make herself understood.

"Father Benito." She kept pointing to a heap of vestments in the corner. Except it wasn't just clothes. It was the priest, unconscious.

"Father!" He was halfway across the room before

it occurred to him. If Father Benito was in here, who was hearing confession?

"Hello, Father Benito. It's me, Claudia Ellison. I know this is an unconventional way for me to talk to you, especially since I'm not even Catholic."

She waited for him to acknowledge her presence, but he said nothing. He was there, though. She could hear him breathing on the other side of the carved wooden grate lined with fabric that separated confessor from confessee.

"Look, I'm not trying to get anyone in trouble. I just want to save Mary-Francis's life. Her husband is alive, somewhere, and I feel like perhaps you know where he is. Or you can at least guess."

Still, he said nothing.

"I promise you, anything you say to me here will remain confidential. I guess only a priest can extend the seal of the confessional, but I'm a therapist. I'm protected by confidentiality, just like you."

She waited. Nothing.

"I know you took a statue from Theresa's house. I suspect it was filled with valuable coins. I know your intention was not to steal them, because you're a good man. I can sense that about you. Perhaps you were only safeguarding them? Anyway, I'm not the only one who knows you took the statue. By now, Eduardo Torres knows. And he's likely to come here looking for his property. Billy and I want to take you someplace safe. And then Project Justice will deal with Eduardo, or his thugs, when they get here.

"Will you do that?"

His silence was driving her crazy. She knew she'd hit him with a lot, but really, they didn't have all day.

"Father?"

It was then she noticed a faint odor that seemed out of place in a confessional. Menthol cigarettes.

As panic welled up inside her, she fumbled with the latch on the door. Only one thought assailed her brain: *get out, get out, get out.* But she wasn't fast enough.

A fist smashed through the screen.

Before Claudia could get out of the way in the claustrophobic little closet, the hand had clamped around her throat.

"You should have left it alone, like Pedro told you to." The voice, harsh and rasping, sounded as though it came straight from hell. Her body tensed as if frozen, unable to move, and her previously injured wrist and hip throbbed. "You could have saved yourself but you wouldn't back off. My wife doesn't deserve the effort you've made to save her."

Claudia couldn't think, couldn't breathe. Eduardo Torres was pressing on her carotid artery, cutting off the blood supply to her brain. She clawed at his hand, but it was like tearing at steel with bare fingernails.

*Think, think, think.* She was not a helpless victim. She could do something, take some kind of action, that would alert Billy she was in trouble.

Her personal-safety alarm! This time, she had one hand free. She reached into her dress pocket and pressed the button on the little plastic device. An earsplitting siren filled the tiny room.

## *CHAPTER NINETEEN*

"CLAUDIA!" BILLY WAS TORN. Help the unconscious priest or help the woman he loved, who was undoubtedly in trouble right this moment?

"Go. I'll tend to Father Benito."

The nun was standing now. She'd retrieved her glasses from Angie, and she looked a lot stronger and more sure of herself than she had a few moments earlier.

She didn't have to ask him twice. "Watch the girl," he warned as he darted out the door. "Make sure she doesn't get loose."

Billy let his ears guide him to the siren. As he reentered the church, it became clear that the sound was coming from the confessional. He leaped across two rows of pews to get there. He tried to open the door, but it was locked.

"Claudia!" He didn't waste much time trying to get her to unlock the door. She was obviously in trouble or she wouldn't have set off the siren. Instead, he took a step back and forced the door open.

The scene that greeted him was as shocking as anything he'd ever seen. The arm and shoulder of a man reached through the screen and had Claudia pinned to the wall. She wasn't moving.

The second he'd burst through, though, the hand released her and withdrew.

"Claudia, are you okay?"

Her hand fluttered. "I'm okay," she rasped. "Get Eduardo."

Eduardo had already exited the priest's side of the confessional, and he was ready for Billy. From a crouch, he sprang at Billy, knocking him to the ground.

But when it came to hand-to-hand combat, not many people could get the drop on Billy. Eduardo got in the first good lick, but before the other man could get his hands around Billy's throat, Billy changed the angle of his body, shifted his legs, immobilized Eduardo's arm for a fraction of a second, and then raised his hips just half an inch, and all of a sudden it was Eduardo who was on the ground and Billy on top of him.

Now would have been the golden opportunity to teach Eduardo a lesson. The man was a beast, beating his wife, putting her through the anguish of thinking him dead, not to mention setting her up as a suspect, the trial, incarceration, even the death penalty. Unfortunately, Billy didn't have the luxury of time. He'd pitted an elderly nun and an unconscious old priest against wily Angie, who even with her hands tied could do a lot of damage if she put her mind to it.

Billy drew his gun and stood, pointing his weapon at Eduardo and daring him to fight. "Turn over onto your stomach and put your hands behind your head."

"Okay, okay, don't shoot." The gangster did as requested.

Claudia emerged from the confessional, pale and shaking. She had a necklace of angry red marks around her throat, and the sight of her injury made Billy want to shoot Eduardo through his heart.

"Are you okay, *cielito?*"

"I'm okay." Her voice was nothing but a whisper. Had Eduardo injured her vocal cords?

"The police are on their way, but I need you to find something to tie Eduardo's hands with."

"How about the belt from my dress?" Her voice was stronger now, but still shaky.

"Perfect."

"I don't think that will be necessary."

Stunned, Billy turned to find Angie holding a gun of her own. She had Father Benito and the nun in front of her, the weapon pointed right at the nun's head.

"Drop the gun, Cantu, or you'll end up with a lot of dead people on your conscience."

Slowly, Billy did as requested. He laid the gun at his feet, then slowly straightened and put his hands in the air. He kicked the gun, sending it sliding several feet under the pews. The last thing he wanted was for Eduardo to get his hands on a deadly weapon.

"Get up, Dad," Angie said. "I got it under control now."

Eduardo was slow to get up, and in fact, he never made it. His right leg buckled under him, and he fell back to the floor, howling in pain.

"You son of a bitch! I think you broke my leg."

"Let's just get the coins and get out of here," she said nervously. "One more time, old priest, where did you put the coins?"

She jabbed Father Benito in the chest with her gun, which would have been a stupid move had she done it to Billy. He'd have gotten the gun away from her in a flash. But he was too far away to do anything.

The priest had a large bump on his head, and he was pale, but otherwise he seemed okay. "I told you already, the coins aren't here."

"Then where are they?"

"In Mexico, where they belong. Your father stole

them from a Mexico City museum. Your mother told me the whole story. Spanish gold and silver coins, recovered from the wreck of the *Margarita.*"

"*You* stole those coins!" Angie shouted. "You took advantage of my aunt being in the hospital and you broke into her house. What kind of priest are you?"

"One who was very close to your aunt, and your mother," Father Benito said calmly. True to his word, he didn't seem to be afraid of dying. "We were all from the same poor village, you see. As a young priest I came to the States, and the Rio Verde elders asked for my help. They asked me to find good American husbands for the young girls, so they could have a better life, free from hunger, where they wouldn't have to have their babies without doctors or hospitals. I thought I was doing a good thing."

"Mary-Francis was fifteen," Claudia said. "Her sister only two years older."

"In rural Mexico, back then, fifteen was considered a marriageable age. Eduardo Torres was a wealthy young man, twenty-four and already he owned a house. He promised to be good to her. If I'd known what he would put her through…"

He couldn't go on.

Angie actually seemed to be paying attention to what the priest had to say. She didn't look as angry as she had before.

"Don't listen to him, Angie," Eduardo said. "He's trying to distract you. Just get him to tell us where the coins are. Shoot him in the leg if you have to."

"The coins are gone," the priest said coldly. "Yes, I took the statue. When I realized Theresa was nearly murdered, most likely because of the coins, I took them—for safekeeping, at first. But then I realized how much evil had been perpetrated because of greed over those coins, and I decided to do the right thing. I returned them to the museum. I took the reward money and I donated it to the school in Rio Verde. Then I set up a shrine with the statue. I prayed to the Virgin every day to heal Theresa, and to free Mary-Francis, who I knew in my heart could not have killed her husband. Though in my opinion she would have been justified had she done so." He looked as though he wanted to spit on Eduardo.

"So there are no coins?" Angie wailed.

"There are no coins, my child," the priest said. "They are gone forever."

Angie's eyes filled with tears. "So it's all been for nothing. All the planning and lying, all the searching. I assaulted a nun, and now I'm going to jail and there aren't any coins."

Slowly she turned the gun away from Father Benito and aimed it at her own head.

"Angie, don't," Billy said. "You haven't done anything that bad. A good lawyer can get you off."

"Conspiracy to commit murder. That's what you said."

"I was lying." He glanced over at Claudia and was surprised to see she had gradually worked her way closer to Angie. Wasn't this her area of expertise? Wasn't she the one who dealt with suicidal patients?

"I was gonna live a life of luxury in Mexico. Just me and Dad. We figured no one would question a nun and a priest crossing the border. The money from selling those coins would have bought us a house in Cancun, with servants. And a Mercedes."

"Put the gun down, Angie," Billy said.

"Billy, duck!" Claudia screamed as she launched herself at Angie—just as Angie turned the gun toward him.

He dived out of the way.

Angie pulled the trigger, but the bullet went wild—and blew the head off the Virgin Mary statue.

The combined forces of Claudia, the nun and the priest wrested the gun away from Angie. Billy, meanwhile, retrieved his own weapon from under the pew.

And that was when, at long last, the police chose to make their entrance.

"Shots fired, shots fired," one of the uniformed cops screamed into his radio.

Next thing Billy knew, another cop was relieving him of his weapon and cuffing him while Eduardo tried to convince the cops he was the real priest. It took a few minutes to get things straightened out, when all Billy wanted to do now was take Claudia in his arms and hold her…just hold her.

Finally, when all of the correct suspects were cuffed and everyone had received medical attention, Billy saw his opportunity. Claudia sat by herself in a back pew, applying lipstick and fixing her hair.

His heart expanded, creating an uncomfortable pressure inside his chest, and he quickly sat down beside her, before anyone could buttonhole him to ask more questions.

"Oh," she said. "I guess this looks pretty silly, worrying about my appearance at a time like this."

"I'm guessing it's perfectly normal, in a time of high stress, to do something to quiet your nerves. Didn't you try to tell me, once, about self-comforting gestures?"

"Very astute of you. That's exactly what I'm doing—introducing an extremely mundane activity into this chaotic scene to calm myself." She put on a brave smile as she put away her lipstick, but when she took his hand and squeezed it, she was still trembling.

Billy couldn't help himself. He put his arms around her and hugged her. "I've never been so scared as when I saw Eduardo choking you. I thought I was too late. And then when you called out a warning and jumped on Angie—you saved my life. How in the hell did you know she was going to shoot me?"

"It was all over her face. She was no suicide candidate—she loves herself too much to take her own life. She was pointing the gun at herself for effect, for sympathy, maybe. I could tell by the way she looked at each person, gauging whether she was getting the reaction she wanted.

"And when she looked at you—even though it was just a brief glance—she showed obvious, strong contempt. She blamed you for ruining everything. The tension in her arm and hand changed and I just knew she was about to strike."

"I will never, ever call your skills voodoo again, I promise." He pulled back so he could look into her eyes. They swam with tears. "*Cielito,* don't cry. It's over now."

"Billy." She swallowed, struggling for words. "I'm so sorry."

"For what?"

"For insisting you tell me about Sheila."

He waited for the crushing pain that always struck him anytime he heard her name or thought of her. It was there, but it seemed more a dull ache than the punishing blow it had always been before. Maybe today he'd broken the curse, or reversed the spell, or something. Today, he'd gotten to everyone in time. He'd saved Claudia from Eduardo.

"You were right," Claudia continued. "Everyone has the right to privacy of thought. I can't stop myself from reading faces and gestures—that's a part of me that I can't turn off. But I don't have to constantly broadcast what I see, or insist on knowing more. That was wrong of me. Very wrong."

"Maybe not so wrong, *querida.* You saw darkness in me, and it scared you. You only wanted to bring my soul into the light."

"That's a very poetic way of saying it, but that doesn't make it right."

"I'm just sayin', maybe I have the right to a few secrets, but you have the right to feel safe when you're with me. And if you don't feel safe, you have the right to leave."

"Then I should have just left, rather than force you to—"

"You couldn't have forced me if I hadn't wanted to talk. I've been tortured by people a lot scarier than you."

She gasped. "You were tortured? When?" Then she slapped her hand over her mouth. "Never mind."

Billy smiled. "That's a story for another day. And I'll tell you all about it, if you really want to know. But about Sheila—I was afraid to tell you because I thought you'd turn away. I killed her."

"You made a judgment call. It might have been the wrong decision—*might* have been. But maybe he would have killed her even if you'd aborted the moment you realized things weren't quite right. Either way, that's not the same as killing someone. I would never turn away from you for that. I…I love you, Billy. I know that's kind of crazy, but I do."

"Claudia. *Te amo, también. Mi trocito de cielo.*" *I love you, too, my little heaven.*

Forgetting that they were in a church, he leaned in and kissed her. And he would have kept on kissing her if Sister Marguerite hadn't cleared her throat. They broke apart guiltily. The nun had been restored to her habit, looking as scary as any he'd faced in school.

He just hoped she didn't have a ruler.

"I DON'T NORMALLY advocate drinking during the workday," Daniel said from his video screen in the conference room, "but since this was Billy's first official case, and he successfully closed it, a little champagne is in order."

Daniel popped the cork of a bottle of Dom Pérignon, and in the conference room, Billy did the same. The conference room was jam-packed with everybody who'd worked on the case, even a little bit, and some people who just liked to celebrate.

"Mary-Francis Torres will be released from prison tomorrow," Claudia announced. "Her sister, Theresa, is improving day by day. She's up in a wheelchair now, and her doctors believe that with physical therapy and other treatments, she'll be going home soon."

"In addition," Billy said, "Pedro Madrazo was taken into custody yesterday. He's facing a long list of charges, including his assault on Claudia in the parking garage."

"What about the priest?" Daniel asked. "He did steal a million dollars' worth of valuable coins."

"Since they were stolen property to begin with," Billy said, "and he returned them to their rightful owner, and he didn't take them for personal gain, no one's inclined to press charges. So he's in the clear."

Billy poured a few swallows of champagne into crystal wineglasses for everyone who chose to imbibe. Celeste was first in line, and when everyone had been served, she thrust her glass at Billy again.

"You only gave me a few drops the first time."

Billy emptied the bottle into Celeste's glass, then everyone raised their glasses and toasted the success of the case.

"Turns out we have a couple more things to celebrate," Billy said. "The first is, I'm leaving Project Justice."

"What?" Raleigh said, along with several others. "How is that a reason to celebrate?"

"Because I'm going back to police work. I've applied to the Houston Police Department, and with Jamie's recommendation I'm pretty sure they'll take me. Working the Torres case made me realize how much I miss wearing the badge."

"That is good news," Daniel said, lifting his glass again. "I knew Project Justice was only a temporary way station for you until you found your way back to law enforcement. And I trust you'll be our ally with the police."

"I'll do my best."

Everyone raised their glasses again, congratulating Billy on his decision.

"You said two more reasons to celebrate," Daniel said. "What's the second?"

"I bet I know," Beth said.

Billy felt his face splitting with an ear-to-ear grin. "Dr. Claudia Ellison has agreed to be my wife."

Spontaneous cheers broke out as everyone rushed Billy and Claudia in an effort to congratulate them. Just when the furor was dying down, and a few people were wondering if there might not be another bottle of champagne somewhere, seeing as they had three things to celebrate, a strange noise came from under the polished mahogany table—a loud snort and a scuffling sound.

Jillian screamed and climbed up on her chair, teetering there in her high heels. Within seconds every woman in the room and half the men were screaming or shouting as the javelina burst from cover, snorting and pawing the ground.

"Good God!" Daniel shouted. "Is that the pig?"

Celeste calmly scooped up the critter. "There, there, Buster, it's okay. You don't have to be afraid, Mama's got you now." She made a quick escape.

"Clearly I need to spend more time at the office," Daniel grumbled. "Okay, everybody, back to work. There are innocent people still in prison."

THE CHURCH OF OUR LADY of Perpetual Hope had never looked more lovely, Claudia thought, decked out in white roses. The smell of them was everywhere.

Sister Marguerite had seen to it that the floor was scrubbed, the pews polished with lemon oil until they gleamed and every cobweb in even the highest corners removed.

Mary-Francis had paid for the Virgin Mary statue to be repaired by an expert ceramic restoration company. The statue held pride of place at the front of the church, looking remarkably like she'd never been damaged.

Billy and Claudia had agreed to keep the wedding low-key. They'd sent out only a few invitations, just close friends and family, but since Claudia didn't have any family, Billy's mother and sisters had jumped in to help her prepare. The Cantus really knew how to throw a wedding, and it took a lot of persuasion to convince them that simple was best.

Claudia wore a plain satin tea-length gown and no veil, just a few flowers wound into her hair. Billy looked breathtaking in a blue suit, crisp white shirt and his boots, of course, polished to a high gloss for this special occasion.

Father Benito did the honors. Mary-Francis and Theresa were there, sitting in the front row, Theresa in her wheelchair but looking five-hundred percent better than she had only a few weeks earlier.

Claudia walked down the aisle to the beautiful strains of the old pipe organ. The love shining from Billy's eyes almost brought her to her knees, and though she swore she wasn't going to cry, she did.

When he placed the gold band on her finger, she knew she'd finally found the place she belonged, and that she and Billy would make a warm and loving home together. They were shopping for a big house with lots of bedrooms, where Claudia intended to shelter foster kids, adopted kids, and maybe a few of hers and Billy's, as well.

They would give those kids all the love and acceptance she'd never had as a child.

"Please join me," the elderly priest said, "in congratulating Mr. and Mrs. Cantu on the start of their new journey as husband and wife."

They kissed briefly, not wanting to incur the dreaded throat clearing from Sister Marguerite. Then, hand in hand, they began their journey.

* * * * *

# HEART & HOME

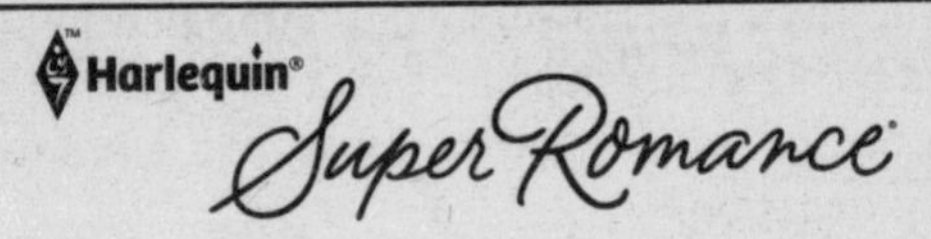


**COMING NEXT MONTH**
AVAILABLE JUNE 12, 2012

**#1782 UNRAVELING THE PAST**
*The Truth about the Sullivans*
**Beth Andrews**

**#1783 UNEXPECTED FAMILY**
**Molly O'Keefe**

**#1784 BRING HIM HOME**
**Karina Bliss**

**#1785 THE ONLY MAN FOR HER**
*Delta Secrets*
**Kristi Gold**

**#1786 NAVY RULES**
*Whidbey Island*
**Geri Krotow**

**#1787 A LIFE REBUILT**
*The MacAllisters*
**Jean Brashear**

*A grim discovery is about to change everything for Detective Layne Sullivan—including how she interacts with her boss!*

*Read on for an exciting excerpt of the upcoming book UNRAVELING THE PAST by Beth Andrews....*

SOMETHING WAS UP—otherwise why would Chief Ross Taylor summon her back out? As Detective Layne Sullivan walked over, she grudgingly admitted he was doing well. But that didn't change the fact that the Chief position should have been hers.

Taylor turned as she approached. "Detective Sullivan, we have a situation."

"What's the problem?"

He aimed his flashlight at the ground. The beam illuminated a dirt-encrusted skull.

"Definitely a problem." And not something she'd expected. Not here. "How'd you see it?"

"Jess stumbled upon it looking for her phone."

Layne looked to where his niece huddled on a log. "I'll contact the forensics lab."

"Already have a team on the way. I've also called in units to search for the rest of the remains."

So he'd started the ball rolling. Then, she'd assume command while he took Jess home. "I have this under control."

Though it was late, he was clean shaven and neat, his flat stomach a testament to his refusal to indulge in doughnuts. His dark blond hair was clipped at the sides, the top long enough to curl.

The female part of Layne admitted he was attractive. The cop in her resented the hell out of him for it.

"You get a lot of missing-persons cases here?" he asked.

"People don't go missing from Mystic Point." Althoug plenty of them left. "But we have our share of crime."

"I'll take the lead on this one."

Bad enough he'd come to *her* town and taken the posi tion she was meant to have, now he wanted to mess wit *how* she did her job? "Why? I'm the only detective on thir shift and your second in command."

"Careful, Detective, or you might overstep."

But she'd never played it safe.

"I don't think it's overstepping to clear the air. You hav something against me?"

"I assign cases based on experience and expertise. Yo don't have to like how I do that, but if you need to questio every decision, perhaps you'd be happier somewhere else.

"Are you threatening my job?"

He moved so close she could feel the warmth from hi body. "I'm not threatening anything." His breath caresse her cheek. "I'm giving you the choice of what happen next."

*What will Layne choose? Find out in UNRAVELING THE PAST by Beth Andrews, available June 2012 from Harlequin® Superromance®.*

*And be sure to look for the other two books in Beth's* THE TRUTH ABOUT THE SULLIVANS *serie available in August and October 2012.*

# THREAT OF DARKNESS

## VALERIE HANSEN

As a nurse and special advocate for children, Samantha Rochard is used to danger in her small town of Serenity, Arkansas. But when she suspects a little boy is in jeopardy, she puts herself in the line of fire...and her only source of protection is old flame and police officer John Waltham. Can they team up again in time to save this child's life?

**THE DEFENDERS**

*Available June 2012 wherever books are sold.*

**Look for a special bonus book in each Love Inspired® Suspense book in June.**

www.LoveInspiredBooks.com

LIS44492